They were on a scarf-finding mission. They strolled purposefully from the bitterly cold, early morning, sun-drenched pavements into the silk-walled casements of luxury. Chanel, Farhi, Hamnett. It was curious being in with the right set in these terrifying shops. When Amy was at the publishing house she and another work experience girl would escape most lunchtimes to meander around South Kensington. They developed a formula for being treated seriously in the shops. Turn waxen with glumness before entering and don't smile. Appear uninterested at all times and express delight, loathing and any greeting merely with your eyelashes. Thus a flicker denotes excitement, a plummeting of lashes disgust, and imploring eyelashes 'I'm trying this on' (no pleases here, I'm afraid). They'd stoically wander between rails in this fashion, suppressing all rapture. Once outside they'd curl over with laughter and 'I must have that's. There invariably followed the adage 'I've got to be rich', chanted so sincerely and with such desperation that Amy almost believed that if she closed her eyes tightly enough the darkness would yield it. Rich boyfriends or cheque-book fraud seemed more likely options, though.

Clare Naylor was born in Yorkshire in 1971. Her peripatetic childhood included climbing mango trees in Zambia and playing netball in Hampshire. She studied English Literature at Royal Holloway College, London University. In 1993 she was a prizewinner of the Vogue Young Writers Talent Contest and after a brief spell writing for magazines and one day in PR she opted for a career in publishing. She currently lives in London with her three flatmates and is writing her second novel.

Love:
A User's Guide

Clare Naylor

CORONET BOOKS
Hodder and Stoughton

Copyright © 1997 Clare Naylor

First published in Great Britain in 1997
by Hodder and Stoughton
A division of Hodder Headline PLC
A Coronet Paperback Original

10 9 8 7 6 5 4 3 2 1

A CIP catalogue record for this title is available
from the British Library

ISBN 0 340 68577 8

Typeset by Palimpsest Book Production Limited,
Polmont, Stirlingshire
Printed and bound in Great Britain by
Mackays of Chatham PLC, Chatham, Kent

Hodder and Stoughton
A division of Hodder Headline PLC
338 Euston Road
London NW1 3BH

For Ada and Arthur Stephenson.

Chapter 1

Orgasm. It was the most perfect word. Eliciting all it could, easing meaning out of every syllable. O . . . a large perfect Oh, the softly parted lips, the promise of the never-ending union. Gas . . . gasp, a shuddering intake of breath, a sensation to savour and the arching curving back as you sink into the mmmmm . . . the bliss. Yes, it was a great word, Amy thought. She'd had a fair few in her time, some deft and delicious, others more hit and miss affairs; she'd been thinking about that word all morning as she basked in the afterglow of sex like early morning sun on her face. What she doesn't know, but we do, is that there are greater and better things to come (as it were) for Amy, more Ohs than she can dream of, enough gasps to take your breath away and an abiding mmmmm of satisfaction that would keep any girl smiling. Yes, there's a lot for her to look forward to, only she doesn't know it just yet.

Amy crawled on the floor looking for a pin to hold together the spare wisps of silk in the model's organza creation. Her boss rushed forward and tugged it from her hand.

'Come on, come on. OK Amy, the shoes are wrong, pass me those blue Patrick Coxs.'

Amy grovelled on the floor a bit more.

'Cloud or Duck egg, Lucinda?'

'Those, those. Here, pass them here.'

Another Monday morning, another undernourished teenager to be got up in the spirit of the lazy days of summer. Amy shivered in the biting February chill of the studio. Carefully ironing between the beads of a pair of Lacroix harem pants, she lapsed to thoughts of herself as a Matisse muse, reclining plumply on a chaise longue, fauvist colours warming her bare breasts, one hand propped above her head, a harlot's smile flickering about her lips and the divine beaded Lacroix creation adorning her gently rounded, golden-tanned stomach. And Luke Harding – she knew it had just been a one night stand but she couldn't resist casting him in the role of libidinous painter (sorry Matisse). When Luke could no longer keep a steady brush he strolled to her side and placed indolent, painterly kisses all over her courtesan form . . .

'Amy, the Lacroix, quick. Today purleasse.'

Lucinda was a bitch from hell on a shoot but then so were all fashion editors. They had the artistic sensibilities of the photographer to worry about – 'more tits darlin' pull it down a bit' (this was *Vogue* by the way, not *Big and Bouncy*) – and the poor model who bit her lip and cried as she exposed an inch more of her pigeon chest; the make-up artist who sulked at the model's spots and shouted if the shell pink of the clothes clashed with the navy blue lipstick he was about to apply; not to give credence to a multitude of hairdressers and PR girls on the end of the phone demanding the aforementioned shell pink number back for a *Marie Claire* shoot in an hour's time. This made for a pretty hellish time for the editor, but it was perdition for the lowly fashion assistant, i.e. Amy, who was the only emotionally balanced person in attendance. Allegedly.

Post-nightmare, Amy and Lucinda sat nibbling the remains of the model's lunch. Cucumber isn't really a square meal but it provided an excuse for them to natter purposefully and wind down from Lazy Days of Summer hell. Lucinda kicked off her scarlet satin Manolos and grilled Amy about the weekend and the smart wedding she'd been to. She was a girl who knew her social onions so a wedding of society pages' significance was always a treat. Who was there? Did Lady Blah get pissed again? What possessed the bride to wear Ozbek and most importantly who snogged whom? Amy deliberately filled in each of the former first.

'Miranda looked like an angel, naturally,' Amy began.

'Naturally,' echoed Lucinda.

'It was at Josh's parents place down in Surrey, there was a kind of wood nymph theme I think, I couldn't quite work it out. I thought the bridesmaids had wings but the woman I sat next to at dinner said they were just weird veils. Anyway, they looked lovely.' Lucinda lapped up the details. 'And the house was amazing but most of us stayed at this hotel down the road.' Amy supressed a smile at the memory of the hotel. 'And Josh cried during his speech which was quite cute I suppose.' They both gave a perfunctory nod on the understanding that, yes it was cute, but not something they'd put up with in their own husbands. Once Amy had exhausted her repertoire of ways to describe lace and hats, she broached the subject closest to both their hearts and blushingly admitted to having a bit of a ding-dong with some guy called Luke she'd fancied for years.

'Woweee, Ohmigod, you didn't? Tell all!' Lucinda exploded.

Amy flushed with pride and hid her delight behind a slice of cucumber. 'Well, his name's Luke Harding, I haven't seen him for years but—'

'Not Luke Harding with the very little bottom?' Lucinda furrowed her brow.

'Well, I suppose so, now that you mention it. Why?'

'Ohmigod, *quel* rat!' darted Lucinda. She was imbued with the spirit of *Breakfast at Tiffany's* and could often be heard shrieking Holly Golightly phrases with a little less grace than la Hepburn.

'Because, darling, he's been living with my friend Kate for ever. Oh. My. God. Poor Kate.'

Amy choked, horrified. She wiped the traces of spluttered Evian from her chin, 'I knew he had a girlfriend, but . . . God Luce, not your Kate.'

Lucinda nodded so hard her rouge noir lipstick became a fuzzy streak of colour against her alabaster face. The effect was like fairground lights from the Big Dipper. Amy felt sick.

'Yes, my Kate. Shit darling.' She paused, sternly contemplating the infidelity. 'Was he good in bed?'

They were hysterical with tears and Evian all over the

place when the photographer walked back in, stifling the deluge of tales relating to Luke Harding's willy. He looked at them, turned round and left. Cue more laughing like drains.

Chapter 2

As she sat in the studio later, picking up pins and Polaroids, Amy mulled over the weekend. It must have been the hat, she thought.

Cecil Beaton, yes, the hat sealed it, a still from the Beaton hall of fame alongside wasp waisted, arched eyebrow beauties of the past. Amy stood back from the mirror and felt pleased with today's look. Her black trouser suit fell around the lean lines of her body; her shoes, a wild black and white animal print, and her new black hat, wide brimmed and striking, invited that finishing touch, two fresh white roses.

Her pride in her outfit would have been frowned upon by her growing coterie of those 'for her own gooders': those friends who seemed rather cross that at the age of twenty-four she was beginning to blossom. Her artistic flair lent her appearance, already fine and aristocratic, a flicker of eccentricity which was at once endearing and glamorous. Her friends, Amy felt, preferred her as the long limbed teenager, bending her knees beneath her billowing skirt to conceal her height, laughing tomboyishly with the lads. Now, they thought, her ego was a little out of control, she was way too involved in the one-too-many novels she'd read and saw life a little too rose-hued for their liking.

She picked up her handbag, fraying at the seams, and shot downstairs to the waiting minicab. Miranda had been a friend for many years, always very beautiful, with luxuriant black locks and lips of such curvature and plumpness that only a handful of mathematicians in the world could have solved the equation of their rare shape and symmetry. Today, Miranda was getting married to Josh, a fitting match for such a sublime young woman.

As Amy stood in the church, her hat obscuring her eyes but her berry mouth duly responding to the emotion of the ceremony – a spectral smile at the gentle fluffing of the lines and a worried retraction of her lips at the prospect of 'till death us do part' – she was only vaguely aware of the attention she attracted. Only vaguely aware in the way that all women are constantly a bit alert to the impression they are creating, the tick tock of self-perception taking up a little corner of their brain. So that as they cry hysterically they dab desperately with a tissue, hunting down wayward smudges of mascara; when pursued by a wailing police car they glance discreetly into the rear-view mirror in order to assume the correct aspect of gravitas. It comes of being brought up to worry first about the cleanliness of your knickers before giving a thought to the fact that the ambulancemen are rushing to gather your limbs up off the road.

After the terrifying soul-searching part of the ceremony was over, the sermon which always dwelt on love and made every couple present reach for one another's hand as a gesture of remembrance, guilt or fear, the part which made one tremble at the magnitude of the vows and wonder at the sanity of the marital pair, Amy glanced around the church and some rows behind recognised a face from her seventeen-year-old past. Luke Harding. A few years ago her younger, lankier self had felt little shame in pleading for invitations to parties where he'd be. She'd sit as alluringly as possible on a sofa somewhere, subtly gesturing to him with her eyelashes or toes, or some such part of her anatomy, discreet enough for her brazenness to have careered over his head. By eleven o'clock Luke was usually ensconced in a nearby armchair with a stouter, more peroxide version of Amy, his wandering hands cruelly drawing her attention to her own comparative lack of voluptuousness. The evenings had always ended thus.

The fact that she was currently receiving significantly more attention from Luke than he was bestowing upon the *All things bright and beautiful* being mouthed by the congregation was satisfying but slightly bewildering. Amy looked behind her to check that she wasn't being shadowed by a Sun-In haired lovely. No. She had his absolute attention, so she turned round and licked her lips seductively? No, she concentrated hard on her songsheet and mimed 'the Lord God made them aaalllll' more convincingly than even the maiden aunts.

Miranda's father had just finished his recounting of his daughter's adolescent peccadilloes (funny how all brides had at least one suitor with a motorbike and indulged a passion for black nail polish at some stage of their journey into womanhood – just as well dad never knew the quarter of it), when Amy, lolling slightly back in her chair and cradling an icy flute of champagne against her burning cheek, felt a brush of warm air behind her left ear. Her facial muscles set rigid as a man's voice whispered his invitation to skip the speeches in favour of a walk in the grounds. Her hand taken hold of, she had little choice but to follow.

Luke Harding, she could hear them now, well that's what everyone's after at a wedding, isn't it? Who could blame him, they would say. Apparently his live-in girlfriend was away, probably just missing her. But Amy didn't care; all those diary entries, the time she rescued his Lucozade bottle from the bin and kept it for two terms, all was vindicated, she thought, just for that soft breath on her neck. But then she would think that, couldn't see the wood for the trees, he wanted a shag, couldn't she see that? They said.

They stood shaded by the imposing grey stone and ivy of the house, drinks in hand, resting against the trunk of an ancient plane tree. Amy could hear occasional bursts of laughter from the open windows of the house as the speeches continued. She could feel her face getting pinker by the second, champagne always did this to her. And there he was, blond, dishevelled in black tie and looking straight at her.

'You broke my heart when I was seventeen, Luke Harding.'

He laughed low, not displeased with the nineteen-year-old self which could have appealed to the heavenly creature who stood beside him.

'No, really.' Amy smiled wanly. A beauty from birth would not have felt the need for such candour.

Luke took her glass out of her hand and kissed her. Just like that. No messing. It was nice, she thought, a warm residue of champagne on their lips, light fingers resting on her bottom, the glass wavering precariously somewhere in between. But it was nothing to how it would feel later, when she played the little details back to herself, rewound the conversation and filled in the bits (champagne glass's whereabouts, envious onlookers, etc.) she had missed due to her participation.

The odyssey through the swirling red carpets of the hotel corridors in search of Luke's room left Amy breathless. Finally, the elusive room 101. Oh hell, thought Amy, a portent if ever there was one. She tried to object but toppled against the door frame instead. The keys rattled the door open and they fell in, giggling as one of the roses dropped off her hat. She bent down to pick it up and he grasped her bottom so firmly she gasped and stumbled forward into the hotel room. Hotel rooms were absolutely her favourite thing, the anonymity which spelled illicit encounters and the joy of pinching little guest soaps, this was the life. Amy dropped backwards onto a bed of such chintzy proportions that for a blurry, tipsy moment she feared herself in her grandparents' bedroom. Luke shed his shoes with purposeful thuds and clambered on his elbows to her side. They held one another's gaze for a few hazy seconds and then continued where they'd left off. He tugged gently at the buttons of her jacket until he could feel the lace edges of her bra and then his hands disappeared beneath the linen in a frenzy of exploration. That old chestnut, Amy half-thought. She felt an ancient flutter of terror as he reached for her breasts, the moment she expected the interloper to sit up and yell that he'd been conned, but that was then – now she was as well endowed, if not better, than the next goddess, so she focused on the pleasant lurching of Luke and felt for his zip.

Chapter 3

Monday night was commonly laundry night in Amy's Battersea abode, the kitchen windows steamed with an excess of clothes drying on radiators and boiling pans of rice. Her two flatmates had done their dark wash before she had time to add her jeans and now she was waiting patiently in a bid to get her whites in before she ran out of underwear altogether. She sat on the floor amidst a heap of washing (she'd been sentimentally avoiding washing what had fondly become her Harding knickers, but the time had come) and, nursing a cup of tea, she related her latest notch to the distinctly moribund looking pair occupying the only two chairs in the kitchen. They egged her on for details, eyebrows rising and plummeting in time to the symphony of her recollections.

'You know, I've fancied him for so long that it had to happen, it was fate. Like Hardy's poem "Faint Hearted in a Railway Station," you know, where he sees a girl sitting on a railway platform and knows if he doesn't get off the train and speak to her he could be altering his entire destiny. Well, we looked at one another and had to get off the train, as it were. Had to know if this was it.'

Cath's eyebrows crashed together as she frowned, all faux bewilderment. 'And was it?'

Amy heard the tone, felt the mockery but chose to shrug it off,

'Well, no. But it was nice and he's got a girlfriend, so we can't. But the point is now we know.'

Cath and Katie sought each other's glance and eye-rolled knowingly at each other as Amy bent down to close the door of the washing machine.

Amy left the Persil and the gruesome twosome and trailed upstairs. As soon as they heard her radio go on in the room above they launched their Waterloo. Cath hugged her knees into her chest.

'Her ego's just gone mad, that's the problem, a few guys show a bit of interest and she's so flattered she jumps into bed with them.'

'Yeah, I read that that's what happens to ugly teen-agers who lose weight or something, they just become intolerable and so lose all their friends.' Katie omit-ted the rest of the article which dwelt on the fact that 'Friends often find it difficult to adjust to the new status ascribed to BTB (beastly turns beauty) as they feel it threatens their domain. There's only so much jealousy a friendship can take before it starts to turn sour'.

'"Meant to meet!" God, she was bad enough with her fantasies when men wouldn't touch her with a bargepole, but now . . . heaven help us. Think of all those years at school when she'd hide behind all those baggy clothes because she was so overweight.'

Katie's subconscious unfairly presented her with a snapshot of Amy in school uniform. She wasn't vastly overweight, in fact she'd been more of a beanpole, but fat was a more heinous sin, so she decided to let it pass uncontested.

Amy pottered around her room for the rest of the evening, listening to old cassettes and sorting out her underwear drawers, one of which was given over to sample pairs of support tights and beige camisoles. Oh the joys of being a fashion assistant. Friends thought your life was awash with complimentary Prada bags and Conran evening gowns, but it was usually all you could manage to beg a zipless pair of canary yellow nylon hotpants (in December). And far from the stylishly groomed environs one might expect of the employee of such a salubrious publication, Amy's room was positively dishabille. Not a Louis XVII clock or bleached oak floor in sight. Merely a well-hoovered but nonetheless thinning beige carpet; a childhood duvet begging to be replaced with Egyptian cotton sheets and chenille throws; an array of Moroccan plant pots from Cambridge market spewing beads and sunflower hairclips; an abandoned set of mini-dumbells from an aeons-old bid to get fit; and the wardrobe of a hopeful twenty-four-year-old. That is, things picked up in sales which will come in handy for *that* cocktail party on the lawn, *that* week on a yacht in St-Tropez, *that* picnic at Glyndebourne. Needless to say most of the outfits hadn't had an airing yet, but we live in glorious anticipation.

Underwear was particularly close to Amy's heart at the moment. It seemed somehow . . . representative. The 'for her' jockey briefs and athletically cut sports bras were an ailing breed. Over the last year or so, as she'd begun to get more confident, less gawky, they had been usurped by mesh and lace and gauzy, flouncy things, mostly white but occasionally black. It heralded a new start for her. She was Madame Bovary and her shoes, thought Amy. When Emma Bovary had wanted to escape her dreary life she wore a pair of garnet-coloured slippers; they elevated her into the lavish realms of her imagination, from the mundane into a world of swirling ballrooms and gentlemen with silver cigarette cases. Her shoes are my underwear. She giggled at the notion, but it was true. Had she not wooed Luke Harding with her 'push 'em up' bra? She certainly knew that if she wore something divine and silky close to her skin she behaved more sexily and was more inclined to wiggle her bottom for the benefit of random strangers. For some women shoes do the trick: in their usual penny loafers they're capable of feeding the cat and rearing seven children but present them with a pair of slut red Manolo Blahnik dagger heels and they metamorphose into a lusty harlot who wouldn't know one end of a potato peeler from the other.

But Amy had never needed many props, or much encouragement, to charge off into wonderland, to follow a fantasy. The artistically gathered dust on her book-shelves bore testament, not to the fact that she didn't read, but rather to the way she felt books should be: worn, old and telling. Outmoded and sentimental some would say. A blade of grass in *The Winter's Tale* reminded her of a summer spent revising at university, flopping on the grass in the quads, trying to memorise soliloquies; a bus ticket in *Crime and Punishment* recalled a gruelling spell of work experience at a publishing house in South Kensington. And now? Now she pulled out a copy of the supremely erotic *Delta of Venus* by Anäis Nin and smiled at the curled pages. During a particularly rampant affair with a photographer last summer she had read this copy in the bath, over breakfast, on the loo, cover to cover.

The written word, the photographic image, both were infinitely more satisfying to Amy than reality. There was a detached beauty about them, a sublime loveliness that made her gasp with almost more pleasure than the most expertly delivered orgasm. She would dearly have loved to mould her life into the cornfield kiss scene from *A Room with a View*, to experience the passion of Elizabeth Bennett as she beheld Mr Darcy or to want to die for lost love like Anna Karenina.

Chapter 4

Lucinda led Amy around Knightsbridge with the awe inspiring confidence of one of a hallowed breed who are met not with disdain but deference when patrolling the upper echelons of Sloane Street's boutiques. There was a type of woman in this part of town whom one imagined wouldn't be able to breathe outside this postal address; place her in an SW11 or an N6 and she'd be reaching for her inhaler, rasping in a bid for her self-respect. Swathed in camel colour, with dashes of Hermes black leather, like some Piebald horse, she walks with balletic steps the length of Walton Street before hailing a cab. Never known to speak or to eat.

They were on a scarf-finding mission. They strolled purposefully from the bitterly cold, early morning, sun-drenched pavements into the silk-walled casements of luxury. Chanel, Farhi, Hamnett. It was curious being in with the right set in these terrifying shops. When Amy was at the publishing house she and another work experience girl would escape most lunchtimes to meander around South Kensington. They developed a formula for being treated seriously in the shops. Turn waxen with glumness before entering and don't smile. Appear uninterested at all times and express delight, loathing and any greeting merely with your eyelashes. Thus a flicker denotes excitement, a plummeting of lashes disgust, and imploring eyelashes 'I'm trying this on' (no pleases here, I'm afraid). They'd stoically wander between the rails in this fashion, suppressing all rapture. Once outside they'd curl over with laughter and 'I must have that's. There invariably followed the adage 'I've got to be rich', chanted so sincerely and with such desperation that Amy almost believed that if she closed her eyes tightly enough the darkness would yield it. Rich boyfriends or cheque-book fraud seemed more likely options, though.

And the scarves: the soft velvet and lace, rich chocolate chiffon, amethyst silk and dense satin. Amy fingered each in turn, draping some over her shoulder, veiling her mouth and nose with one so she looked like a Turkish Delight temptress or just inhaling the trace of perfume and opulence of the fabrics. Amy pondered but Lucinda knew.

'Fifteen of these and seven of those,' she instructed a willowy blonde in a pinstripe trouser suit who had previously just drifted like flotsam amongst the shop's various *objets d'art*. The girl encased the spoils in tissue paper and a serious paper bag for them to carry away.

To reward a successful scarf purchase Lucinda took her to lunch in Daphne's, following her doctrine of never look an expense account in the mouth. The pair sat in the conservatory, the icy sunshine pouring through the windows, the occasional waft of basil or warm bread whetting their appetites. Lucinda was pale and ethereal and beautiful; she'd risen effortlessly in the fashion world partly because she was universally adored and partly because she could couple a Philip Treacy hat with a Saint Laurent suit in a way which women would lay down and die for. Amy thought she was the last word in glamour and was fast becoming her best friend. Lucinda loved Amy because she was witty and charming and ever so slightly gauche, and what a pleasure it was to have someone so fresh around in the airless sometimes stale world of fashion. Lucinda was also stable and clever and the perfect mentor for a would-be heroine. Mutual appreciation was the name of the game. Amy was about the youngest person there, and, if we're being truthful, the most beautiful. She was naturally super-seded in grooming by each and every woman in there (her nails harboured rare cultures, and possibly whole undiscovered tribes, beneath them) and her hair was more crap than coiff, but still, thanks to a beauty routine which was one part witchcraft and two parts tap water, she managed to look fresher than the rocket salad and considerably more appetising. That is, if the appreciative leers of the film moguls and all the fat-walleted (and, all too often, fat-bottomed) men lunching there were concerned. Some, probably the English, gave that coolly arrogant stare which said, 'You may think I wouldn't mind a bit of rumpy with you young filly, but you're sadly mistaken, I'm far too important to fancy you.' Then there were the obviously Latinate appraisals of unadulterated pleasure and the terrified Americans, all PC paranoia: should they smile or would it clash with their Calvin Klein, and what will his wife think and what would his therapist say? Amy smiled inwardly at her cornflake packet guide to national character delineation and decided that it was not crass to generalise, in this instance. Serve them right, pervy bastards.

'So, has Luke called yet?' Lucinda ravished a roulé of goat's cheese without injury to her lipstick.

'No, but I really wasn't expecting him to, and I'm really not too bothered, y'know. It was just a kind of finishing off. Smoothing over. He's not really my type.'

Lucinda smiled sympathetically, wholly believing Amy to be putting a brave face on her misery.

'Lucinda! I don't care, honestly.'

'OK, sweetheart. Why don't you come to a party with me tonight, get out your glad rags and find yourself a bigger fish than Luke to fry? There'll be tons of people there.'

Amy nodded weakly. She wanted a night to catch up with herself after a manic week at work but knew better than to offend Lucinda when she had her charity hat on. 'Luce?' she looked up from a vinaigrette-laden frond of curly endive. Lettuce, let's face it, endive, rocket, raddiccio, bloody lettuce. Amy winced at the stupidity of her fellow diners, paying through the nose for vegetation. Still, as they rationalised it, at least they stayed slim.

'Luce, you do see, don't you, why I'd rather just, y'know, sleep with these guys than go out with them. There's so much more romance in the moment, in some bubble of perfection than ending up wearing jogging pants and stopping shaving your legs.'

Lucinda smiled with as much mother earth compassion as a woman who dictates other women wear hipsters can muster.

'Darling, if you love someone, eventually it doesn't

matter that you've eaten garlic or have furry armpits, really, it becomes more than that.'

Amy squirmed with disgust. QED, she would stick to glossy unreality, faint hearts and all.

'That's your trouble, darling, you want too much – you want a Ralph Lauren ad for a life, but those boys are all gay and babies vomit all the time. It's not so pretty in reality.'

Chapter 5

When was the last time you went to a party which lived up to your expectations? Parties, let's face it, are a metaphor for dashed hopes. By far the best bit is the getting ready. Keats got it right, thought Amy, pushing her toe into the tap to stop it dripping. 'Sweet fancy melteth like bubbles when the rain pelteth.' The anticipation is all, the reality just never seems to come up to scratch.

The steaming lilac vapours rose around her and she sunk beneath the waters as oh so handsome men swirled in her head and her evening built up before her into the glorious technicolour of late 1950s' films. Her head became a rainy Saturday afternoon in front of the television. All ladies in pistachio gowns removing themselves from the whirl of the ballroom to a balcony of orange blossom and cool air; moments later a devilishly good-looking man would emerge onto said balcony and there'd be a brush of skin or proclamation of love. Or perhaps some film noir of rainy nights and cruel, red mouths and dark encounters. Whatever, it had to be better than real life, she thought, rising from the bubbles and simultaneously drenching the floor.

The party was a champagne and oysters affair in Holland Park, at a magazine editor's house. This particular editor loved the world to know she had exquisite sofas and perfect cornicing so was altogether happy to have a relative nobody such as Amy there, as an apostle for her interior decorating. This editor was also known as the worst bitch in London, and a total nutter to boot.

'We call her Dagenham, because she's one stop up from Barking,' a journalist who laboured under the dictatorship of the hostess proudly informed Amy. He sniggered as though he'd just stuck his tongue out to his school teacher. He gave her a whistle-stop run down of the assembled luminaries. Most of them seemed to inhabit the strange cloisters of daytime television. Take a vow of non-entity and you too can retreat there to atone for some long ago sin on prime-time ITV. Amy remained a paragon of unimpressedness as these besweatered men and fluffy women were introduced to her. She bore with fortitude the slings and arrows of insult as they addressed her just beyond her left ear, one eye trawling the room for someone more interesting, or at least more wealthy.

Lucinda was one of life's believers in social self-sufficiency; you picnic on conversation, mingle with ease and charm and flatter effortlessly, or else why were you invited? Amy came from the school of thought which preferred a girlfriend to weld herself to as a permanent source of security, a safety valve for difficult conversations and the human equivalent of a T-shirt declaring, 'Hey, it's OK, I know someone here.' Thus Lucinda bellowed with laughter by the fireplace with a group of curtain designers and Amy stood alone. Lucinda's boyfriend Benjy spotted her, much to her shame and relief.

'I take it you're Amy, I've heard lots about you. Benjy, I go out with Lucinda.' He proffered his hand.

'Yeah, I'm Amy, nice to meet you.' He was very handsome, blue black hair and china blue eyes, slim and slightly wasted looking. Very man-of-the-moment. But Lucinda had obviously been ahead of the game, spotted his fashionable potential three years ago before he was a glimmer in a style guru's eye.

'What do you do?' asked Amy, knowing full well he was a script writer but opting for perfunctory rather than inspired conversation.

'Oh, I write scripts, mostly documentaries right now, but I'm doing the odd project of my own, films of obscure Russian novels, par for the course stuff.' He smiled self-consciously, aware of the pretentious edge. 'How are you finding life as a Voguette?'

'Oh, you know, ups and downs. I've had my fair share of tears in the loos but otherwise it's fun. Lucinda's fantastic.' Amy tried not to wince as she downed an oyster.

'Yeah, she has her moments.' He drifted off into love thought, gazing at his beloved across the room. Amy looked on enviously. Why can't a man look at me like that? she lamented. They were joined by a film producer who snapped Benjy up into industry conversation and Amy found herself on the periphery again. She just smiled on cue and surveyed the room.

In the corner, in the midst of some particularly fine parquet flooring, the editor squealed her objection to various minor royals (they obviously hadn't RSVP'd) and slunk up to the only gorgeous man in the room. Amy instantly recognised him as the rising young star and recently divorced ('It's hard to keep a relationship going when I'm filming in LA and he's on stage in London,' quoth actress wife predictably in some glossy magazine) actor ... she couldn't remember his name. Seth? Gus? Tudor? Something faintly ridiculous anyway. He was so beautiful, Amy had seen him as Mr Rochester and he'd won her heart.

'Forget bloody plain, dull Jane Eyre,' she'd wanted to say, 'I'm here and won't give a damn about the dodgy woman in your attic.' He was the epitome of the man Amy wanted, brooding yet sensitive. And he was talking to the editor who evaporated in a combination of lust and a bustier one press stud too tight whilst he was cool but charming, courteous yet aloof. Amy felt cross and desperate. What was she doing here? There was no real fun in living a glamorous life vicariously. She wanted to belong, but knew she wasn't even approaching gossip column material, let alone *Harpers* cover status (as The Actor, naturally, was). Her legs were too funnel-like, her bank manager had a vendetta against her and she hadn't yet made it to the inner sanctum of fashion where fey men air-kissed her and pleaded with her to wear their velvet jodhpurs. God she was depressed.

Amy the wallflower was in full bloom, her tendrils climbing the russet rag-rolled walls, her leaves clinging to her bucks fizz with all her might. Amius Wallflowerus. All those old insecurities seeped from beneath her newly glam façade. She stood with her legs twenty inches apart in an age old bid to look shorter and less conspicuous. In her mind her lacy g-string became a pair of maroon nylon gym knickers and her hair distinctly stringy. From her

Love: A User's Guide

hideaway beneath a potted lime tree she attempted conversation with a bespectacled columnist (poor eyesight, a definite blessing as he couldn't see her hideousness) but she just sounded like John Major, all *Spitting Image* grey and nothing more riveting to discuss than crudités. Vegetables for heaven's sake. After the third Samaritan (those charitable types who can't bear to see a lone someone fiendishly stuffing twiglets in their mouth in a bid to look busy) had tried to salvage her social reputation and fled in defeat, she thought it kinder to everyone if she went home.

'Don't look so glum sugarplum.' It was the photographer. Memories of her very nice, Anaïs Nin summer came churning back. Art gallery openings and lessons in aperture. Cool Martinis in sweltering bars and not quite as many phone calls as she'd hoped for. In a panic Amy looked down to check that it was actually her red velvet trousers she was wearing and not the brown, holey leggings she'd mentally dressed herself in.

'Toby, my God, hello, what . . .'

He kissed her on the lips and smiled. 'Good to see you, Ames.'

'What are you doing here?' she said, wondering if she could somehow surreptitiously put some lipstick on before their conversation. She settled for licking her lips.

'I'm Dagenham's new favourite. I have to go to all her parties and look the part, foppish Bohemian, neo-Bailey. She fancies herself as a new Jean Shrimpton, albeit twenty years too old.'

Amy was horrified. 'You mean, you and her?' Her nose crinkled in barely concealed disgust.

'No, you darling dummy, I just have to laugh at her jokes and wear velvet scarves a lot.'

Amy thought back to her early impressions of the photographer, so dashing and creative, she had almost fancied herself as Jean Shrimpton. She'd worn a few short floral print dresses and combed her fringe down. Then she'd realised that she was more in love with herself than Toby. She'd spend all her time thinking about how she looked, what she said, and when she wasn't with him she barely remembered what he looked like. And she'd been wildly turned on by his camera. He'd photographed her naked brushing her teeth and she'd soared on a wave of sexiness. But the photographer was not really boyfriend material, and at the time that was what she'd longed for. His lens was sexy but he was just a bit too elusive; she'd finally stopped calling him and hadn't heard from him since.

But tonight he was her saviour and his hallowed position in this inner sanctum made him even more appealing.

'So, shall we go, petal?' he brushed his hair back from his face and she remembered his appeal, brown eyes, long lashes, never quite clean shaven.

'What? Why?'

'Well, you were, I presume, leaving, as you're wearing your coat?' Amy nodded.

'So why don't we go somewhere we can have some fun? The beach?'

'Toby it's eleven o'clock at night in February.'

'OK then, Battersea Bridge.'

They clambered into his Mini (it didn't really do the

trick for her, she had to be honest) and juddered their way to the embankment, laughing at the party guests and breathing the air of silliness. No more best behaviour, they were like children let out of class early. They left the car on some double yellow lines on Cheyne Walk and hopped out. In the wind the little waves of the Thames fluttered against the sides of the houseboats. Amy marvelled at how cosy it would be inside until Toby pointed out the lack of showers and central heating and more dry rot than the Mary Rose.

'You're so boring, Toby, don't spoil everything.'

'I'm your knight tonight doll-face, be careful.'

Yes, Amy thought to herself, knowing that she didn't really want to be doing this. She wanted to be going home with the Actor, to his Mayfair home with deep duckdown pillows and a grand piano like the Robert Redford character in the *Great Gatsby* and then he'd ask her to stay, forever. Instead she held hands with Toby and they walked along the riverbank. Amy wrapped herself in a little dance around the lamp-posts with dolphins swimming down them, he followed her with pretend camera pops, her own little feature film. Her own paparazzo.

They went back to his flat in Chelsea, a studio hangover from the eighties, lots of floorboards and coffee tables strewn with prints, negatives, contact sheets and bits of lenses. She sat on the edge of a leather chair and flipped over the pages of his portfolio. He poured two mugs of whisky and sat on the table in front of her.

'Well, who'd have thought it. What a happy twist of outrageous fortune.'

'We had fun, didn't we?' Amy wasn't sure whether

she meant tonight or last summer, but the whisky tasted nice and Toby's hair flopped gorgeously forward into his eyes. She couldn't resist brushing it away. This time a whisky-tasting kiss. She was drunk enough to forget her boobs on this occasion which made for an altogether happier half hour (not bad going). The photographer took his time and interspersed licks and kisses and enjoyable stroking bits with his own personal slant on lovemaking which was to film the process. (Now whilst your average mum of three in Surrey can generally get away with cavorting before a video camera without more than a select few blokes at the local squash club having a butcher's, a young aspirant like Amy has to be more wary of who films her pert bottom looking positively buoyant. Heaven forfend, only this very evening she'd mingled with the celestial habitués of TVAM.) When Amy saw Toby fiddling with his equipment (please forgive) her initial thought was of her mother, who would have dissolved in a glut of Catholic cursing ('Jesus. St Anthony. Child. What were you doing?'). Her second thought was 'hmmmmm, rather like the sound of that,' so with her best breast forward she abandoned herself to the glories of voyeurism and lust.

Chapter 6

In the pale Sussex light of Monday morning Amy found herself humming in a faintly hysterical manner. She hummed as she removed cowpats from a field. This morning she was in no mood to marvel at the ridiculous nature of her job, she hummed in the way we all tend to do when there's something we'd rather not think of. Hum to escape your horrible faux pas. Manically and with acute embarrassment. Amy dumped another cowpat into her bin liner and hummed a bit more.

'Great job darling, nearly there.' Amy yelped with horror.

'Bloody hell Lucinda, don't do that you'll scare the cows.'

'Ouch, touchy, what's wrong with you?' The affront soared over Lucinda's head and in galumphing Sloane style she carried on regardless.

'What happened to you on Saturday? I saw you leave with Toby, are you two on again?'

In no mood to discuss her sin, shame and downfall, Amy shrugged and mercifully Lucinda ran to the aid of the model startled by a rabbit. (Or could it have been the other way around?)

We should probably address the cowpats first. Cow-pats, because in an ideal world fields don't have them; they have cows, naturally, but not ugly plops of dung. On any other morning Amy could probably have waxed lyrical on the joy of the cowpat, the rural idyll rather than some bucolic, Capability Brown-type excuse for one. She would have persuaded the stylist to leave the cowpats in. But today she was more concerned with her own downfall.

'*Paradise Lost*, with me as Eve.' Oh sin, depravity and video cameras. Oh Shame.

Amy is, as we should perhaps know by now, at least as far as matters of the flesh are concerned, a woman of the nineties. We've witnessed the Harding episode and left her in pre-Lapsarian bliss with Toby. So whence all this guilt? Well, not guilt at all actually, that wouldn't be very nineties. More disappointment and terror. She wondered if sado-masochists (real ones, not stockbrokerish, silk cord and velvet blindfold types) felt ashamed of themselves the next morning. Or did they have the courage of their sexual convictions? Was she a pervert for enjoying the camera bit? Probably, she obliged her conscience. (Catholicism!) Well, now she was paying. Divine Retribution. (Like every Catholic caught out by fluke she put it down to Divine Retribution. Tripped over after making a nasty comment about someone's thighs? Divine Retribution. Migraine whilst enjoying the fantasy of credit card fraud? Yes, you've guessed it.) Amy was just feeling like a cowpat because she was horrified that right now, as she loaded poo into a bin liner, a group of pseudo-Bohos smoking Gauloises and sipping

Mexican beer might be leering at her hips, thighs and heaven forbid, she couldn't bear to think about it, her tits! (It was eight o'clock on Monday morning but it was perfectly plausible that a group of grown men with satellite TV of their own would hot-foot it round to Battersea to make a meal of her in flagrante.) Or, oh Lord, even worse, it wasn't beyond the realms ... the photographer was a friend of Damien Hirst. She pictured the Tate, the Turner Prize, queues of people waiting to see not Mother and Child but Photographer and Floozy. All disparate, abstract televisual images of her body parts, swilling around in formaldehyde. Fuck!

The cows snuffled and Amy sat on a crumbling stone wall, her binliner at her feet, bathed in the milky winter sunlight. The models frolicked and the photographer yelled at them as Lucinda hopped on the wall beside her, and whispered, 'When this is over let's pop down the road to Charleston, the Bloomsbury group place, you can cadge a lift from me back to London.'

Amy, in her emotionally precarious state, was overcome with fondness for Lucinda and kissed her on the cheek before shedding a little tear. Lucinda gave her a hug and together they sucked on the models' Marlboros and watched with horrified objectivity as the lunatics took over the asylum.

They slammed the doors of Lucinda's battered sports car and tore off down the meandering Sussex lanes, narrowly avoiding decapitating curious farm animals. Lucinda was a brisk driver to say the least. Amy feigned a relaxed demeanour but all the while dug her nails deep into the upholstery. Charleston was just the thing for a guilt trip. Whilst Amy was feeling all seedy and disgusted with the late twentieth century she was slowly seduced by the goings on in twenties' and thirties' Sussex. The passage of time lent them a certain air of glamour, but there was no escaping the fact that the Bloomsbury Group, purveyors of great art and literature, had been distinctly seedy themselves as far as sexual antics were concerned, and Amy began to feel in better company with her debauchery.

She drifted around the house marvelling at its freshness. The walls a harlequin pattern of sundrenched colours, yellows, muted blues and greens. The bedrooms where great economists and artists had formed love triangles as colourful and bizarre as the decoration, and where Virginia Woolf had lain in bed listening as the occasional fish flipped over with a splash in the lake at the front of the house. The lake was more of a puddle but in the overgrown grass on its banks was scattered statues, classical men and a curious levitating woman. Amy lounged amongst the winter jasmine in the fast fading light of late afternoon and slowly recovered.

Restored and reassured by Lucinda and the lascivious Bloomsbury Set that her life wasn't totally crap and that her lusty languishings weren't going to end up as headline news in the *Sun* tomorrow, she faced her return to London with fortitude and a Vanessa Bell print plant pot from the local shop.

On the drive back Lucinda and Amy nattered and chomped Maltesers, sniggering about models and lamenting London life.

'Benjy and I should just get a little place out here,

paint a bit, do something freelance and cook. I could have a garden and grow flowers the colour of boiled sweets, we'd have little fluttering muslin curtains, with a cupboard for our wellies . . .'

'Luce, you'd be soooo bored, you'd hate it. And what would you do freelance? Dress the local Women's Institute for its annual fête?'

'No, I had these friends who moved to the country and made papier mâché things.'

Amy laughed. 'Like what, for heaven's sake?'

'Well, I think it was cows, or it could have been mushrooms.' Amy spluttered with laughter. 'No, like toadstools, huge bloody toadstools with red spots.' Lucinda redeemed herself.

'And?'

'And they made money out of it, enough to buy a goat and go to Morocco every six months.'

Amy shrieked at Lucinda's quite obviously trustafarian notions. 'And then they inherited the parental stately home and the goat had its own wing and they called the child-product of their liaison Bicester after their time in rural paradise?'

'Don't scoff, Ames, I'm surprised you're not dying to go and live in the shadow of the Rude Man of Cerne Abbas with some Florizel-type goatherd, play Perdita and copulate madly, Druid fashion.'

'And how did Druids copulate?'

'You've seen the penis on that thing, use your imagination,' smirked Lucinda.

'Anyway, don't scoff, I loved Florizel. I once went out with an Etonian just because when they go rowing they wear those straw hats with flowers all over them. He was like a blond angel, all flowers, princely notions but innocent peasant love.' Amy smiled with self-consciousness at her overly romantic ideas, but she had loved him a bit and the memory made her quite nostalgic. Then she caught him in the cloakroom at a ball snogging his best friend. Exit Florizel. By the time they'd arrived back in London Lucinda had persuaded Amy that there was life after homemade pornography and that she should come to Dorset next weekend to stay with Benjy's sister who had a place. As one does. There'd be a few people and they could all paint and have walks, smoke some grass and relax. Amy nodded in consent and went home to bed, totally knackered.

Chapter 7

Amy didn't have a clue what Dorset had in store so she packed her *that* weekend in the country wear, thrilled that at last her life was catching up with her wardrobe. This particular outfit was the result of many a Laura Ashley sale and consisted of Little Lord Fauntleroy hats and waistcoats and some sludge coloured wool socks. The other guests would all be undoubtedly trendy and Lucinda's will would reign supreme, with every woman in hipsters, but what the hell.

The car tooted in the street and Amy ran out, her small suitcase swinging in her hand. The car was an assortment of Benjy's friends. They were all quite sweet. One was a scriptwriter, one a cauliflower-eared accountant and the other an Irish ex-pop star. Amy was introduced but immediately forgot their names since she was so busy trying to look pretty as she shook their hands. Not because she fancied them, just because pretty is as pretty does, whatever that meant. They whizzed along with the radio blaring, squashed into the back like a packet of sausages.

The road leading up to the cottage was so strewn with stones and potholes that they emerged rubbing their buttocks for dear life. The cottage was a rustic pink colour that wouldn't have looked out of place nestling away in the Umbrian Hills. The winter light gave it a warm glow and tucked away behind huge teracotta pots of bay trees and strange cacti was a tiny front door with a huge lion's head doorknocker. On closer inspection the paint was weathered and flaked to the touch and Amy could just make out the etchings of a Renaissance fresco above the downstairs windows. In fact Lily and friends had laboured over this last August but hadn't accounted for English winter besetting their Italian *palazzo*. Wow, Amy gasped in barely audible admiration. They piled out, myriad carrier bags and shabby paperbacks and an army of sleeping bags. At an upstairs window appeared the aforementioned Lily, Benjy's sister. Her plaited hair hanging forward, her face covered in—

'Yoghurt, I was out this morning and got windburn, yoghurt does the trick,' she yelled.

The boys exchanged bewildered-by-women glances as she disappeared and ran downstairs to open the door. Everyone got a kiss, despite, or perhaps because of, the yoghurt, and she ushered them into her living room cum studio.

The various merits of strawberry versus mango yoghurt were discussed at length by the assembled company, nine in all. Not so scary as Amy had expected but all a bit older and a bit cooler than her own friends. They decided that a walk was number one on the agenda and anyone not on for that could meet them in the local pub in an hour or so. Amy tugged on a tweedy peaked cap and, gratified by the 'ooh how divine' from Lily, walked off down the rubbly driveway with a little skip. She discovered from

Benjy that Lily was a painter with a bit of pottery thrown in who'd absconded from the City two years ago in favour of the good life. Well, she had two chickens, one of which acted as her alarm clock and one for eggs, but she was basically besieged every weekend by friends so she couldn't be classed as a true country dweller.

Amy tried to take up this conversation with Lily, whom she took to instantly because Lily was not only exceptionally pretty but the epitome of the Girl Men Fall in Love With, so Amy thought she'd watch and learn. Or at least Amy perceived this to be true; not to be too convoluted she was The Girl Women Want Men to Fall in Love With, because women liked her and believed in her. She was pretty, eccentric and fun. But we all know that these virtues, not being anatomical, don't necessarily count for much with men, so women go on getting it wrong. And in their own way it's the women who fall in love with these women because they're what men so often aren't. Gorgeous and nice.

Lily, though, seemed more intent on waving at the stony-faced passengers on the train to London than making small talk, so Amy, spurred on by the howling wind, joined in. Such abandonment was wholly uncharacteristic for Amy who only really let go in her imagination. But here she was, running shrieking around what she thought must be Hardy's Egdon Heath with the grace of a deer and the lungs of Pavarotti. Lucinda watched with amusement, gratified that all was going according to plan. She'd known she had to do something about Amy, she just wasn't sure what. What she did to fashion spreads she liked to do to life, the odd hitching

41

of a hemline to create the perfect silhouette here, a bit of excitement for her friends there. It was what she was good at. What she did know was that a weekend in Lily's company was never going to do anyone any harm, and certainly not Amy.

On the way back to the pub they discussed their favourite Hardy novels. Hands went up for *Return of the Native*, the dour Irish pop-star backed *Jude the Obscure* and Lily spun round and opted for *Tess*, 'Don't you think that Amy has lips like Tess? Come on boys, you could pop strawberries into that mouth very happily.' Amy flushed with delight and the boys turned away, embarrassed and grunting whilst Lily smiled straight at her.

They commandeered a green velveteen corner of the pub for most of the afternoon, consuming Guinness in indecent quantities and staying on to beat the locals in the pub quiz that evening. Amy's head swam with a creamy deluge of Bailey's and whisky. In an effort to get home they all linked arms for stability and trundled through puddles and ditches.

'It'll all be OK,' Lily soothed. 'I've fallen asleep behind the hedgerow before now and got a lift home on the milkfloat the next morning, so all is most definitely not lost . . .' she trailed off with a little slur. They stumbled all the way back to the cottage and numerous bruises later tumbled into the irrelevant sleeping bags.

The morning was too painful for Amy to bear to move. She lay as still as possible knowing that if she lifted so much as a fingernail she'd be sick. And I just can't be, she told herself, I'm not fourteen anymore, I can't be running to the loo to throw up, it's way too embarrassing. But the room had a vague smell of turps and the more Amy thought of it the iller she felt. Eventually she leaned over and lifted the sash window. Ice cold air blasted in and the flimsy cotton curtains were caught up in a frantic dance with the wind. Hastily closing it and flopping back onto the bed with the exertion Amy gazed blankly at an array of canvasses stacked up against the wardrobe until Lily peeped her head around the door.

'You look as rough as I feel,' she ventured.

'Hmmm, could be right there.' Amy winced, not daring to breathe.

'I'm so sorry, you're only a child, we shouldn't have been so rough on you.'

'Lily, I'm not a Mormon, I have been pissed before.'

Lily threw herself down onto the end of the very soft bed. Amy's stomach leapt and lurched. Don't bounce, she pleaded silently. Please.

Lily sat there looking so pretty that Amy couldn't quite bear it. Even her dark circles were poetic and a smattering of pale freckles made her look all daisy-like, an advert for fresh, ice cold milk next to Amy's wan, 'malaise before Nurofen' look. She sunk into her pillow feeling that life had dealt her an unfair blow. Lily clambered in next to her and they huddled under the duvet together groaning gratuitously, born-again teetotallers.

Lucinda walked in bearing mineral water and vitamin C tablets, but seeing the writhing, grumbling duvet almost span on her Birkenstocks and left.

'Stop right there, Gunga Din!' yelled Lily, her head appearing over the parapet of the duvet. Lucinda sheepishly walked towards them with her mini pharmacy.

'You weren't worried that I'd seduced poor Amy were you?' Lily grinned.

'No, of course not Lil, I just thought you were sleeping.' Amy had never seen Lucinda, veteran of the social exchange, look so flummoxed before. She wondered at the cause, shot a puzzled glare at Lucinda and gratefully quaffed her water and Redoxon. Then the fog and pain lifted a little and it began to dawn on her that the reason the men weren't swarming round Lily was that everyone perhaps knew something she didn't: i.e., Lily preferred women to men. Amy felt Lily's bare legs next to hers. Amy was naked (except for Chanel No 5? No, except for Mum deodorant and last night's *eau de* pub) and Lily had a lacy vest and shorts on and indecently golden limbs. She reasoned soberly – what a joke – that (1) Lily probably didn't fancy her anyway, (2) Lucinda was there and if she did fancy her she'd be more discreet than to make a pass whilst her brother's girlfriend (and Amy's boss!) was in the room and (3) Lily was much too pretty for Amy and she should be so lucky, basically. Having established these points Amy felt no better at all. She remembered her legs were prickly and she hadn't cleaned her teeth. She sat brusquely upright and jabbered with an inanity which baffled even Lucinda.

Assorted bodies in various states of disarray sat around Lily's enormous kitchen table. All pretext of glamour had been abandoned. Faces were unshaven, contact lenses were replaced by unappealing spectacles and painterly pretensions were superseded by naff jogging pants. Needless to say everyone felt much more at home and bonded over sizzling bacon and boiling kettles. Benjy had burnt his fingers on some toast and shaking his hand in annoyance turned to Lucinda.

'You did tell Amy, didn't you, Lucinda?' Lucinda looked sheepishly into her coffee.

'Well, no, but what's there to tell? "Oh by the way Lily's gay and has a penchant for young innocents?" Don't be ridiculous, Benjy, anyway I actually think it'll be good for Amy to be flattered a bit, looked after. It'll also broaden her horizons and keep her away from accountants like Luke Harding. Sorry Craig [he of cauliflower ear and calculator], but Amy needs some real life experience.' Benjy looked at his intended with horror.

'Luce, you're a monster. Amy's fine without a splash of lipstick lesbianism to enhance her life, and Lily's not gay, she just thinks it's glamorous and Sapphic to kiss women.'

'Precisely. She and Amy can fuel each other's romantic imagination for a while and I won't have to pick up the few little pieces of self-respect Amy has left at the end of her liaisons.'

'You're weird, Luce,' he said, sitting on a sofa in the corner and gazing at his emerging blister.

The male guests looked baffled by the notion and hid their heads in the Sunday papers whilst tucking away the image of the two lithe temptresses entwined into the recesses of their minds for a little rewind later. The females sulked inwardly that they hadn't been singled out by Lily. Though of course that wasn't their thing, it would have been nice to have been asked.

Upstairs ears were too sleepy to burn. The girls lay

Clare Naylor

somnolent and languid on the bed, dozing and dreaming in a Bailey's induced haze; Lily's hand resting softly on Amy's shoulder. Thus they lay until midday when Lily's deeply unreliable rooster-alarm took it upon himself to rally the hung-over from their slumber. The household twitched and winced with pain at the shrill intrusion; Amy opened her eyes to find Lily's pert nose wrinkling awake. Her tummy did a little jitterbug of anxiety and she tried hard not to shake her pins and needles ridden limbs for fear of startling Lily who let out a baby sigh and cautiously opened one eye.

'Ooooh, morning,' she cooed, smiling with her eyes screwed up against the light.

'Hi,' said Amy, a gnaw of nerves tightening inside her, trying to confront her new found knowledge of Lily.

'How lovely to wake up next to such a pretty mouth,' Lily mused to no one in particular. Amy felt like she was watching a French art house film with few words and an erotic edge lacing every look. The tightening in the pit of her stomach melted into warm tingles and spread down to her toes. Lily's smile coerced Amy to follow suit. Amy didn't manage the smile, but the darts of heat assaulting her body gave her the courage to lift her eyes and look at Lily. A nod is as good as a wink in some circles. Lily lifted a finger to Amy's lower lip and, tracing it gently, softly pushed it into her mouth. Amy was torn between fear and an overwhelming desire to taste Lily's plump peony-petal lips. Tilting her face towards Lily's their lips collided full and gently. The soft skin of the encounter surprised Amy, no coarse

46

cheeks grazing her own; the downy symmetry of their curves caused their bodies to brush, Gemini-like, against one another. Amy's fear evaporated. How divine, she thought.

Chapter 8

Amy let the water in the shower scald her; she lathered up an old cracked cake of Imperial Leather all over her and sneezed at the smell. She felt fully fledged, extremely sophisticated and she grinned like the cat who'd eaten the canary. And a ruddy pretty canary at that, she smirked. Like Vita Sackville-West, Sappho and a Georgia O'Keefe flower all rolled into one. Yum. The brimming embodiment of femininity stepped out of the shower into the steaming condensation of the minuscule bathroom and dried every limb with histrionic *tendresse*.

In the kitchen everyone sat around peeling feathers from freshly laid eggs and shelling peas in a quaint but pointless way. They'd already decided to have fish and chips on the quayside for lunch.

'Guys, please don't do too many. Every Monday morning I'm left with a colander full of the bloody things and every Friday I throw them out,' begged Lily as she bent over to feed her cat.

'Why don't you make soup or something?' Lucinda advised helpfully.

'Because there's a Marks and Spencers in town and they do it for forty-seven pence a tin.' Everyone saw her point but carried on shelling peas anyway. Amy made her entrance. Gone were the tweeds and in their place was a sort of lavish sarong garment, all the colours of the rainforest with a couple of parrots for good measure. She was barefoot and satisfied. Hmmm, pondered her audience. Hmmm, pondered Lucinda. Did her the world of good, obviously.

In town they browsed around all the haphazard china shops and whiled away an hour in a second-hand book-shop. Amy's mind was half on the day, half on her new found glow. It wasn't really to do with Lily, not in the way that having a man made you all focused on that man. Amy was thinking of herself and what a sexy individual she was.

Lily and Amy broke away and made their way along the windswept quayside, down some fearsome steps and, sitting just clear of the water, munched their vinegar-sodden chips, chirping about boats and books and chick-ens and . . .

'It's been fun having you here Amy,' said Lily. 'Come again in the summer when we can have candlelit picnics in the wood at midnight.' She held her hand on Amy's thigh; Amy visualised wood nymphs and moon bathing.

'Love to.' She coaxed the last chip from the bottom of the soggy bag.

She was interrupted by a pair of navy blue trousers towering above Lily. The trousers slowly bent down and kissed Lily's cheek.

'Good God woman, you'll be the size of a tank if you carry on eating those things.'

Lily's shriek scattered the seagulls padding around beside them.

'Orlando Rock, well he-low!' Amy puzzled at the name – she'd heard it before, a thousand times, but couldn't place it. School? Male model? My dentist? She was craning her neck around to see who Lily was hugging so furiously when she caught a glimpse of his profile. My God, it's Mr Rochester. Her heart stopped beating and she stopped chewing her chip. The Actor. Here. On the beach. But how on earth does Lily know him? The pair stopped cavorting and Lily introduced them.

'Amy, Orlando. Orlando, Amy.' And? willed Amy.

Mr Rochester, alias Orlando Rock bent down and shook Amy's hand firmly.

'Always a pleasure to meet one of Lily's friends,' he breathed huskily and stared her crash bang in the eye. Amy gulped and smiled.

'Hi.' Feeble, Amy, you can do better than that.

They stood around awkwardly for a couple of seconds before Lily pulled Amy to her feet and, one arm around Orlando's waist, marched them off to an olde tea shoppe. They sat amongst women of a certain age whose little fingers cocked as they sipped Earl Grey. They ordered cream tea and iced buns with a cream horn for good measure.

'Lapsang Suchong, please,' requested Lily.

''Aven't got none, luv,' said an elderly waitress, her yellowing lace apron somehow not managing to convey much olde worlde charm.

'OK, Tetley's then, please.' The lady was clearly not impressed.

'We 'ave Earl Grey, English Breakfast or Rose'ip.' This struck Amy as a curious array, but given the take it or leave it tone it was presented in Lily conceded and opted for rosehip. She and Orlando chatted about an assortment of glamorous topics, when they were last in Chile and my God we haven't seen each other since the Warhol party in New York. The more Amy thought of to say the less she was capable of contributing to the conversation. She just smiled periodically and sought out the fragrance of Bergamot in her Earl Grey, carrying out a little experiment to see if when you held your breath and stopped sniffing, you could still taste the Earl Greyness of the tea. You couldn't. Then she noticed the horrible peeling border of the wallpaper and the swirly patterned carpet. She'd prefer to have high tea in Claridges, she decided. Looking around at the clientele she suddenly became aware that more than one middle-aged lady was glancing in their direction, in one case accompanied by a whisper to her companion. Amy heard the buzz in her head,

'Isn't that whatshisname, terribly handsome?'

'But not nearly so tall as he looks on the telly.'

'Yeees, you're right Jessica, now what is his name?'

Orlando Rock. Amy filled in. His eyes were inordinately blue and his features so aquiline and delicate he looked like a Roman God. And he was sitting at her table tucking into a cream horn. They barely exchanged a glance, but when they did his was warm and friendly.

A stout figure in pink bouclé loomed over the table, peering down at them from her hornrimmed spectacles.

'Hello Mr Middlemarch.' She nodded, very pleased with her memory and casual wit.

The actor looked up and smiled kindly.

'Hello,' then turned back to Lily and Amy for conversation.

'You were ever so good, would you mind signing my lottery ticket?'

He obliged and she puffed back to her table like a Trafalgar Square pigeon.

'I wasn't even in bloody *Middlemarch*,' confided Orlando. The trio burst into repressed olde tea shoppe laughter and devoured the rest of the scones. When the time came to leave, Amy had ad libbed a few entrées into the chit-chat and even raised a smile from her God.

'Amy works with Benjy's girlfriend at *Vogue*,' Lily informed him. Amy smiled weakly and resisted saying 'for my sins'. Her job sounded so stupid. Yes, I'm a multi-dimensional person who knows about hemlines and can spot Versace leggings at fifty paces.

'So how long have you and Lily been together?' he enquired sensitively when Lily had leapt up to go to the loo. No. Please God No. It's not like you're even in with a chance Amy, she told herself. But Oh No. He thinks I'm gay.

'Oh, well, we're not . . . umm exactly . . .'

'It's OK, I've known Lily for years. It's hardly a secret,' he reassured. I'm trying to flirt with him. I have a God of stage and screen. Mr Rochester. Mr Middlemarch. At my table. And he thinks I fancy women. Fuck.

'We've only just met. Yesterday in fact. I'm only here for the weekend.'

He chuckled throatily.

'Lily always was a fast worker.'

Lily reappeared at the table, shaking her hands dry.

'Shall we go, guys? The celebrity angle's getting them confused, the waitress just asked me if I was Goldie Hawn.'

They said fond goodbyes outside. A Gargantuan hug for Lily and a polite pair of kisses for Amy. Good going though, she thought, from a mega-star.

'Lily, let's have supper mid-week, I'm filming just round the corner, I'll give you a ring. And Amy,' he turned his attention to her. She felt ridiculous in her Amazonian sarong ensemble, as though she were wearing a brightly coloured paper napkin. 'Amy, it's been a pleasure, and who knows, *Vogue* have asked me to do a shoot for them, maybe now I'll oblige.'

Puff. Amy was Trafalgar Square, Leicester Square and any other pigeon you cared to mention. Pre-historic and Post-modern pigeon. Her feathers puffed proudly and her chest burst with pride and excitement. She pushed the gay thought to the back of her brain and longed to be back at work where the actor could call her, as she knew he must.

Chapter 9

They drove back from Dorset late at night and Amy fell asleep in the back of the car, her head lolling on the Irish ex-pop-star's shoulder. She occasionally woke with a start to find her mouth hanging open and quickly closed it and dropped off again. When they pulled into her street it was past midnight and she barely had the energy to utter her goodbyes.

Needless to say another Monday morning found her feeling less than raring to go. But she tugged herself from bed and by nine o'clock was picking at a flapjack and diet Coke behind her desk. She was doodling ideas for a feature on Council Estate Glamour when the phone rang. In her best Judi Dench voice she leapt to answer it.

'Hello, fashion.' What a ridiculous thing to say.

'Amy it's me, Cath. Where were you this weekend, you dirty stop-out?'

Her stomach plummeted. Not the actor. She'd known it wouldn't be, but Cath. Oh God, what did she want?

'Cath, hi. I thought I'd told you I was going to Dorset.'

'Of course, sorry, forgot. Anyway, I'm having some people to dinner tonight, will you be around?' Amy wasn't sure whether this question meant she was invited or expected to disappear.

'I'm in I think, but don't worry about cooking for me, I can just have cheese on toast in my room or something.'

'Oh, well if my friends aren't good enough . . .' Cath 'joked'. But she wasn't joking. She was chippy.

'Cath, if you're inviting me I'd love to come. Shall I?'

'OK, I'll buy extra broccoli then,' volunteered Cath grudgingly. That Girl! fumed Amy. And broccoli, I hate broccoli.

Girl dying her hair in the kitchen sink. Two neighbours, mules and dangling fags talking over the fence whilst hanging washing out. Lots of rollers. Amy was jotting down her views on Council Estate Glamour when Tash, the features editor, burst into the office in search of a thesaurus.

'Tash, I've been meaning to ask you, are you interviewing Orlando Rock?'

'Trying. He's very elusive, I suppose I'll have to go down to the set in Dorset to seek him out. He's also avoiding journalists because of his divorce.' Amy winced at the mention of his wife, ex or otherwise.

'What's he doing in Dorset?' Amy ventured, still doodling and trying to sound nonchalant.

'Hardy. *Return of the Native* I think.' Tash pushed her cuticles back with a pencil and lost interest in the conversation and thesaurus and left. Amy returned to her brief. Model looking seductive in satin slip as man sits in vest with beer cans in armchair behind her. She chewed her biro and daydreamed about having to return to Dorset for a photoshoot. Then she could wow him with her loveliness and convince him of her heterosexuality.

Or at the least bisexuality, she purred, still proud of her new found status.

All day she sat at her desk with one ear listening for the phone, trawling the newspapers for snippets about her new paramour. But each time she came across one she was plunged into despair as she saw his leading lady. All raven locks and creamy skin. When Lucinda came to rescue her at lunchtime the trough of her depression was river deep.

'Lunch, darling?' Lucinda called up from reception where she'd been gossiping with some girls from *Homes and Gardens*. Making sure the office answerphone was on, just in case, Amy went down to meet her. Huddling under the security guard's umbrella they headed through the swing doors out into the noise and drizzle of Hanover Square. It was much too wet to contemplate a lunch hour browsing in Bond Street so they opted for smoked salmon and cream cheese bagels in a café across the road. Amy slumped over her coffee. Lucinda too hung her head over her lunch. Benjy hadn't spoken to her since last night when in a fit of tiredness she'd accused him of ogling a girl in the petrol station on the way home.

'I know I overreacted, in fact I'm sure he barely noticed her, but I couldn't help myself, Ames, he barely looked at me all weekend.' She dropped another two sugarcubes into her coffee.

'Steady with the sugar, Luce. Look, anyone can see he loves you, but it's not easy after so many years to be all over each other all the time.'

'I know, but sometimes I just have uncontrollable banshee moods. I just yell for no reason, and I quite enjoy it, it's the only way of getting a response sometimes. I don't think men are capable of loving as much as women.' Lucinda swirled her spoon in her still untouched coffee.

'I know, you just have to look at literature. Anna Karenina couldn't find anyone who'd love her enough so she had to jump in front of a train.'

'And Eustacia Vye in *Return of the Native*, "To be loved to madness is my one desire" she said, and she ended up dead too because all the men in her life were hopeless.'

Amy winced at the mention of Eustacia Vye and the delectable actress in Orlando's film flashed into her mind. Oh God I'm obsessed, she thought. I think I love him. The thought of Orlando sent her appetite scuttling for cover. The girls morosely picked the paper tablecloth apart and Lucinda stabbed her fork into a huge piece of chocolate cake until she was about to pop.

'And I've got to go to one of Cath's dinner parties tonight.' Amy stared out of the window onto the grey pavements slopping with rain.

'I've no idea why you don't move out, Ames. Those girls are poisonous.'

'Yeah, but I was at school with them and they're not so bad most of the time, they're just pathological bitches.' She shrugged with resignation.

Cath's dinner party was hideous. More bankers than was necessary crammed around the small dining table dropping risotto and red wine on the tablecloth that Amy's dead grandmother had made. Clever people who should have known better did their best to be boring and right wing. The house smelled of broccoli and Amy was taunted because of her vapid job.

'Yes, I know but I just don't think I'd enjoy working in the City,' she apologised. Why the bloody hell am I allowing these idiots to bother me, she fretted. But she knew it harked back to a long time ago, longer ago than she cared to address and so she let them taunt her as they had done when she was the skinniest girl in the third form. She volunteered to wash up as she knew that none of the Hoorays would set foot in a kitchen and skulked to bed without saying goodnight, although she knew there'd be hell to pay for her 'rudeness' tomorrow.

Chapter 10

'Amy darling it's me, mum. Ermm. Are you there? No? Well, it's just that I've got these tickets, well actually daddy got them, only he's ... well, he can't come. So we thought maybe, if you're not busy, perhaps you'd like to go ... with me ... oh darling, there's a strange bleep, does that mean I've run out of time? Well, maybe I'll phone you later, lots of love darling. Bye.'

Thus it was that Amy's mother, in a round-about mother-not-quite-getting-to-grips-with-this-answerphone-lark way invited her to the theatre on Thursday night. Now the laws of stage and screen dictate that one can't be both on stage and on set at the same time. But Amy's world and the excuse of a charity event attended by the Princess of Wales dictated otherwise, so for the Gala performance of *Henry IV Part I* with Orlando Rock as Hotspur, Amy and her mother had seats in the stalls.

Amy is a bright girl, and she knows in a vague way that the stalls are not really visible from the stage, but she's also an optimist, so she left work at three o'clock on Thursday afternoon to indulge her optimism fetish. She exfoliated and lathered, waxed and waned, creamed and preened an excessive amount. She put her make-up on in the nude (very important for that oh so sexy frisson in one's gait) and combed her hair with the loving strokes of a seven-year-old grooming her pony. She slipped into her exactly-the-green-of-her-eyes silk shirt and her oldies but goodies trousers. Veeerryy nice, she thought as she assessed her appeal. Not a hint of the lesbian, just lots of lipstick.

She stood in the foyer beside the rows of jelly babies and KitKats looking ravishing amongst the red velvet and living in a little daydream of being Orlando's lover. She looked alluring and the second someone caught her eye she shyly and conspiratorially lowered her head, convincing them that, yes, she was the great woman behind the great man, but let's just keep that between you and me Mr Theatre-goer, don't want the press crawling all over the place do we? Don't want to upstage the tiaraed one in the stalls. Her status as the new woman in his life was a fact she was sure she had convinced everyone in the crowded foyer of until her mother rushed in. Her raincoat sodden, panting and delving into her abyss of a handbag for the tickets, her mother cried,

'Darling Amy, I barely recognised you. You look lovely,' to the assembled theatre-goers, a few of whom turned to witness the transformation.

'Thanks mum, do I usually look so awful?' Amy mumbled, her chin buried in her chest.

'Now don't be so sensitive, I just said you looked very nice. Now where are those tickets?' She foraged some more, a truffle pig let loose in the foyer.

They sat back in their seats as the pprrrinngg of the bell sounded in the theatre. Amy's stomach lurched with churning motions usually reserved for first dates and job interviews. She practised different poses: coy, ebullient, nervous (a theatre wife should always have sympathetic stage fright for the one she loves), tragic (it was *Henry IV* and Hotspur's death was imminent). As she and her mother flicked through the programmes she, ever so casually, let slip that she'd in fact had tea with the phenomenally famous Orlando Rock on Sunday (just enough volume to impress the neighbours), but her mother wasn't deeply thrilled.

'And what were his parents thinking of do you think? Sheer cruelty to give a child such a ridiculous name. Was he nice, dear?'

Amy gave up but felt suitably elevated in her neighbours' esteem so resumed her careful countenance. You never know, he just might look up during a soliloquy and see me.

His performance was impeccable and the actress playing his wife was attractive in a RSC actress type way but really nothing to write home about, and certainly not someone you'd invite to share champagne in your dressing room afterwards, she reassured herself. When the time came for Hotspur to oh-so-heroically die she was barely consolable.

'"Food for worms ... etc ... Fare thee well great heart."' Dies. She could hardly bear it. God, she fancied him in his thigh high boots and poniard thrusting in a Shakespearean fashion. Pure animal sex in chainmail.

In her mind she was whisked onto the stage at the end and kissed and thanked: 'I couldn't have done it without the love of this wonderful woman,' crooned Orlando, his poniard pressing against her thigh. The audience cheered as she wowed them all in her imaginary diaphanous Ophelia dress, as light and pale as baby's breath. And then onto the Oscars and a whistle-stop charity tour of the Czech republic, Amy handing tickets to culturally starved theatre-goers at the door, Orlando pacing the stage with the passion and majesty of Olivier. Shakespeare Around the Globe they'd call their project, Orlando Rock and his wife.

Actually her coat was trodden on by sniffy people impatient to leave and her mother couldn't find her handbag. People tried to get past and huffed and sighed, Amy crashed calamitously to earth, and, bruised and unhappy not to have been spotted on her cloud in the stalls by Orlando Rock, caught the last bus home.

Chapter 11

Amy was chatting to the security guards in the reception of Vogue House, an injustice of models sitting on chairs around her, as thin as knicker elastic, their portfolios perched on their Prada-encased knees, and their flawless complexions and minimalist nails leaving every woman in the vicinity feeling as made-up and froufrou as Zsa Zsa Gabor. Amy was used to this particular drawback of working in the fashion industry, but she wasn't used to feeling as though every woman she saw would be more likely to go out with the actor of her dreams than she was, including the fifty-year-old lady who worked in the accounts department (could be fantastic in bed – all maturity and experience). On her way up in the lift she scrutinised herself in the cruel mirrors. Yeuch, she thought, even if I see him again he won't want to know; he's so glamorous and talented, I just pin hems and ply bulimics with sandwiches for a living. The lift doors opened and Amy was greeted by an infantry of Vuitton luggage and a rail of clothes, plus several scuffling fashion editors.

'Amy, thank Christ, we had no idea where you were. Help me with these, we're off to Dorset,' Nathalia yelled. Nathalia was pure Eurotrash. Blonde, perma-tan, father owned Germany or something, and Amy was terrified of her.

'What are we going to Dorset for, I'm supposed to be working on my Council Estate Glamour shoot,' Amy protested, dreading spending the day with this monster who wouldn't know a council estate if it got stuck to the bottom of her shoe.

'I'm styling Orlando Rock and I need you to iron his gear,' she said in her mid-Atlantic drawl. Amy bristled proprietorially, like a tom cat marking out her territory.

'Oh, Olly,' she improvised. 'Yeah, he said he'd be down there, *Return of the Native*.'

'You mean you know him?' Incredulous.

'Mmm, we had tea on Sunday, lovely, he's a darling.'

Amy, what are you doing, you'll be caught out, embarrassed. Shut up. But it did the trick. Nathalia was deferential until they reached the motorway and she realised she'd forgotten her lipstick and fell into a sulk.

In the chasm of Nathalia's silence Amy was suddenly struck with fear at the enormity of the situation. She was wearing a cardigan she'd had since sixth form, she was in love with the man she was going to see, he had her down as not-the-marrying kind, to put it mildly, she'd just lied to Nathalia who would be sure to show her up and . . . and Amy glanced at the brief for the session.

'. . . Orlando Rock . . . blah . . . Versace . . . blah . . . stylist Nathalia . . . photographer . . .' No! It can't be him! She looked again. No! It can't get any worse. A nervous rash crept up her chest and onto her neck . . . it was worse. Toby Ex, Battersea's answer to Hugh Heffner, was the photographer and Amy had broken out in spots. Oh my God, what if he says something, what if he mentions the video, tries to blackmail me. Never mind Christmasses, all her nightmares came at once.

By the time they pulled up outside Hardy's cottage Amy's rash had made her look like a giant raspberry. She saw the photographer outside the front door, engrossed in light meters and polaroids and braced herself for the inevitable.

'Amy, hello dearest.' He kissed her fruity cheeks and smiled kindly. Anyone that can come within a mile of me and my rash, let alone kiss me, can't be that bad, she sighed.

'The ubiquitous Toby,' she managed with a grin. They exchanged sympathetic, vows-of-secrecy glances and buried their dubious sexploits beneath a duvet of professionalism. Phew! number one, thought Amy gratefully. Which was of course tempting fate. Nathalia came tearing out of Hardy's garden like *Jude the Obscure* on acid, all maniacal depression and misery.

'Where's the make-up artist? I can't face Orlando without lipstick. Amy, you haven't even begun to unpack those clothes, you're bloody useless.' She spun off again. Amy's tearducts pricked and she looked heavenward with her eyes wide open in a bid to prevent the tears rolling down her cheeks and spoiling her blusher. I hate her, she chanted, kicking about two thousand pounds' worth of suitcase until it bore the imprint of her shoe. And I hate bloody Orlando Rock, he's just some rich git who'd fall for the fake charms of Nathalia and her crass jet-set friends. Inwardly she gave up, that moment when for self preservation you know it's better to believe that it will never be. Optimism is not only misplaced but idiotic and masochistic; why hurl yourself off the cliff of rejection headfirst? We're from different worlds, thought Amy with a hollow pit of misery inside her. Even at the party I knew there was never a chance, I should never even have entertained the thought. She sat on a little bench at the bottom of Hardy's garden, early spring birdsong drifting from woods nearby. She was calmed as she leant down to stroke a cat curling himself around her feet and she made a private bid to be more sensible. Life's not like books, she told herself, I'm not Anna Karenina or even Holly Golightly. From here on I'll set my targets in the real world. Maybe Cath and Kate are right. But one small thought peeked through her gloom. Maybe Orlando will come up behind me now, sit down and in the still garden, we'd laugh and chat. Stop! She pushed the last of the romantic thoughts to the back of her mind and faced grim reality.

Grim reality was ironing shirts for most of the afternoon. Amy presented a curious sight beside her ironing board amongst the trees. She solemnly eased out the creases and derived a little therapy from her task. Within earshot the photographer coaxed steely glances and heroic stances from Orlando Rock. Amy had thus far avoided him as though it were he and not she who had a rash. She watched the scene through a break in the trees, Orlando sitting on a log, a shaft of sunlight highlighting his beauty, singling him out like some Olympian god of long ago that had just wandered into this modern day forest by accident. He was like a sad and lonely sculpture, a breed apart from the men surrounding him and untouchably beautiful. She caught a flicker of muscle in his thigh as he changed position and a broad boyish smile at the pretty make-up artist who puffed powder onto his cheekbones. She could just stand and watch all day, hear his distant chuckles and easy banter. So ordinary and affable, but my God so special. She felt safe just watching and dreaming of the night she would be the one to meet him with a kiss after a performance or accompany him to a dazzling premiere. But she had to stop daydreaming, the time had come for her to dole out tea from her flasks and supply the troops with ham sandwiches. She wandered around gazing at her feet, avoiding everyone's glance.

'I wanted vegetarian Amy, not pig,' snapped Nathalia. Amy winced at the mention of her name and delved back into her lunch box for an alternative.

'Amy, hello, Lily's friend. It is, isn't it?' asked the god. A smile superglued itself to Amy's lips and her heart sprinted.

'Orlando, I've er ... been ironing,' she floundered, trying not to seem impolite for not saying hello earlier.

'I had supper with Lily on Wednesday, she's very well.' He winked. Amy's mortification was concealed behind her grin.

'Good, that's nice.' Jesus I'm so boring, why on earth is he wasting his breath? Get a grip Amy.

'How's the filming going?' Amy attempted, trying to resuscitate her brain, but she was felled by a shriek from Nathalia as she bit into roast beef and horseradish.

'Are you totally stupid?' she shrieked, spitting her sandwich all over the floor. Amy turned away from

Orlando and glanced at Toby looking for some sign of solidarity, but he pretended not to have noticed her and carried on with his lens-fiddling. Amy fled, tears and her rash competing to make her face as red and blotchy as possible. If she'd stuck around a bit longer she'd have witnessed Orlando's newly chilly handling of Nathalia. As she stroked his hair into place over the collar of his coat he brushed her hand away, as she fawned he glowered. Nathalia, of course, didn't seem to notice.

Chapter 12

Taking the view that you have to pick yourself up, brush yourself down, etc., Amy faced Saturday morning with a schizophrenic blend of utter misery and eternal optimism. She flicked off the shipping forecast because she wisely knew it would depress her, all those lonely little boats in gales and wives sitting sadly at home. Instead she put on that anthem for female empowerment, '*I Will Survive*', and had it blaring from stereo and tonsils. Nine in the morning and she was dusting her room in her pyjamas. She flung her arms and duster tunelessly around, feeling better now. Thanks Gloria, you've done a lot of women, and many a gay man, a great service over the years.

She decided that retail therapy was just what the doctor ordered for this particular brand of nagging pain. The pain of humiliation and professional catastrophe. She burned lavender oil to lift her spirit and slipped her emergency only credit card into her purse. On the bus to King's Road she read glossy magazines, mentally noting her purchases: new nail polish, a must; shampoo for thicker fuller hair, could transform my life; fennel tea to kick the demon coffee. She hummed her anthem the length of Sloane Street and felt content in the morning sunshine. In Harvey Nichols food hall she picked up some black olives in basil, she sniffed a scoop of Chinese green tea and ran her fingers through a barrel of shiny black coffee beans. She bought a bag of watermelon-flavoured jellybeans and meandered her way back downstairs via bedlinen and le Creuset saucepans. This is the life, she smiled to herself.

Pottering down the Fulham Road she popped into the Conran Shop, past the array of flowers and lobsters, stroking rosewood tables and, catching a glimpse of herself in a knotted wood Mexican mirror, looking good for a girl low on love, Amy reassured herself. Self-love is the first step to loving others, she had once read. As she picked up a giant starfish which would look exquisite in her bathroom she saw the familiar profile of Orlando Rock browsing amongst the pot pourri. Oh no, it can't be. I spend my life not seeing a single famous person and then in the space of two weeks they begin to reproduce asexually all over the place, like those spores I learned about in biology. Except that this was one famous person cloning himself all over her life. She decided to ignore him; he'd hardly be offended that a person whom he'd met for a grand total of an hour in his entire life decided to snub him. She slunk behind the bathrobes and disappeared into candles, surreptitiously glancing in mirrors to make sure he wasn't behind her. Just as she was about to disappear up the stairs and make her exit she felt a hand on her elbow.

'Hello trouble.' Shit. She stopped dead, caught in the act. Turning slowly she helloed with fake surprise,

'Orlando! We have to stop meeting like this!' Did I really say that?

'I never usually come to such smart places as this, but I have to get a present for someone.'

'Your girlfriend?' Amy spilled out without thinking.

'No, just divorced. For my mother actually.' Expect the unexpected, Amy, isn't that your perfume's motto?

'They have some fantastic things, for gifts.' Get a grip, Amy.

'I know, there's this amazing sofa, come and have a look.' He led her up the stairs by her fingertips and flopped down on a vast, fat leather sofa.

'Veeeryy nice. If you want to get laid,' offered Amy. He laughed.

'No pulling the wool over your eyes, eh?'

'I prefer this one, jewel coloured crushed velvet. Jimi Hendrix would buy it.'

'They should have a sticker saying that on it. In tests eight out of ten dead rock stars would buy this sofa.'

'What about actors?' Amy queried.

'No sense of style at all, just take on board the life wholesale. Y'know I might just buy this place intact, rhubarb leaves in wine glasses, that kind of thing. No imagination of my own, just method furnishing.'

'I sometimes think that one day I'll have a magnificent dinner party with all this stylised stuff, serve pebbles in bowls with a few red berries for colour, goldfish in the soup tureen,' Amy ventured. They both got the giggles and invented a fantastical life in the day of the Conran Shop shopper.

'Pyramids of oysters and a banana tree,' he offered.

'A bed you could live in, like that Evelyn Waugh character, Sonia Digby Vane Trumpington, who just drank black velvet in bed all day, entertained all her gentleman friends from the bath and let her pekes keep her feet warm. Darling.' Amy put on her best Noel Coward voice and they spun through the chic splendour of the shop until they'd constructed a fantasy around every teaspoon and assumed parts of Italian countesses, reclusive starlets and East End gangsters shacking up on the Costa del Sol.

'What about this one?' Orlando said hurrying over to a filigree lace hammock.

'I don't think it would hold me,' said Amy, assessing its delicacy.

'Rubbish, it would hold both of us. It's for some South Pacific island where you could swim with turtles by day and lie beneath the Southern Cross at night.'

'Tied between two palm trees,' Amy mused, fingering the white lace.

'No, mango trees, then you could pluck them handily for breakfast.'

'I should think if I decided to plant a farm at the foot of the Ngong hills, I'd like one of these.' Amy put on her best *Out of Africa* voice and patted a large mother of pearl encrusted tea-chest.

'But watch out for syphilis,' warned Orlando.

'Why syphilis?' Amy asked.

'Because, my dear, the Happy Valley was positively alive with it, that and elephants and the sound of us all making love to our best friends' wives. See what I mean old girl?'

'Absolutely darling. Neville was the most handsome man I ever had the pleasure of committing adultery with.'

Amy smoked an invisible cigarette and tilted her head to one side.

'Almost as good as me in bed?' asked Orlando, holding her gaze and falling silent.

Amy didn't say anything. For a half second they looked at each other and she held her breath, then a shopper with a large palm tree walked between them. Barely remembering who they were they collapsed, exhausted, on the sofa where they'd begun.

'I still don't know what to get for my mother.' Orlando frowned.

'Hyacinths,' said Amy confidently. 'Mothers always go on about how divine they smell and "what a beautiful blue" they are.'

'Settled,' he said, heading for a vast terracotta tub of bulbs.

They stood in the queue to pay.

'All this talk of grand lifestyles has made me feel like Neanderthal man, never cooking, never entertaining. Why not come round for Sunday lunch tomorrow? I can't promise olive groves but I can buy some cashews from Sainsburys.'

'Love to,' said Amy. They shook hands.

'Done.'

'Here's my address.' He scribbled on a taxi card and handed it to her. 'One-ish.' Amy nodded.

As she was leaving she noticed the girl at the till noticing him. She was pouting and fluttering like a drag queen. Never mind, Amy shrugged, I'm sharing roast chicken with him, not her. That-a-girl Amy!

Chapter 13

Amy pulled up on Orlando's doorstep just a few minutes past one. Ish, she told herself, one-ish, this'll be fine. She contemplated doing another couple of laps of the street on her bike to waste time but then she'd already done three and might start to perspire, or was it glow? She knew ladies didn't sweat. A little flummoxed, she checked her already much scrutinised piece of paper. She'd done some amateur calligraphy on the loops on his g's and was quite pleased with what his capital letters told her about his temperament. Yup, right address. A little run down, she thought, glancing at the peeling window sills, but perhaps in that clever south London way its scruffy exterior denoted smart home contents. Probably. She wiped her glowing palms on the jacket she'd borrowed from Lucinda in a fit of panic last night and after a few yoga breaths pressed firmly on the doorbell. Clatter clatter down the staircase, fiddle with keys. Help, what am I doing here? Door flung open.

'Amy, hi.' Kiss Kiss. Nice Sunday smell drifted down the stairs.

'Something smells good,' she remarked, with all the originality of a seasoned (if dull) house guest.

'So it should, I've been up since dawn scrubbing floors

and basting dead animals, look – dishpan hands.' He held his beautiful, long fingers out for scrutiny.

'You're obviously using the wrong brand of washing up liquid. Men always do.' She sniggered, he huffed with a camp toss of his head and led her through to the kitchen. Amy noted the bachelor feel to the flat, a tidy but drab kitchen, lots of scrubbed pine but not a vase of flowers or cleverly arranged rug in sight. Behind the house was a tiny veranda leading onto an even tinier lawn. It wasn't really Mayfair, she thought, feeling sure that actors must get paid enough to live north of the river in somewhere a bit more palatial. Maybe though he just hadn't got round to it since the divorce, maybe his ex-wife had the penthouse.

'Very sweet,' said Amy, 'Did you decorate?'

'Nah, I've only lived here for about six months. I try not to invite anyone round because they think I should have some hell pad with shiny floorboards and revolving statues of nudes.'

'And black satin sheets and a water bed.' Amy perched on the edge of the worktop, getting into the swing.

'Oh I've got those. My only indulgence though, I find money's never wasted where good taste is concerned.' He handed her a glass of red wine. Amy looked up from his hand to his eyes. Shit. Reality check. Looking straight at her was Orlando Rock. God of stage and screen with all the sex appeal but minus the poniard. Her mind flickered to Orlando in the woods, the superstar surrounded by admirers. Then her stomach flickered. Her hand almost didn't grasp the stem of the glass and for a second it wavered between their two hands.

'Do you think we're destined to talk about interior decoration for ever?' said Amy finally managing to secure her red wine.

'Yes, 'fraid so. I made a pact with the devil: I can be famous and successful but in my private life am condemned to talk about home furnishings for all eternity.'

'Shit. Well, I think I'd better be off, perhaps you can have the chicken in sandwiches for lunch tomorrow, I wasn't terribly hungry anyway.' Amy made to leave the room, picking up her coat on the way out. Half of her longing to really leave so she could have time to adjust to this peculiar twist in her life.

'Stop, you're my only hope, I need the blood of a beautiful virgin and some eye of newt for a potion I was planning. Only then can I break Satan's hold over me.'

'No can do. I'm sure you can get eye of newt in Asda but you're about six years too late for the virgin's blood.'

'Bugger. And you look so innocent too. Mind you, so does Lily.'

Amy was plucked back to reality. I can't go on letting him think that Lily and I are an item, it's not fair to him, she told herself, when what she really meant was: if he wants to kiss me later, which he won't, he has to know that I'm straight, or bi, or whatever.

'Orlando?'

'Amy, there's no need to be embarrassed, it's cool about you and Lily, really.'

'No, you see, well, that was my first time, with a woman. I've never really felt attracted to them before and, really I think I prefer men, but it was nice, and . . .'

'There's a first time for everything,' he interrupted sympathetically, ready to counsel his pretty young guest that 'if it feels good – do it'.

'No really, I fancy men. Lily was lovely, but it was more of an erotic thing, a backlash against crap men.'

He nodded and refilled her glass.

'Well, if you say so. I'm sure the male population will launch a collective cheer at that news.'

Phew! number two, thought Amy. Better late than never.

They chatted late into the afternoon. He told her about his recent divorce and a bit about 'the pressures of acting'. Amy was surprised to find he didn't sound like an actor at all, even though he told her he missed his wife but they'd both changed a lot and really, actresses weren't his cup of tea. Amy was almost convinced that he didn't fancy the raven-locked temptress in *Return of the Native*, but when she slipped off to the loo and pondered this thought in a moment of relative sobriety she decided he was just deceiving himself. Who wouldn't be in love with her, especially as she got to wear a jet black velvet cape. As she pondered the Hogarths on the wall of his downstairs bathroom she was suddenly beset by panic. She'd been too nervous to have breakfast and the wine had gone straight to her head and she thought she must be making a total fool of herself. There is just no way in a month of Sundays that he'd invite me here because he fancies me, or even likes me vaguely. Maybe he thinks I'm the editor of *Vogue* and can get him a good review for his next play? No, that's it, he needs a new cleaner, the place is looking a bit grubby, someone probably told him I need the money. At this thought Amy almost stayed in the loo. She didn't want to go out there and be ritually humiliated. Then she realised that she'd probably been gone for much too long so, after scrubbing the red winey flaky purple bits off her lips she ventured out.

Orlando was stretched out on the sofa cradling his glass in the palm of his hand, watching the liquid swirl around. When Amy appeared at the door he looked up but didn't speak.

'Nice Hogarths,' she said, taking care to perch herself on the chair furthest away from Orlando where he couldn't possibly imagine that she'd misconstrued his motives. Still he didn't speak but just looked at her.

'Could do with a bit of a dust though.' She smiled cheerfully. This broke his concentration and brooding look. He frowned.

'I don't doubt it,' he said, breaking into a smile. Amy kicked off her shoes and stretched her legs out in front of her. The wine lulled them into a haze and they made a bet as to who could eat the most roast potatoes.

'Loser does the washing-up, how's that?' he bargained.

'And the drying,' added Amy, confident of her ability to demolish an inordinate number of spuds.

'I don't have Irish blood for nothing,' she warned. 'All those years of famine are in the genes you know. I see a potato and eat it.'

And she did. She ate nine, he managed seven.

'You wouldn't have let me do the washing-up anyway, you're too much of a gentleman.'

'Don't you believe it, you've yet to see the dark side of my soul.'

'Oh, I read about that in the *Tatler*: the demonic actor. It convinced me of your serious, scary nature. I'm truly stunned you even eat roast dinners, you sounded as though you just ate Derrida for breakfast and Sartre for dessert. Can this be true?'

'Don't wind me up, you saucy young thing. What about you?'

'I'm a much misunderstood and oftentimes maligned personage.'

'And verbose,' he nipped in. Amy slapped his arm and continued,

'You have no idea what it's like working on fashion shoots all week. I just want to recreate beautiful scenarios from Keats poems, full of velvet and pre-Raphaelite lovelies, and instead I have to be hip and have models who look like heroin addicts in bondage gear.'

'Sounds good to me, can you introduce me?' he teased. She slapped him again and in a mock sulk refused to utter another word.

'Come on, tell me, what do you really want to do?'

'I want to write.' Amy confided her deepest darkest secret. It was loosened from her by a good deal of *vin rouge* but more by trust. She was quite shocked and unprepared for her disclosure and tried to backtrack.

'Tell me more.'

'No, I'm not sure. I just want to create beautiful worlds. Nothing clever, just kind of Enid Blyton for grown ups, lots of imagination.'

'Bit like acting really,' he pondered. It was getting

much darker outside and Amy realised with misery that she'd come on her bike and her lights didn't work. Orlando stood up to light the fire and she sunk her head back into the cushions on the sofa, closing her eyes, all heavy and soporific.

'I think I have to go,' she said.

'I've just lit the fire, you can't.'

'God I hate Sundays. When I was younger I used to think it was because I'd never done my homework but now it's like real life has to start again tomorrow. Burst bubbles.'

'That pit of the stomach feeling when you know it's all hanging over you. At least you don't have to go to the wilds of Dorset away from civilisation and reasonable human beings.'

'You're forgetting that I work in the fashion industry, Orlando.'

They both fell silent, accepting the inevitable. The day was over and Amy had to leave. They exchanged goodbyes on the doorstep, Amy hopping from one foot to the other to keep warm.

'Well, that was lovely, thank you,' she said, not knowing whether to offer to reciprocate the invitation and just a bit too shy to do so.

'No, thank you, I haven't had such a fun time in ages.'

Kiss kiss. A bit more hopping from foot to foot, fiddling with bicycle lights. Goodbye. Goodbye.

Chapter 14

For the next two days the phone lines in London were burned up by Amy. She increased BT's profit margin singlehandedly and developed a crick in her neck. But she didn't tell a soul about her afternoon with Orlando Rock. She heard her friends' problems, talked about last night's episode of *Men Behaving Badly* and systematically phoned her way through her Filofax. Somehow, though, she could never find the right words: 'Oh, by the way, I'm seeing that hugely successful actor Orlando Rock,' or 'Have you seen *Henry IV* at the Haymarket? Yes, I had a remarkably intimate roast with Hotspur yesterday. *Actually*.' It just didn't sound right. And do I really want them to know? To know what, anyway? We just had lunch, gorgeous, but – no, nothing happened. Amy hadn't really thought the whole thing through, which was why she needed to tell someone, anyone. But not. Oh God, another pickle. So she toyed with her thoughts alone. Until Lucinda phoned her and shrieked, 'I hear you have something to tell me!'

'Lucinda, what are you talking about?' Genuinely wondering what she meant. There was no way Lucinda could know.

'Excuse me, I just thought we were friends.'

'Luce, settle down. What are you talking about?'

'Benjy just called to say that you're going out with Orlando Rock.'

'Benjy? But how? Don't be stupid, of course I'm not.'

'He spoke to Lily who'd seen Olly, he said you'd spent Sunday together.'

'Which does not constitute "going out with",' rationalised Amy, somewhat out of character.

'I want to hear all about it. I'll buy you supper in the oyster bar, meet me there at seven.'

Amy pulled on some halfway decent trousers and lipglossed her mouth into a mini ice rink. Once at the oyster bar, she sat waiting for Lucinda for the customary twenty minutes. She was used to this facet of their friendship. But it left her rewinding her encounter with Orlando, dissecting and analysing, until she saw his ghost walking through the foyer into the Conran Shop where she'd bumped into him. Serendipity if ever it was, she romanticised. She thought back to him on stage, strutting Hotspur in his thigh high boots; saw his face on an infinite number of magazine covers; recalled how she'd felt at the party for the magazine editor. He was in another league. Sunday had been a fluke. Maybe it never happened. Lucinda turned up and two glasses of Chablis later they were still chewing over the conundrum.

'You see I just can't reconcile his public image with the man I had lunch with. I kind of expected him to be so aloof, so beyond. But he wasn't, just lovely.'

'Have a ciggy, darling,' proffered Lucinda.

'I've given up, Luce, I don't smoke.'

'I think you probably do tonight.'

So like two fag-ash Lils they huffed and puffed and Lucinda was quite disappointed with the non-event that Amy had painted. No snogging. No drugs. No sex. And not even Amy's usual embellishment of the occasion, just roast chicken and red wine. No 'God I love him's. No 'I think this is it's, which she was so used to with Amy. Something must have gone wrong. She determined to find out what.

'Nothing, Luce, I just had a lovely time. But y'know he's very ordinary, more ordinary even than that accountant friend of Benjy's with the funny ear.'

'Don't you believe it, darling, it's just a test. If you like him when he's ordinary then he can safely show you the high life, sure in the knowledge that you love him for himself.'

There could be some truth in that, thought Amy, now starting to get confused about the whole situation. And I suppose he did say he had a dark side, made sure I knew that, even though it didn't show through.

'You could be right, Luce, but the thing is I don't even know if he likes me. He invited me thinking I was Lily's lesbian partner, I'm sure it's just platonic.' Amy depressed herself at the thought.

'Plato never had it so good darling, just you wait and see.'

After the three-day Nirvana period when you're happy just to bask in the hormones of the last encounter an unsettling feeling begins to creep in. Will he? won't he? call again. Amy was even less sure than most of us at

this point because there were only her own hormones
to bask in as they hadn't exchanged body fluids of any
sort. She threw herself into finding marabou mules for
her council estate shoot and tried to avoid the nagging
little voice in her head: Will he? Won't he?

At the same time as she was choosing just the right
shade of marabou Orlando Rock was frolicking in lots
of heather on what passed for Egdon Heath. His leading
lady, a beauty of note, was developing a crush on him.
She pressed herself a little closer to him in the love
scenes than nineteenth-century etiquette demanded. She
cleaned her teeth three times before a kiss and tasted
like a peach. All this didn't go unnoticed by Orlando
Rock. Like any other red-blooded male he found this
siren infinitely desirable, but somehow she just wasn't
his cup of tea. An actress, you see. He was also quite
taken with a certain young lady he'd found eating fish
and chips on a Dorset beach. He liked her haphazard
eccentric beauty, her funny cardigans and her strange
imagination. Yes, we can safely say he was very taken.

On Friday afternoon the phone rang in the fashion room.
It rang and Amy was buried beneath a pile of crumpled
Armani shirts. She yelled to anyone to pick it up.
   'Amy, it's for you,' called Amelia.
   'Who is it?' the crawling pile of Armani yelled.
   'Who's speaking? OK, I'll just get her. Amy it's
ORLANDO ROCK!' pointedly. Subtext being 'you sly
old fox, what's he doing phoning you?'
   The heap of shirts gave birth to a tall girl in jogging

pants who, shaking them off, clambered towards the phone. Amelia held the receiver to her chest, refusing to hand it over until Amy had acknowledged her quizzical raised eyebrows. Amy tugged it from her, smiling conspiratorially.

'Orlando, hi.' Very nonchalant, well done, he'd never guess at the seven hours Lucinda and Amy had spent deconstructing him, the very peculiar dreams Amy had had about him and the twitter of excitement he was causing in the fashion room.

'Yes, that sounds great, where shall we meet? OK, under the lion, two on Saturday. Take care. Bye.'

Aaargh! The fashion cupboard erupted with little shrieks and volcanoes of excitement. Romeo Gigli skirts came to life and danced a samba, Prada shoes tap danced across the floor and Amy was accosted by a huddle of Voguettes dying to know 'everything darling'.

By lunchtime she was a minor celebrity throughout Vogue House. The lady from the library offered to let her have a look at all Orlando Rock's press cuttings and the security guards winked as she left the building. A fully fledged date with Le Rock. Yeee ha! She swaggered home on the tube, ensuring that her bottom swung in a jungle manner. She went to M&S for supper instead of Tesco and bought a Chinese meal for one and a French beer, girls' beers she called them. Heaven. She used all the hot water without worrying about the wrath of her flatmates and ate a whole box of champagne truffles she'd been saving since Christmas. Sheer irresponsibility. Divine.

Chapter 15

Saturday lunchtime found her beneath a lion in Trafalgar Square. She was sure she was under the right one but had a glance at the others just in case. Then she saw the silhouette of Orlando approaching, backlit by the glaring March sunshine, his thick brown hair and in-character beard barely concealing his heartbreakingly beautiful bones, his terrifyingly intense eyes. She was filled with fear. My God what am I doing here, he's beautiful and meeting me. Maybe I've overslept, maybe I'm still dreaming, Amy had dreamt of moments like this since she was thirteen and hoped that George Michael was her long lost brother and all manner of television detectives were her boyfriends. But here she was meeting famous actor person on a dream date. I'm OK as long as I don't look at him, she told herself. So, kiss kiss hello she avoided eye contact and addressed his grey fisherman sweater.

'Hi, how's it going?' casually, deeply, and deeply sexily, Orlando asked.

'Hi, good, fine.' She overegged it.

'It's one of my all time favourite places and I never get to come, so I thought it'd be perfect. Is that very selfish?' he asked, leading her up the steps of the National Portrait Gallery.

'No, I absolutely love it here,' Amy gushed.

Clare Naylor

They were on nodding acquaintance with most of the mon-
archs, speculating on Elizabeth I's sexuality, prevaricating
over which of Henry VIII's wives was the most beautiful.
Amy hummed 'Greensleeves' and proclaimed that any
man who could write tunes like that couldn't be all bad,
even if he did decapitate several wives. Through dark
Tudor chambers they emerged into the airy portals of
the pre-Raphaelites.

'Ellen Terry was a radical feminist, you know,' she
informed Orlando.

'I hate to sound like a philistine, but, who's she?'

'One of your professional forebears, dummy, the great-
est actress of her day. She was mad about her career
and wouldn't give up acting for anything, that's why
her husband painted her here. *Choosing*, some horrid
Victorian allegory, she's sniffing the camellia of worldly
success rather than the violets of domestic harmony, or
something like that.'

'And what happened to her?' asked Orlando.

'Divorced within a year,' Amy stated. A warning to
men.

He watched her squinting at the thick swirls of oil
on canvas, smiled to himself at her strange titbits of
knowledge.

'I thought I was the expert. I brought you here so I
could impress you with my wealth of esoteric knowledge
of history and you're beating me hands down. I resign.
How do you know all this stuff?'

'Aha! I did a curious degree called English Literature
which means that I went away and studied everything
I liked for three years, dabbled in Victorian allegory,

92

went shopping a lot and learned how to crack a joke in Anglo-Saxon.'

'You speak in riddles, Amy, that doesn't explain a thing.' He placed his hand on the small of her back and guided her through the door. She shrieked inwardly with delight. They wandered the halls lined with stern men in costume clothing; huge gilt frames hung heavy and austere and Orlando provided a commentary on many of the assembled luminaries.

'Hogarth hated foreigners, and a few years ago they x-rayed his self portrait and found he'd painted over a bit of canvas with his dog cocking its leg up, peeing all over some foreign drawings,' he explained.

'What a weird thing to do. I guess he never anticipated technology.'

As they alighted on the longed-for Romantics room Amy paid homage to *real* men.

'Oh Byron,' she swooned.

'Can't think what you see in him, he had a gammy leg,' muttered Orlando, replicating a conversation that many a man must have had with his wife when the great poet was alive.

'But Shelley was lovelier, more ethereal. And Keats . . .' she fell silent before his portrait. Orlando indulged her excessively romantic nature and misquoted 'She walks in beauty' at her.

'And Constable, I always vowed I'd make my bride-groom wear this outfit, black silk cravat and nineteenth-century frock coat.'

'Well you'll be lucky to find yourself a husband then won't you?' said Orlando cheekily.

'I'll have you know there are many men in the world who would wear that for me,' she boasted.

'If you say so, dearest. Shall we go and get a slice of cake? I'm famished.'

'Just one more,' pleaded Amy, leading him past Nell Gwynn with her nipple revealing attire.

'They don't make orange sellers like that anymore,' Orlando remarked.

'Look,' said Amy, tugging his sleeve and craning her neck heavenward, 'John Wilmot, Earl of Rochester. The wildest man around. Rake, cad, libertine, all round bad boy. Every woman's fantasy.'

'Pervert.' Orlando grinned, leading her by the hand to the coffee shop.

Post-gallery they strolled up to Covent Garden. Amy felt particularly queasy going past the theatre where she'd seen her companion tread the boards just ten days ago. He held her hand firmly, manoeuvering her through cobbled streets smelling of alehouses and steak and kidney pies, her arm tugged insistently in her socket. 'Masterful' she labelled the faint ache. She struggled to keep up her end of the conversation *and* take in the admiringly envious looks of passers-by. People just don't realise how multitalented you have to be to date a celebrity and remain coherent, she lamented. But she barely had time to think 'woe is me' to herself before she was being marched into a stone-walled dairy ponging to high heaven of divine cheeses.

'I always expect Tess of the D'Urbervilles to come out

and serve me,' said Orlando, swiftly falling into Amy's pattern of a literary hued world.

'Sod Tess, let's get the whiffiest stilton imaginable and some of this brie,' instructed Amy. Orlando looked slightly perplexed.

'Don't look so offended, it's just that you've discovered my Achilles heel.'

'Cheese?'

'Yup, oozing brie and the smelliest blue cheese, but it has to be with port.'

They walked away with two brown bags brimming with oatcakes and Cornish wafers. Blue marbled bliss, thought Amy. Curiouser and curiouser, thought Orlando.

Chapter 16

'How was your weekend, Orlando?' breathed Tiffany, alias Eustacia Vye.

'Good, thanks.' He continued tugging on his boots and doing up a multitude of brass buttons on his jacket. Amy would probably love this get-up, he thought warmly, grinning at the memory of her weak-kneed before salacious heroes of the past. Tiffany mistook his smile for encouragement and called him over to help her to rearrange her bustle.

'We'd better be careful,' she giggled, 'People might talk.'

'Can't think why,' Orlando mumbled, striding off.

If Amy could have seen him she would have marvelled at his Mr Darcy moodiness, his lack of grace with others, but his gorgeous warmth and attentiveness towards her. But the logistics of the Dorset-London scenario meant of course that she didn't see him. She couldn't read his mind, so she agonised instead.

'You mean you feasted on stilton and port, on his bed, and he didn't kiss you?'

'Correct.' The girls had worked late and were rewarding themselves with margaritas in the Hanover Grand.

They found a quiet table in the corner and sat back to dissect Amy's date.

'You spent the whole day together, he told you about his horrid years at boarding school and his divorce, and nothing happened?'

'Lucinda, you're making me feel like a freak.'

'I'm sorry, sweetheart, but I don't really understand it. What time did you leave?'

'Eleven o'clock,' said Amy timidly, terrified about what this hour would denote to Lucinda. Was he a vampire? A priest? Gay?

'Hmm. Well, I'm puzzled, I have to say. Maybe he's just feeling bruised after his divorce.' She plumped for the sensible option. 'Did he ask to see you again?'

'It's not 1953, Luce,' she said, giving in to temptation and reaching for one of Lucinda's cigarettes.

'Imagine if he asked if he could kiss you.' Lucinda leaned over to offer a light.

'Oh God, that would be so horrible. Luce, people don't really do that do they?'

'I don't know, I've had the same boyfriend for years, but it does happen in films.'

'I'd die, Luce. Or, even worse, imagine if he said "make-love!"'

'What?'

'I hate it when people say "make-love". It's such a horrible euphemism, like women are too sensitive to know about sex. Yuck!'

'Or like "family planning". That's so stupid. I don't go to the family planning clinic because I want to have six babies, two blonde, four dark, I go because I don't want any at all,' added Lucinda.

Mercifully for Amy the conversation veered away from Orlando and onto less awful topics. This wasn't one of those things she could romanticise or rationalise. She had a really nice time with him, he hadn't kissed her yet and she was too nervous to think about it anymore.

Arriving home and thinking the flat monsters would be in bed Amy automatically went to the fridge and picked at an apple strudel that'd been there for a few days.

'Who's a dirty stop out then?' Cath appeared in a pair of men's pyjamas, her gesture to prove to the world that there had once been a male in her bedroom. Kate was not far behind.

'Hi kids,' Amy mumbled through apple strudel. 'I hope that wasn't, like, an important apple strudel.'

'Well actually I was going to take it to work for lunch tomorrow,' Kate said, putting her head around the fridge door to check how much Amy had devoured.

'Sorry. I'll buy another one tomorrow to replace it.' It was bloody horrible anyway, Amy thought.

'OK. Anyway, where have you been?' Cath persisted.

'Oh, just for a drink after work with Lucinda. Just a gossip.' Amy poured herself a glass of orange juice and plopped down on one of the chairs, leaving the she-devils to fight over the other.

'And what's news?' Kate said, hastily claiming the spare seat. Amy's tongue was loosened by the margaritas and a healthy desire to tell the world her exciting news. She also knew that if she didn't tell them they'd probably spike her shampoo with Immac.

'Well not much really. I've kind of met this guy though.'
The flat monsters tightened their lips and watched her.
'He's quite nice.'

'Oh yes?' The Amy Inquisitions always followed this
pattern. Sneering questions with Amy feeling compelled
by ancient loyalty to divulge all.

'Yeah. You might know him actually.' This was bait
for the piranhas.

'Really? Who?'

'A guy called Orlando Rock?' She didn't want to
presume.

'What? Orlando Rock the actor?' Cath didn't miss a
beat. Deadpan. Not a flicker of excitement.

'Yeah, I suppose so.'

'So how did you meet *him* then?' No girly shrieking
and hearty congratulations. Hey, our friend's sleeping
with a love god, let's open that bottle of tequila. Well
done Ames!

'I suppose I met him that weekend in Dorset. We've
only been out a couple of times.' She played down her
conquest.

'So this has been going on for a while then?' The
accusation was levelled straight at Amy's conscience. And
why didn't we, your oldest and dearest (ha bloody ha)
friends, know about this?

'Not really, it's not a big deal. You'll have to meet
him.' Amy offered this encounter with Orlando as an
olive branch. She'd no more want him to meet them
than she would have liked to have been reincarnated
as a Christian in Roman times. Their eyes were narrow
and their derision much more hideous than being fed to

the lions. Suddenly Amy couldn't be bothered any more, she emptied the rest of her orange juice down the sink. 'Anyway, guys, I'm really knackered, I'll fill you in on all the gory details in the morning. Sweet dreams.' Like hell. Their idea of sweet dreams was to spike a toddler's sherbert dip with arsenic. Amy fell into her own Orlando dreams with the ssssshhhhhing of the witches' whispers in the kitchen below.

The phone rang and Amy jumped out of the bath, a deluge of her favourite lilac bubbles settling in pools around her ankles. She grabbed a towel and hurtled herself down the stairs to catch it before the answerphone did.

'Hello.'

'Hi, could I speak to Amy?' drip drip, bubble bubble, melting sensation in tummy.

'Orlando, it's me.'

'I didn't recognise your voice.'

'I've just got out of the bath.' Pause so Amy can imagine him imagining her in her glorious state of undress.

'Oh. I was just wondering, I won't be around this weekend so thought maybe you'd like to come round tonight, have some supper?'

'That'd be lovely, but I think it's my turn. Why don't you come here? My flat monsters are out and we could get a take-away.'

'OK, I'll be there in half an hour.'

Orlando Rock, have you no sense of decency? No shame? Don't you know that it's a cardinal sin to allow a girl a meagre half hour to get ready? We're not just talking 'See you in the pub in half an hour', which can be accommodated. A few miracles with concealer and some mousse and all could be well. But here? In half an hour? Gottabejoking. Amy coped womanfully with the task. She deposited all dirty laundry in her sportsbag, hid her tampax and contraceptives in a drawer, turned round her clipboard with twee photos of herself in mutton-sleeved ball dresses myriad ex-boyfriends all over it, chucked *Hello*! under the bed and replaced it with *Trainspotting*, no, on second thoughts, too hip and grim. *Fear of Flying*, that'll do, very retro but seminal and sexy.

She plunged a bottle of white wine into the freezer (mustn't forget or I'll end up with an exploded mass of frozen peas and white wine all over the place), took the pair of black lacy knickers someone had hung on the noticeboard down and hid her council tax demands. Good. Nearly there. Oh my God. Me? She looked down at her deeply unsexy towelling dressing gown and hurled herself back up the stairs. No time for nude lipstick application. Powder, Japanese silk dress number? Nope, too try-hard. Jeans, T-shirt, nice and tight. Fine. Barefoot? Yes, very Bardot. So, within twenty-seven minutes Amy was perched at her kitchen table perusing the arts section of the *Telegraph*, sipping wine with Sting at low volume as though she'd been born there. As though she always wore full make-up and shaved her legs just to sit at the kitchen table.

She'd read most of cinema and a bit of the television guide when the doorbell finally rang.

'Sorry I'm late, terrible traffic coming over the bridge.'

A vision in pale lilac cotton, damp hair and a shy smile stood on her doorstep. Ohmigod.

'That's fine, come in.' She sprinted up the stairs before him, careful not to let his eyes dwell too long on her bottom which followed her at what felt like fifty paces. They retrieved a dial-a-curry menu from the wastepaper basket and ordered enough kormas and nan bread to satisfy a maharaja. When it arrived they laid it out on the living room floor and sat cross legged with their plates on their knees. Amy watched Orlando as he helped himself to more rice, mesmerised by his hands. They were large and slim with the merest dusting of blonde hairs, and his watch, a brown leather strap and solid face. But it wasn't the watch that held her transfixed, it was the way it sat on his wrist bone, the tanned and powerful wrist, the forearms and gentle curve of muscle beneath the creased rolled up cotton of his shirt. She'd never seen anything more suggestive of good sex in her life. She shifted in her seat with anticipation and distraction. Get on with it, Orlando, I'm losing patience.

'How's the Hardy?' she asked, trying to suppress her urge to jump on him.

'Good. I can't say I'm having the time of my life, but I think it's working well.'

'What about the rest of the cast?' Amy attempted to extract salient information about his luscious co-star.

'They're fine, we all get on pretty well.'

'And your leading lady?'

'Fine, she's a great Eustacia.' He had women a little wrong in this respect. Whilst Amy longed to hear how dull Tiffany was and he longed to tell her, he thought

103

it would just make him seem crass and misogynistic. Oh crossed wires.

'Actually, that's part of the reason why I came round.'

Oh God he's having an affair with her. He's perfectly entitled to, of course. It's not as though we have anything going on, but . . .

'I have to go away to finish the filming.' Amy's heart sank like a stone into her stomach and she felt nauseous.

'Really?'

'Not for very long, just a month. We're going to New Zealand. The light in Dorset's really bad so the producer thought we should go to Auckland.'

'Excuse me for pointing this out, but Auckland and Dorset aren't awfully similar.' Amy came over all acerbic.

'It's a popular ploy amongst crews who feel like a trip. Pretend the light's better on the other side of the world and heigh ho off we all go. I'm sorry.'

'Don't be sorry. I mean, not to me. It's not as though anything's going on, is it?' There. She'd done it. Voiced her paranoia and made herself sound like a bitter spinster.

'Amy, I don't know what to say. I thought things were going well. I thought that when I get back from New Zealand we could see a bit more of each other, if you still want to.'

Amy was unconvinced. I've heard some elaborate brush-offs in my time but heading for the Antipodes at the first sign of trouble seems insane. But then all actors were insane. Professional weirdos. Amy's warmth plummeted to room temperature and below. Icy spells.

'You don't owe me some debt of gratitude, Orlando.

You're a free man, you can go to the other side of the world whenever you wish.' Poor bloke, and he thought it was all going so well.

'Amy, I'm not asking your permission to leave, I'm just asking if we can see each other again when I get back.'

'Just as long as you don't ask if you can kiss me.' In her general hysteria Amy got uncontrollable giggles and couldn't believe what she'd just said. He smiled in bewilderment, not getting the joke.

'It's just something Lucinda and I were laughing about the other day, men who ask you if they can kiss you. We weren't sure if they existed anymore.' She wiped the tears from the corners of her eyes before erupting again. Orlando sat still, smiling benevolently and waiting for her to calm down.

'I take it I don't have to ask then,' he said, leaning over and taking her wrist. She fell silent and they kissed.

Post coital *tristesse*. Amy couldn't understand who'd coined this term. *Le petit mort*? No don't get that either. The French are so morose about sex, take it far too seriously, she thought, experimenting with little kisses on Orlando Rock's shoulder. It was definitely a turn-on having a sex symbol in your bed. But he was Orlando too, kind Orlando, gauche Orlando who'd looked so hurt when she pretended not to care. Cute. She kissed his chocolaty dark nipple and wished it were chocolate. Forget the old joke about women turning into pizzas after sex; if men turned into chocolate she could die a happy, very fat woman. Forget *petit mort*. Fat *mort*, more like. She bit his nipple to test if he was awake. He groaned a bit and ruffled her hair with his hand. Amy remembered a saying she'd heard about men thinking women didn't masturbate and that they had to be kidding, God only made men fall asleep after sex so women could get on with it. Well, I'm not complaining about this man's ability to deliver, she purred. After she'd looked at his lips from all angles, their almost indecently large, succulent form, she decided she wanted him to kiss her again. She slipped her hand around his bottom and pinched it lightly. His eyes flickered open and Orlando Rock, sex god, woke from his slumber. He bit her lips and she raked her nails across his back, they shook the house to its foundations and Amy bumped her head on the wall. He screwed his face up tightly and her neck stretched out, her muscles tensing. Mmmm, better than a Cadbury's flake, she declared to herself, and sucked his earlobe.

Chapter 17

Her mood wasn't so sassy, though, a week later. She'd been there, had the hormones to prove it, basked in them and was now officially 'missing him'. Orlando Rock's flight from the country had been detailed in the tabloids, Tiffany Swann not far away in the background. Bollocks, she thought. If only, she thought. But he was now firmly ensconced in the land that invented bungee jumping, had lots of sheep and who knows what else? Who cares, frankly. He was there and she was here. And she could just see it in that tart's eyes, she was hankering after him, would probably get him in a month too. No man can wait that long till he has sex again. Amy knew about such things. Or so she thought.

She dragged her feet around the house and refused to wash her hair,

'It's good for it, after six weeks it'll start to wash itself anyway, and I'll never have to waste money on shampoo again,' she justified it to Lucinda.

'You'll stink.'

'Natural oils, they're very pleasant, I could probably market them, they're full of pheromones.'

'You'll smell like a sheep,' Lucinda protested. Amy

took herself into hibernation mode. The girls at work tried to prize her from her moribund state, come out with us to this new bar they chorused.

'I'm making coleslaw tonight, I can't.'

She stayed at home and wrote letters to long forgotten aunts except she never really started one, let alone finished and posted one. Instead she drew flowers in the corner of the paper and chewing her pen gazed over at her bed. He's been here, in this room. He's kissed me. He's on the cover of *Esquire*. We've had sex. But the facts didn't stick. Maybe he's an imposter, some bloke who looks like Orlando Rock and hangs around bars picking up women. But I didn't meet him in a bar did I? And Lily knows who he is. So he's real. She felt sick at the thought of how amazingly handsome, in fact, just how amazing, Orlando was. *Was*, because she knew that she would never see him again. She was just one of those bints who these guys could have all the time, any time they wanted. She still wasn't convinced as to why her number had come up in the lottery rather than one of those ravishing creatures you see on Friday nights on Fulham Road. Maybe I remind him of his mother? Amy nearly chipped a tooth she was chewing her pen so hard. Shit. I guess it happens all the time, famous person sleeps with normal person and they never set eyes on them again, except on the cover of a magazine or on the rare occasion that the fortunate bint gets pregnant during her encounter and she can establish a link, albeit via the tabloids, with the man she'll never forget. Never forget even after she's married an investment banker and now lives in a very nice house thank you very much in Virginia Water. God I'm pathetic, thought Amy, finally giving up the fight with the pen and paper and wandering downstairs to watch telly instead.

In her exile she even tried to mend fences with the flat monsters who grilled her incessantly about Orlando and provided her with an excuse to talk about him.

'What did you talk about?' queried Cath.

'Oooh, allsorts,' said Amy, reeling off the little jokes they'd shared and not shutting up when she should have known better. But at least they were interested, everyone else she knew tried to make her forget it, take her out of herself and enjoy herself.

'I don't want to bloody well enjoy myself, Lucinda, I'm miserable. I've been deserted by sodding Orlando who quite obviously just wants to get into that tart's knickers and I think my heart's broken.'

'You're not, you're just being a drama queen and you've got to get a grip. You look like something the cat dragged in.'

'Thanks for the support,' Amy snapped and put down the phone. Right now she didn't deserve friends, particularly not ones as nice as Lucinda.

On Saturday afternoon she went to the video shop and bought two cans of Pringles and three videos: *Carry on at Your Convenience* (the one about the toilet factory), *Cyrano de Bergerac* and *Breakfast at Tiffany's*. She cried at all of them – she even cried at the *Carry On* because she thought Sid James was lovely and he was dead. She ate her coleslaw out of the tub and munched her way through the Pringles. At six o'clock she was filled with self-loathing and fortified herself for an evening of Cilla Black and *Inspector Morse* repeats. Not a terrible prospect ordinarily, but with seven hours of viewing under her belt and enough sloth and greed to make the devil himself recoil in horror she thought maybe she should go for a run or something. As she contemplated going to her room to find her trainers the phone rang. In her apathy she let it ring until, answerphone . . . beeeep:

'Amy pick up the phone, I know you're there.' The strident tones of Lucinda. 'Amy I mean it . . .' Amy tripped over the mess and lurched towards the phone.

'Lucinda, what on earth do you want?'

'I'm coming round in half an hour to pick you up. Pack your case, I'm taking you to my mother's.'

'Luce . . .' Whine, whine.

'Just shut up and get ready.'

Half an hour to get ready may be a spur when a famous actor's coming for a curry, but when it's your best friend the motivation isn't quite there, especially when she's taking you to her mother's. Amy wondered what on earth Lucinda's mother could be like. Lucinda's received pronunciation and sergeant major qualities should denote an army background, but rumours abounded that life was nothing of the sort *chez* Luce. Oh well. Amy packed her little suitcase, the one she'd last used for her (in her pining eyes) ill-fated weekend in Dorset. I wish I'd never met bloody Orlando Rock.

Amy had avoided mirrors for a few days now but

collecting her toothbrush from the bathroom she was confronted with the horror that was her face. It was the same face she'd always had, she supposed, only today her eyes looked smaller, those lashes a bit more stubby. And her eyebrows didn't arch in a come-hither fashion as she'd come to imagine. And the lips – nothing rosebud about them, fast-fading geranium, maybe. But she knew what the problem was: she'd spent so long in magazines over the past few days – studying the face of the inhumanly nubile Tiffany Swann, and scouring the visage of Orlando's ex-wife for something as deeply unattractive as laughter lines (to no avail, I'm afraid) – that she felt that she should be on a par with these divinities, that somehow her own facial misfortunes would vanish under the Midas gaze of Orlando Rock. Not so, babe. She took a step back and was about to examine her body but the Spirit of Self-Preservation spoke up, 'You're not even gonna go there, honey.' She warned. Instead Amy stabbed her toothbrush into her soap bag crossly and balked at the packing of shampoo, but for decency's sake she thought it better that she did. All Lucinda's fault, she thought petulantly. Bloody bossy cow.

The bloody bossy cow rang the doorbell. Trog trog down the stairs.

'Amy you look a fright. My mother will wonder who the troll is I've brought home.'

'Fine, then I'll stay here.'

Lucinda pulled Amy's arm.

'Don't you dare, come back here.'

The ill-matched pair squashed into the car, Lucinda

looking like a packet of opal fruits in the latest spring colours, all glossy hair and fruity lips. Amy looked like something she'd salvaged from a skip. They sat in silence most of the way to . . . heaven knows where.

'Where are you taking me?'

'To my mother's.'

'Where does she live?'

'Norfolk.'

'Oh.'

Scintillating. Eventually, and not a moment too soon for either party, they pulled up along a very muddy lane. Amy stepped out into a puddle – at least she presumed it was as it was so dark and she couldn't see. It could very well have been the swimming pool for all she knew. Lucinda carried the bags to the house and they were greeted by two bounding Labradors. Unsurprising so far, thought Amy.

Some daughters do 'ave 'em, as the saying goes. But Lucinda's mother surpassed expectations. Tart with a Heart sprung to Amy's mind.

'Now come in darling.' That's where Lucinda gets it from. 'I've made up a bed in the scullery.' Do people have sculleries anymore? What is a scullery? And why put a bed in there? Amy puzzled. But she was more agog at the rest of the scenario. Lucinda's mother was blonde, but not maternal blonde, mind you. Slut blonde. Teased and lipsticked to the nines. She was beautiful in a survivor kind of way, been there, done that. But warm and lovely, caring and barmaidish. Not a mother though, and not Lucinda's mother, surely. Meeting parents usually means that the jigsaw begins to fit. This one didn't, but Amy was so wide eyed for the next hour that she clean forgot about Mr Rock and his strumpet in New Zealand.

The house was a glorious mix of Colonial horrors, things like Zebra rugs and ivory ashtrays and Aga paraphernalia, racks of drying clothes and packets of organic cornflakes. And Labradors, called Zeus and Iggy. Wooooh, thought Amy. Am I really here, this is too much of a trip to be true. The girls were fed couscous salad and garlic sausage and packed off to bed.

Amy woke and nearly screamed at the bison head above her campbed. She was brought to her senses and remembered firstly that she was at Lucinda's mother's, secondly that she was there in her capacity as disaster victim and presumably was in for some hefty TLC and counselling. But right now all she wanted was to see Orlando. She see-sawed between *knowing* that she would never see him again and feeling sick with longing. She wanted to relive the afternoon in the gallery, the walk through Covent Garden, the Sunday lunch at his house, all of it. She wanted to go back and appreciate, to be more stunningly beautiful, wittier and lovelier, and now she'd never get the chance. And something smelled strange. She twitched her nostrils and realised to her horror that it was her hair. Amy stood up and cursed cold stone floors. Probably a common feature in sculleries, she told herself. She half remembered the previous night's directions to the bathroom and after a minor detour into a room that looked like an Edwardian bordello but was probably Lucinda's mother's bedroom found herself tackling her dreadlocks.

'Good lord darling, I thought you were a rastafarian last night,' chortled Mrs Lucinda, Amy couldn't remember her name, but Lucinda came to her rescue just in time.

'Anita's just been telling me that there's a foal in the paddock. We should go and have a look after breakfast,' said Lucinda. Who's Anita? thought Amy, some long lost sister/aunt/neighbour?

'Yes, I told Lulu that weather permitting we should have a ride too.' It all became clear as day. Anita was Mrs Lucinda. How sixties, thought Amy, in awe of the coolness of calling your mother by her first name.

'Amy, how about some breakfast?' Amy nodded to toast and 'Linda McCartney's'. She had no idea what 'Linda McCartney's' were until she caught a glimpse of the packet of faux sausages, with Linda grinning widely on the front.

'Anita loves animals, rescues cats and stuff,' confided Lucinda when Anita had wafted outside in her Gucci kaftan. Amy thought it better not to point out the virtual zoo of dead things adorning the house and devoured her very tasty soya inventions instead.

The three of them donned wellies and hats and slopped around all morning cooing over the foal and picking bluebells. Amy was introduced to an assortment of chickens and rabbits and the village stray cats. She wondered if there was a patriarch lurking somewhere in the family, in an undiscovered study or suitably patriarchal place, but the female spark was just a bit too bright to convince her that there was. Then she remembered the bordello and was sure there was no man about this house.

*   *   *

114

They shook the crumbling mud off their wellies and sat down to a lunch of taramasalata and white wine.

'I remember when I was little I used to long for real tea-time,' reminisced Lucinda. 'I wanted to come home to baked beans and fishfingers at six o'clock.'

'Oh darling, don't be so hard bitten, there was always food in the fridge. It was my ploy to make you the wonderful, self-sufficient human being you are today,' laughed Anita, not remotely fazed by the accusations of dysfunctional family life.

'I hated tea-time, it meant I couldn't move until I'd eaten carrots and peas. Think yourself lucky.'

'Thank you Amy. This one wouldn't know the good life if she won the lottery,' Anita quipped, stroking her daughter's cheek fondly.

'Anyway, I was working to keep you in ra-ra skirts.'

'What did you do, Anita?' asked Amy.

'Oh, very predictable I'm afraid. I was a model.' Amy could see it, the bones behind the tizz of hair, the startling blue eyes.

'She was also an actress,' Lucinda said proudly.

'No, I was just in one film, a very sixties thing where I wandered round looking half stoned. Very dull.'

'Actually, Anita went out with a few celebrities in her day. Didn't you?'

Anita looked crossly at Lucinda.

'You have absolutely no tact, Lulu darling.' Amy began to smell a rat.

'Amy, I just thought mum could offer you some advice on coping with a famous beau,' said Lucinda timidly.

'Luce, my problem isn't that Orlando's famous, it's that he's on the other side of the world.' And probably sleeping with Tiffany Swann, she didn't add. Amy sniffled, her emotion suddenly getting the better of her.

'Oh sweetheart, don't cry. Now Lulu, you can go and check on the donkey. Amy and I will have a cup of tea in my room.'

So Amy was whisked off by the lissom Anita who doled out tea and sympathy on her colossal four-poster. They snuggled into the huge feathery duvet and while Amy sobbed Anita told her about the time she'd followed Mick Jagger to Morocco.

'Marianne and I packed bags no bigger than that little Prada creation of Lulu's and hopped on the plane to Morocco. I was so in love with Mick and Marianne was in love with at least three of the boys so we figured you should go after what you want. Had the most fantastic time, days in the souk, evenings by the pool. Sheer bliss.'

Amy giggled through her tears at Anita's stories. She decided that Lucinda was probably Bill Wyman's daughter and Anita's spirit began to infuse her.

'You're right. It's only been a few days, and it does take twenty-four hours to get there. If he doesn't call while I'm away I'll phone myself. After a whisky.'

'Darling, you should get your bottom on the next plane and go and show him what he's missing.'

'What happened after Morocco?' Amy asked.

'Oooh, more of the same really, in New York, London, all over the place, and we're still terrific friends. Mick sometimes comes with Jerry and the little ones, they love the horses.' God how lovely, thought Amy, crying all over again.

'Lucinda's really lucky to have you,' she sniffled.

Cheered by Anita's pep talk, Amy pranced around like a young foal herself for the rest of the weekend. She taught Anita how to make coleslaw and the three of them played gin rummy after lunch.

'I nearly forgot,' said Anita, jumping up from her seat. 'Wine.'

'I'm fine, thanks Anita, and I've got to drive back later.'

'Not any old wine Lulu, my wine. Homemade wine.' Lethal.

They sipped their way through elderberry and dandelion, apricot, victoria plum and then progressed to sloe gin.

'I think there's a hint of asparagus here,' said Amy, in her best wine snob voice.

'No, no, it's most definitely carrot,' Lucinda said with a flourish.

'I think you'll find it's horseshit,' Anita squealed, and they all exploded into laughter, pink-cheeked and sozzled.

Chapter 18

Inspired by Anita, Amy arrived back in London a new woman. She had clean hair and was determined not to be so wet and bourgeois about everything in future. She became a walking proverb: make hay while the sun shines, a watched kettle never boils and a stitch in time saves nine. She wasn't sure what the latter contributed to her current predicament or even what it meant, but it followed the general 'the future belongs to the risk takers' trend of her new resolve, so she adopted it as part of her life philosophy.

As testament to the power of positive thinking, and because you've got to give a girl a break sometimes, Amy arrived back at her flat in time to catch the phone ringing. She skedaddled up the stairs just as the machine took it.

'Amy, it's Orlando, I called earlier but you weren't there . . .'

'Hi.'

'So, how are you?'

'Great, thanks, where are you?'

'New Zealand. It's six o'clock on Sunday morning and I thought I'd just say hello.'

'That's nice. Thanks.' Not terribly inspired, Amy. Think Anita.

'And,' he said cautiously, 'and that ... I've been thinking about you.'

'Thinking what?' she asked, dying to be flattered. What? That you can't live without me? That I'm the most beautiful woman you've ever met and that we should get married in Bali this weekend? Women can't be content with 'thinking'. We need details; a one thousand-word essay would be nice but failing that a few salient details will suffice. Orlando didn't fare so badly.

'Just that we had a nice time and ... New Zealand's quite lonely. I miss you, Amy.' Well stone me! Steady Amy ... fools rush in and all that ...

'Gosh, thanks.'

'I know it's not very likely but ...' He was very reticent, or was it the time delay? 'Why not come out here for a week or so? I could arrange the flight. It's quite beautiful.'

Shit, thought Amy, he can't mean it. He doesn't mean it Amy, don't get too up yourself. He's Orlando Rock, you're Amy. Plain Amy. Don't give anything away.

'That's really kind but, well I have to work and ...'

'I know, it was a ridiculous idea, never mind,' he floundered sadly. Morocco. The Rolling Stones. For God's sake woman *carpe diem* ... he wants to take you away. But what if I don't have time to have a bikini wax? He might take bitch Tiffany instead. That sealed it.

'But I suppose I'm owed some holiday. What would I do all day?'

He perked up. 'I've given it a bit of thought,' (a lot of thought Olly, confess!) 'and if you like we could just skip

Auckland and meet in Sydney. I'm not needed on set for a couple of weeks ...' Cor blimey guv, ooo-er matron, thought Amy in her best chirpy cockney Sid James voice. Try stopping me. Bikini wax or no bikini wax.

Amy begged, borrowed and mostly stole the relevant goodies for her sojourn in Sydney. She swiped some sun cream from the beauty cupboard at work, sewed a zip into her yellow canary hotpants and cadged most of Lucinda's summer wardrobe. Vaguely hot was her impression of the weather in Australia at this time of year. She'd never been to Australia, but as an erstwhile *Neighbours* fan thought she pretty much knew her stuff. She was automatically upgraded because of her Vuitton luggage (albeit dented and courtesy of *Vogue*) and sipped Perrier in the posh VIP lounge before the flight. She mistook the olives that businessmen like to have in their Martinis for nibbles and caused a minor olive shortage amongst the airline, but on the whole could have passed, if not for a very important person, at least for a vaguely important person.

The flight was deeply glamorous to begin with. She followed all Lucinda's advice and changed into casual wear, used a cashmere wrap as a blanket and drank only mineral water. She slathered her face in moisturiser until she resembled an oily salad and sat back and watched the films. It was only after the stop at Bangkok airport (horrid place, couldn't buy chocolate for love nor money, just pointless pink orchids) that the travel sickness began to kick in. She scoffed ginger tablets as though they were going out of fashion and when the herbal option didn't work took some emergency valium Luce had kindly given her. Thus she slept the remaining twelve hours. Thus she arrived in Sydney looking like a used handkerchief.

Orlando didn't seem to notice her crumpled state, or the watch strap imprinted onto the side of her face where she'd fallen asleep, but just gave her a huge hug and carried her bags. The heat was rising from the ground in the way it only does in deliciously hot countries, all wavy lines and blinding sunlight. She screwed up the cashmere number, thinking it a little excessive. In the daze of brightness and chemical comedown of valium Amy was a bit too woozy to take in much of what was going on around her; Orlando was still handsome and looked hot in his beard and he was talking a lot about heaven knows what.

'Orlando, I'm sorry but I feel a bit giddy.'

'Probably just jet lag, sweetheart.' Hmm, that was nice, she liked being called sweetheart, even if she couldn't really see straight.

They pulled up outside a white house which Amy thought must be a petrol station or a shop, merely a temporary stalling point, because she knew that they'd be staying in a white marble palace of an hotel. One that shimmered on the harbour front. But then Orlando started to get her bags out of the boot and opened her door, expecting her to get out too she supposed. No can do, she thought, her head flopping forward onto the dashboard. The last thing she could remember slurring was, 'But Olly darling, we can't stay here,

Lucinda said we absolutely must stay at the Regency Hotel.' Then she passed out. For twenty-four hours.

'I will never touch valium again as long as I live,' Amy vowed, sipping her orange juice and slicing into a mango. They were sitting on the verandah of the most divine house imaginable, she'd been quite wrong about the petrol station part. The front lawn was shaded by frangipani and it was filled with white flowers and exotic fruit; the rooms were light and airy and if you stood in the garden you could see the Harbour Bridge. She leant over and kissed him.

'Thank you. It's so gorgeous, I can't begin to tell you.'

'You all ready have told me, now would you like some more orange juice? Are you sure you're feeling better?'

'Yup, no more drugs for me.'

'I'll get you some Melatonin next time I'm in LA. Much better for jetlag.' Orlando put his feet up on a chair and reclined in the early morning sun. Next time you're in LA. My God, a future. We have a future!

'Aren't you awfully hot in your beard?' A far safer topic than their future.

'No choice, I'm afraid. Don't you like it?'

'I think it's very distinguished but it feels like I'm kissing my father, or at best my art teacher at school,' said Amy.

'The *Sydney Morning Herald* journalist said that I was sex on a stick with a beard.' He laughed self-deprecatingly.

'Probably just wanted to get into your knickers.'

'Very likely,' he said teasingly. She threw her mango stone at him and he caught hold of her, wrestling her to the floor. They had sex *al fresco*. They'd now had it indoors, in the shower, beneath the stars and in about six other variations, and Amy had only been awake for four hours.

'I was right, you just got me out here for the sex.'

'I could have paid a hooker and saved on the airfare.'

'You could have slept with your leading lady.'

'You can always tell whether someone's good in bed by the way they kiss.'

'You've kissed her?' yelled Amy, pulling on her hot-pants and jumping to her feet.

'It's called acting, my love, par for the course, you knew that.' Of course Amy knew that. It didn't stop her turning grass green at the mention of it though.

'I know but it's not fair,' she pouted. 'I can never see any of your films, I'd freak with jealousy.'

'No you wouldn't. Anyway, I said she was a hopeless kisser.' Amy took this as an invitation to prove her own oral prowess, so casting all images of her father and her art teacher to the back of her mind, she kissed him again.

And so their baptism of the picturesque little house continued, upstairs, downstairs, in the laundry room and in the flowerbeds. Amy came over all remorseful after the flowerbed and fed the flowers extra water the next day, but their stems were snapped and they were beyond hope. On the third day the teeming bundle of hormones left the house and made its way down to the beach. Orlando had to wear a hat for fear of being 'recognised', which Amy found highly prima donnaish, chiding him,

'It's not as though you're Michael Jackson or Take That, you're just being silly.'

'Trust me, it's better to be safe.'

'Well, let's not take any chances then, best change your name. How about something to blend in with the landscape? I know, Bruce.' She still found the notion hysterical and called him Bruce all day, just in case someone heard the name Orlando and mobbed him. They attempted to body surf, but Amy kept getting dumped by the waves. So with more sand than is funny in her bikini bottoms she gave up, sitting on the beach drinking melon juice instead. Periodically, Orlando would rise from the ocean like Botticelli's Venus and torment her by flicking water all over her.

'Bruce, stop it!' she screamed, 'I'm warning you!' then settled back into her Emily Brontë.

'You can't read the Brontës on an Australian beach, you turnip,' cried Orlando.

'Well just what would you suggest then, Jeremy Paxman?'

'Something local. Something Australian, get into the spirit of the place.'

'Bugger off, Bruce.'

She shook her sandy towel onto him and returned to the Yorkshire Moors. They rubbed more oil into one another than was remotely necessary, just so they had an excuse to be touching. As if they needed one.

'Disgusting,' remarked one old lady as she passed by. 'They look like a couple of slugs, all over one another. This is a family beach,' she pointedly informed her companion. Amy and Orlando collapsed laughing and started to lick one another's face in an exhibition of mock lewdness. The old lady hurried away.

That evening they took their calamine-encrusted bodies to a lovely seafood restaurant on the harbour front. They cracked lobster and let oyster after oyster slide down their throats, although Orlando was hesitant at first.

'They just taste like the sea,' Amy reassured him.

'I don't like the taste of the sea.'

'Not like real sea, just essence of sea,' she tried to describe it.

'Watch, just swill it round a bit and chomp once or twice, like this.'

'I thought you weren't meant to bite it?' he said.

'You're not, but if you don't it's too revolting.'

'So you don't really like them, you're just trying to pretend you're sophisticated.'

'I do like them. Anyway you have to have them, for their special properties.' She winked.

'I don't think I like what you're implying.' Orlando smiled.

'Well Deirdre, it's just that my partner seems to have lost all interest in me, if you know what I mean.' She put on her best Worried of Tunbridge Wells voice. He squeezed her knee under the table until she yelped. 'It's just that we haven't had sex for, ooh all of three hours.' Orlando purposefully devoured another oyster.

They stayed on until all the other guests left and finally managed to lift their seafood-laden carcasses down onto the beach beside the restaurant. They sat in silence on the beach watching the lights in the distance, listening to the boats knock against the jetty. It was the first time since they met that they'd felt a comfortable silence. For Amy it was as soothing as the cool breeze on her sunburn. Accustomed to mulling over all the minutiae of her love life she had been caught breathless by this encounter with Orlando. She couldn't actually believe that she was sitting on a beach on the other side of the world with a man who made her laugh, someone clever and talented and someone she fancied the pants off. Not to mention someone that every woman in the western world wanted to go to bed with. Not bad going. What surprised her even more was that she wasn't more freaked out by the thought. She was actually just taking it in her stride, at least in the way that Amy ever took anything in her stride. A bit of neurosis here, a glimmer of paranoia there, but nothing out of the ordinary, except maybe contentment. He was sitting there with his arm draped lightly over her shoulder and right now everything was fine. She didn't wish they were somewhere else or that he was someone else. If she weren't a cynic she might say it was perfection.

Their sexual gymnastics were somewhat quelled that night by severe sunburn. Every ooohh and aaah was punctuated by an ooucch, so they sought solace in massaging aloe vera lotion into one another's tender parts.

Chapter 19

After a few days in Sydney they flew up to the Barrier Reef for some snorkelling. The reef and its multitude of inhabitants convinced Amy that there must be a God.

'Orlando, how can you see all those amazing fish, with totally pointless markings, purple dots and green stripes and odd shapes, and not believe that God was having fun when he made them?'

'It's just evolution and camouflage, darling.'

'No way, there's nothing orange with yellow zig-zags for them to camouflage themselves against. And what about Dalmatians?'

'Can't say I've seen any yet.'

'No, dogs with spots. That has to be God in creative mode, you must agree,' she said, pulling on a T-shirt to stop the midday glare.

'OK I give up, I believe in God. OK?'

Amy settled back, relishing her victory. They tried every cocktail in the bar and at night were so hot that they lay on top of all the sheets and kept having to take cold showers. Amy ran chilled cans of beer over her arms and chest to cool down and Orlando finally conceded and shaved off his beard, revealing white skin.

'Oh my God, you're piebald. It'll be like sharing a bed

with a horse,' she squealed as she brushed her hair in front of the mirror.

'Flattery will get you everywhere, darling,' he breathed in her ear, taking her hairbrush from her hand and kissing the back of her neck.

Very early one morning they got up for a walk and saw turtles coming up to lay eggs in the sand. Amy shrieked with delight and sat next to one mother turtle for an hour to encourage her through labour. By day they saw manta rays leaping from the water and Orlando swore he saw a shark as he swam out on the reef. He snapped it with his underwater camera and they had another of their bets as to whether, when developed, the photo would prove him wrong or not.

'A Cartier watch,' pledged Amy confidently.

'You're joking, I'm an impoverished actor.'

'Liar. OK then, whoever loses is the other's sex slave for a week.'

'Can't wait,' he said, rubbing his hands together like a dirty old man.

Heaven on earth. Orlando and Amy were the only souls on a vast white stretch of beach, tattered palm trees and turquoise water were all the horizon had to offer. Orlando watched Amy prod sea cucumbers with a stick and felt a surge of unprecedented happiness. If Amy thinks she's a cynic wait till she finds out about Orlando. Sitting here in his faded blue board shorts, his tanned legs stretched out in front of him, one hand on a cold beer, peering over his sunglasses at this woman in a bikini who at his bidding will stroll over and kiss him, in fact do anything he wishes. Men have killed for less. Except of course that Amy won't do anything he wishes. He has to try, he has to amuse her. His life was usually a case of too many chocolates in the box to choose from. And not just one box, the whole bloody factory. But really what he felt like was an olive. Yes, he likes that image, Amy is more of an olive. A different ballpark. She wouldn't call him if he didn't call her, she wouldn't thrust her phone number into the pocket of his jeans. In short she was real, a bit more like himself. She was a great restorative. Somehow she transcended most of the women he knew, in beauty and in her funny ways. And he wanted to hang on to her. Yup, we're looking at a very happy young man.

Their final two days in Sydney were spent getting fatter and fatter. They ate their way through roast peppers and goat's cheese salads, barbecued shrimps in garlic, sundried tomatoes and cumin bread, fricassees and soufflés, sorbets and meringues. They moved only when necessary, that was leaving and arriving at restaurants and the continuing sexual tour of every room in the house.

'My continuity person will shoot me,' moaned Orlando, looking in the mirror. 'I'm six times larger than when I was last on set.'

'You'll have to buy another plane ticket for my stomach,' said Amy.

'Billy and Bessie Bunter,' announced Orlando as he and Amy stood side by side. Amy suddenly started to cry.

'This is so lovely, I don't want to go back.' He stroked

131

her hair and kissed the top of her head as her body shook with sobs against his.

'Darling, it's OK, we can come back soon.'

'No, I've got a feeling about it, we'll never come back here.'

'I'll teach you an old African trick. Kiss all four walls of the house and then you'll be sure to come back one day.' They ran around the house interspersing kisses to the walls with snogging each other and Amy seemed soothed, for the time being, but Orlando knew that goodbye this time would be hellish.

It *was* hellish. They clung to one another in the airport, each waiting for their separate planes to carry them back to real life. Amy wasn't upgraded; she looked like a package holiday maker with her patchy pink skin and too-tight trousers. She didn't care, she'd probably overdose on the remainder of her valium on the plane home, she told Orlando morbidly.

'Then I shall die too,' he pronounced in impeccable Shakespearean tones. They reeled off a list of dead lovers: Tristan and Iseult, Romeo and Juliet, Hero and Leander.

'Sid and Nancy,' he put in.

'Oh you have to spoil everything,' she rebuked him. 'Junkie punks aren't really in the same league are they?'

'As a one-time punk myself I'm inclined to disagree.' Amy looked incredulous and then curious.

'Were you really?' That meant that whilst I was still dressing my Sindy doll Orlando was out chasing women in leather mini-skirts; she had a brief moment of concern for the added six years of living and lusting he had over her.

'Yup, turned my nose septic with a safety pin,' he said proudly.

Amy fell about laughing and tried to find the scar, then stopped.

'There's so much I want to know about you. In fact I don't know anything.'

'When we get back we'll make a concerted effort to get to know each other better, and then who knows, we might even feel we know each other well enough to sleep together.'

'Oh, I don't think so,' said Amy gravely, 'I like to wait at least three years and make sure the man in question is accepted by my priest and the other members of the sect.' So they went out laughing instead of crying and in the general hilarity didn't really get to say anything 'meaningful'. Amy lamented this for most of the way home and the next two weeks.

Chapter 20

'He was a punk and I didn't even know it,' said Amy sadly to Lucinda one lunchtime shortly after her return. They were packing shoes away in boxes in the fashion cupboard.

'That's OK babe, there's lots of stuff he doesn't know about you either.'

'No, I think he knows everything. He knows I'm ordinary, work in fashion, want to achieve greater things, have two parents and a brother.'

'Darling, everyone's ordinary underneath,' consoled Lucinda.

'No, I'm just not glamorous enough. I have no world-renowned talent, look average and am as poor as a church mouse. You see, Luce, at least you have your slightly unusual homelife, your mother and stuff.'

'Yeah, and you've got a father which is something I've never had. Why do you think I cling to Benjy so much? I have no idea what men are supposed to be like, apart from the odd itinerant pop-star who stayed for a few months before leaving us again.'

'Luce, I'm sorry, but Anita's so lovely. I really envy you that . . . eccentricity. Do you know who your father is?' she ventured.

'Yup, but he doesn't, so we have to be terribly hush hush about it. That's not eccentric, that's just horrible.'

As she and Lucinda shared their worries Amy suddenly felt incredibly selfish.

'Luce, I'm sorry, I'm such a crap friend sometimes,' she said.

'You're not at all, it's gorgeous having you around. That's why Orlando likes you, you're as mad as a snake in a jar,' said Lucinda, squeezing her feet into a pair of buttersoft tangerine loafers she'd found in the pile.

'I'm not, I'm useless. I never realised you felt so bad about your father.'

'I don't. I've lived with it all my life. It's fine really. Promise. Now what's all this problem with Orlando business?'

'I don't know, it's just that we had such a laugh, which is lovely, but . . . but we always seemed to be play acting, role playing, maybe he just spends his life acting, it must be so easy for actors to pretend.'

'Yes, but why get you out to Sydney? He must like you.'

'I'm sure he does, a bit, but I don't know anything about him, and I've never seen him as he is when he's famous, y'know in public. Maybe he's ashamed of me.'

'Maybe he's just a very private person.'

The phone rang in the office and Lucinda went off to answer it, leaving Amy in that interminable pit of angst popularly know as the salad days.

Now she was back, the familiar worries started to wrack her brain. Now, when she walked down the street, he wasn't there holding her hand. When she woke up he didn't kiss her neck. The lack of his physical presence made her wonder all over again. Could he resist Tiffany Swann? Surely all he had to do was snap his fingers. For once Amy was right. Would the only thing he couldn't resist be temptation? And what about the acting? What about a man who makes his living playing great lovers? Maybe emotion doesn't even register on his scale of important things. If only he'd given more away . . . if only he'd said he loved me.

Amy talked constantly about Orlando. She dusted her face with bronzing powder to prompt the question,

'Oooh, been on holiday have we? Anywhere nice?' Which was her cue to reveal all, to people at dinner parties, the lady in Marks and Spencers, her aerobics teacher. Any excuse. The developing of the photos turned into a momentous cause for celebration. She'd persuaded Orlando to let her take the films with her because you couldn't beat Boots' one-hour service, and certainly not in some New Zealand backwater. Thus at the first available opportunity she took her precious cartridges, parting with them only after she'd insisted that the man took not only her name but her phone number, address and postcode too. Then she loitered outside the automatic doors for about an hour. The women at the No 7 counter became very distracted as Amy to'ed and fro'ed, sending the doors into paroxysms of indecision. Finally she arrived at the photo counter to claim her inheritance. By the time she'd insisted on checking all the photos individually and laying the ones of Orlando carefully out on the top of the till for less fortunate Tampax-purchasing customers to inspect, even she was surprised that someone hadn't pointed her in the direction of Prescriptions and her obviously uncollected Prozac supplies.

At home that evening she showed Cath and Kate her photos, cooing over each one and then falling about laughing as she found the one of the shark.

'Oh my God, now I have to be his sex slave for a week,' she informed them. They purred a catcall of 'do tell all's. Amy elaborated and they laughed hollowly.

'So what will he ask you to do?' said Cath, tilting her head interestedly to one side.

'Yes, we're all ears,' mewed Kate. They made Amy think of two Siamese cats, all sly and smug, but she'd started so she thought she'd better carry on.

'Oh just something peculiar, he's quite an unusual person,' she dismissed as vaguely as possible.

'He must be a bit unusual I suppose, being an actor and all. We all know that they don't have any emotions of their own,' Cath mumbled. Amy suddenly felt like she was in a kangaroo court but dismissed her misgivings as paranoia due to love.

'I think that's a bit strong, he's a very original person, quite into little fantasies, y'know, just stories. He's got a great imagination, we just go off on a tangent together and there's no stopping us.'

'Sounds great,' sang Kate, her voice reedy and thin.

Amy excused herself and went to phone her mother who was dying to know what Australia was like and whether Amy had had time to visit aunt Melinda in Victoria.

'Mum it's a really long way away, I just didn't get chance.'

'Oh dear, and Melinda was so good to us when she went to stay with uncle Henry in Birmingham. She came all the way down to Hampshire for tea.' Amy's mum was laying on the guilt-trip, without intending to.

'Mum, Victoria's a thirteen-hour drive from Sydney.'

'Nooo, I think you must be mistaken darling, even Scotland doesn't take that long to get to.'

Amy left her mother disbelieving of the size of the Australian continent and went to her room to unpack the rest of her things.

She plagued herself so incessantly with her views on the state of Amy and Orlando that even she, with her degree in fantasy, dissection and analysis, was feeling quite worn out. But it's just that she was so confused. There was a stream of problems coursing through her head. She took out a piece of paper and decided to list them, a time honoured way of sorting your life out she'd heard, but it had never seemed to work before. She once tried it on a boyfriend she was going to chuck, fors and againsts. The thing was she knew before she put pen to paper that she wanted to chuck him, she just couldn't think of an excuse, so pen and paper didn't really help.

But Orlando was a trifle different, she did fancy him, so she listed them:

Nagging Worries about Orlando
1. Too much fun – sounds disingenuous but we didn't ever talk seriously about 'us'.

2. His divorce, I've never been out with a divorced man before but can't imagine the ex-wife factor would be much fun. Ex-wives are also supposed to be weathered – her absence of wrinkles is disturbing.
3. His current leading lady – have bad feeling about her and she's very beautiful.
4. *Celebrity Squares* – can I play this game? How does he feel about being famous? Why hasn't he taken me out 'properly', i.e. to a premiere yet?
5. Do I just like the Hotspur/Rochester side of him, am I in love with 'the real Orlando'?

Amy pondered her piece of paper, doodling little flowers around the edge and realising that they weren't really 'worries', not like famine and the homeless, so feeling self-indulgent and rotten vowed to buy the *Big Issue* tomorrow.

Orlando Rock was in his hotel suite, lying back in his chair and flicking over the sports channels. He was meant to be learning his lines for tomorrow but was too exhausted; the heat was suffocating and he'd spent all day acting out a furze cutting scene. He knew Amy would probably have some highly romanticised notions about the physicality and raw sexuality of furze cutting but he thought that to earn a crust he preferred acting. There was a knock on his door.

'C'm in,' he said, not being bothered to move.

'Orlando, it's me.' The syrupy voice came over and

sat on the table in front of him, obscuring his view of the rugby.

'Tiffany, I can't see the telly,' he moaned. She giggled.

'You can't watch telly, there's a great party tonight at a gallery down the road.' Her baby blue satin slip dress made it quite clear to anyone who chose to notice that she wasn't wearing a sliver of underwear and that she had remarkably pert breasts, thank you very much. Orlando craned his head around her to watch the game and refused to notice her even perter nipples straining their way through the fabric like a line in a Jackie Collins novel.

'I don't think so Tiffany, I'm shattered and still have to learn my lines.'

'That's OK, we can just make the love scene last all day and then you won't have to say a word.' Tiffany and her slip slipped all over the table, her legs crossed and uncrossed and she turned into a parody of a seduction scene. Too long in the business, thought Orlando to himself as she wound a stray raven lock around her finger.

'Olly, I'm your leading lady and you haven't paid a bit of attention to me off set since filming started,' she pouted, as if he would suddenly see sense and make frantic love to her.

'I'm going to crash early, Tiffany. You go. There'll be loads of men there dying to mark your dance card.' She looked puzzled at the dance card bit and in an enormous flick of hair and satin slunk out of the room without a word. He rolled his eyes and leant forward to watch a particularly exciting try.

The phone rang. Bollocks.

'Yup?'

'Olly, what the bloody hell do you think you're playing at, upsetting Tiff? We've all gotta work together on this, and if she's unhappy we're all unhappy.' It was the director.

'Sod the amateur psychology, Bill, I've got lines to learn.' Blast, another try missed.

'Olly, I'm warning you, we need pre-publicity. You go to that party, get in the papers and make this film work.' Orlando was too pissed off to argue. He finished his beer, and tying a jumper round his waist, went to the party.

The party was hideous; not since the magazine editor's party in Holland Park had he witnessed such a spectacular display of vulgarity. Women in turbans sauntered round pointing at pictures of what looked to him like flowers but must instead have been genitalia or no one would have given them gallery space. The men wore dinner jackets and Orlando with his beard and jeans looked like he'd taken the wrong turning for the pub. He half expected to be asked to leave but to his dismay everyone present knew who he was, along with his birthsign and favourite colour. The only consolation of fame was that when he asked for a beer rather than champagne the entire kitchen staff ran to find one. Cameras popped and he stood on the periphery not knowing a soul. Not even any twiglets to keep him company as all the nibbles rotated on the arms of waiters, so he couldn't even stare soulfully into the guacamole.

'Orlando Rock, you sly sausage,' treacled Tiffany, slinking up beside him, slipping her wrist through his arm. 'I thought you said you were staying at the hotel. I knew you couldn't really resist.'

Orlando felt as though he'd eaten one too many Mars bars.

'Yeah, well,' he blustered, wishing she'd take her hand away. The eyes of the room were on them and Tiffany was very well aware of this fact. She popped an olive between her cherubic lips and whispered in his ear,

'We could be the next Bogart and Bacall.' A camera flashed at the other side of the room and Orlando saw boxes of light dancing before his eyes. Extricating himself from her he said, 'Tiffany, I've really got to go, no offence but I don't feel too great.'

'Poor baby,' she lisped, kissing him on the cheek as he put his jumper on and left.

Chapter 21

Amy, like most of us, had never before woken up to find her boyfriend's infidelity on the front cover of the newspapers and we can't pretend she found out this particularly nasty piece of information in a gentle, cushioned manner, because she didn't.

The Siamese pawed their way around her bedroom door at eight o'clock on Sunday morning and perched on the end of her bed. Cath carried a cup of coffee and Kate the newspapers.

'We brought you these,' said Cath, placing the coffee on Amy's dressing table.

'And this . . .' said Kate, passing a bleary eyed Amy a copy of the *News of the World* and the *Mail on Sunday*. Amy rubbed her eyes, thinking maybe it was her birthday and to wake her at an ungodly hour was their idea of a treat. No such luck, Amy.

'I think you'd better read this,' said Kate gravely, pushing the rolled up paper under Amy's nose.

'Thanks,' Amy croaked, trying to sound grateful for this unprecedented 'treat'.

They sat in deafening silence, watching as Amy pulled her pillows up behind her and, yawning, looked at the front page. There, clear as day and twice as vicious, was Orlando Rock, and a woman was kissing his cheek. Not quite comprehending, Amy looked again, half catching the caption: 'Top Actor ... Rock ... Tiffany Swann ... On the Town.' The flat monsters sat there ogling her, waiting for a response. Amy turned white and her coffee cup shook in her hand, but she didn't say anything. She read and re-read the short caption but it made no sense. Eventually the flat monsters went away purring with satisfaction at their triumph.

Amy lay in the bath and let the water lap over her head. She heard the swirling sounds of the pipes beneath the water and felt minute tingles as the bubbles of air rose from her hair to the top of the water. She couldn't really focus on what was happening. Orlando was in New Zealand and kissing Tiffany Swann. She looked at her pink striped body where her swimsuit had been as they'd snorkelled on the reef and felt chilled. Back in her room she tossed the newspaper off her bed and straightened the sheets. Bastard! she growled, and kicked the desk.

The phone rang and she was nearly sick. She crept towards the door and stood on the other side, dreading it being Orlando and preparing insults and accusations, but even more dreading it not being him. She held her breath.

'I just want to talk to Amy,' Lucinda yelled down the phone.

'There's really no need to shout, and I don't think she wants to speak to anyone right now,' said Cath, her philanthropic tone serving only to piss Lucinda off even more.

'If you don't get her at once I'll break both your legs.'

Cath tramped up the stairs and knocked on Amy's door.

'Someone on the phone for you.'

'Who?' asked Amy, desperate for it to be Orlando so she could at least scream at him, or he could explain the terrible misunderstanding.

'That woman you work with,' spat Cath. Amy opened the door and greeted Cath red eyed and pale.

'OK, I'll take it. Lucinda. Hi.'

'You've seen it?'

'Sure have,' she said bravely.

'I'll come and pick you up.'

'No, look, it's better if I stay here.'

'Amy, if he calls the bitches can give him my number.' Lucinda anticipated Amy's worry.

'OK.'

Sitting at Lucinda's kitchen table Amy allowed Benjy to read out the salient horrors of Orlando's indiscretion.

'They were at a party for the launch of one of New Zealand's major artists ... Tiffany Swann, Rock's co-star in the forthcoming film of Hardy's *Return of the Native*, wore a stunning blue dress and the couple were spotted chatting intimately. A fellow party-goer said, "They couldn't keep their hands off one another. The relationship seemed more than just professional."'

'Enough!' shouted Amy. 'I should have known better than to trust an actor, especially one with a reputation for womanising. What a bloody idiot I am.' Lucinda put her arm around Amy and Benjy made some more tea.

'Screw him!' Amy yelled, kicking the table. 'Why can't I just find someone nice? Just a boyfriend, no bells, just a bloke.' They all knew that Amy wouldn't just settle for any old bloke, but humoured her and Benjy took his cue and left the room. Better not to be a moving target when there's a general down-on-men vibe darting around and one of the women present is virtually mainlining Bach Rescue Remedy.

A few nights later Amy's anger had hardened like lava on the side of a volcano. Molten Amy she thought. Mount St Amy. She was still grinding her teeth ferociously but staying with Lucinda and Benjy was a comfort. They'd fed and watered her and in between bouts of dying to see Orlando just so she could hit him she also felt as though she was getting over him. We'll let her live with this delusion too, if it helps the healing process. Eventually the resident carers, Benjy and Lucinda decided that what she needed was to dance. Shake it, strut it and let go a bit. Lucinda came into her room wielding a secret weapon in the form of a laughably tiny corset and some PVC trousers.

'Oh my God it's a glittery boob tube! You're never going to wear that Luce, you'll fall out of it,' Amy shrieked, perking up at the sight of this wonderful garment.

'No, sweetheart, you're going to wear it,' said Lucinda, with no fuss and no room for manoeuvre. 'We're going to a club, c'mon.' The sergeant major diction worked a

treat and ten minutes later Amy was suffocating herself
into the corset and zipping up the trousers. She wiggled
her bottom to herself in the mirror and felt a bit of a
Gloria Gaynor coming on . . . ba na na na ba na na naaaa.
Amazing what a new outfit can do for a girl.

The club was beneath a market stall in Camden Town,
seedy and packed to the rafters with hip young things.
Two transvestites stumbled around crashing into furni-
ture and revellers.

'Off their tits,' muttered the guy on the cloakroom.
This struck Amy as amusing since they didn't even have
real tits. In another corner Boy George was holding court
in a denim jacket and it was rumoured that Naomi
Campbell was upstairs. Amy doubted it and hoped not.
The last time she'd seen Naomi had been on a shoot and
she'd bought her the wrong kind of muesli bar and as
everyone knows, hell hath no fury like a supermodel given
the wrong kind of muesli bar. Amy could only afford one
beer so asked Benjy to babysit it in between spells on the
dance floor. Lucinda and Amy were in their element: they
gyrated and writhed, their hips swung giddily from side
to side and they looked fab.

'Are you feeling better now, darling?' Lucinda leant
over and yelled in Amy's ear, causing her eardrum to
vibrate.

'Yup,' Amy mouthed. And she was. The best outfits
on the floor, the coolest dancers and a bevy of ardent
admirers waiting on the sidelines for the girls to come
up for air, but they didn't. Breathless and hot they carried
on dancing. All that coaxing models into funky positions

had left them both with a variety of stunning poses to strike, and they struck. The music pulsed through Amy's blood and she felt strong and resilient. Even as they stood at the bar the aura of ferocity about them warded off all but the most die-hard suitors. Benjy made himself known as Lucinda's must have accessory, but Amy was easy prey. She sipped at the warm dregs of her beer and watched the men watching her. The *femme fatale* in her came to the fore. And the crueller she looked the more they hankered after her. If only it was always so simple, but the general nature of men is one of perversity, so unfortunately it's not. Benjy and Lucinda went back to the dance floor and Amy was left seductively handling her beer bottle. It didn't take long, that's the great thing about nightclubs, it never does take long. No intellectual pretexts are needed, just plain old,

'You dancing?' a voice behind her drawled. Amy was tempted to run the gamut:

'You asking?'

'I'm asking.'

'I'm dancing.' But she put her Liverpudlian accent on the backburner and turned to face the face whence the invitation had come. Not a bad face, thought Amy. Male modellish. Yes, nice. And not Orlando Rock. Not remotely like Orlando Rock. Blonde and Australian-looking, longish hair, brown eyes. Highlighted hair then? Probably. Don't think I like the idea of that. Oh come on, Amy, beggars can't be choosers, and he looks nice, not like a pervert or anything. Not like he'd chop you up into little bits if you went home with him. That's a relief.

'OK,' said Amy.

So she slunk about and the male modellish looking person put his hands on her hips, he closed his eyes and danced a bit like Jim Morrison. Not bad. After a while her hips obviously weren't doing the trick for him so he moved them up a bit. Amy sped up her dancing so that his hands couldn't keep up with her. She wasn't nearly drunk enough to be doing this, she told herself. But then the image of Orlando's cheek, the cheek she'd stroked and pinched, the one she'd watched as he slept, flashed into her mind, with that tart's lips all over it. She braced herself and let her nameless blonde take hold of whatever bits he wanted. She pulled his shirt collar down and kissed him. They danced close, he pulling Amy against him, against the unabashed hard bit in his trousers. Amy kissed him lots more and was reminded of seventeen-year-old nightclub kisses that were all you could manage because you had to go home to your parents. Their faces slipped sweatily against one another and he tasted of beer and cigarettes. It was so like her first forays into sex that she was quite turned on at the thought. But not enough. I can't. I just can't. She pushed his shoulders away gently and, smiling said, 'I'm just off to the loo, back in a minute.' He nodded dumbly, Amy pegged it to the ladies.

'Shit shit shit.' She splashed cold water all over her face and looking up saw herself in her gold corset and smudged mascara.

'What *do* I look like?' she said under her breath. A six-foot transvestite lurched out of the cubicle behind her in a figure hugging Vivienne Westwood dress and winked a false lashed eye at her.

'You look gorgeous honey, too nice for this place,' he rasped wisely.

'Thanks. You're probably right,' said Amy, blow drying her hands.

'Men, eh?' he smirked, wiping some lipstick off his front teeth.

'Exactly,' she agreed.

She went outside in search of Lucinda, keeping her head down, trying to avoid the Australian. Spying Lucinda and Benjy at the other side of the room she wound her way around the outside and grabbed their arms.

'Guys, I've got to go.'

'We thought you were enjoying yourself,' said Benjy.

'I'm much too old for this kind of thing,' she said, hanging her head for fear of being spotted. Oh God, there he is, he's looking right at me.

'Luce, help!'

'Borrow Benjy,' said Lucinda, quick as a flash, 'Benjy, kiss Amy, now!' Benjy looked flabbergasted and far too nervous to move; time was running out and the Australian was on his way over, practically groping distance away. Lucinda grabbed Amy and kissed her smack bang on the lips, they wiggled their faces around a bit in their best imitation of a snog. Benjy looked on in admiration at Lucinda's ingenuity. The Australian lumbered around, looking quizzically at Benjy. Benjy just shrugged his shoulders. Realising his luck was out, The Australian gave a some-you-win toss of his head and went to seek out the next sure thing. Amy and Lucinda kept up the charade all the way to the cloakrooms, looking lovingly into each other's eyes and holding hands. Then, when they'd all had their jackets safely returned, they tore up the stairs of the club and collapsed laughing in the street outside. Benjy wandered around doing his best 'women, what are they like?' impression, but they all knew that he was feeling proud, if a little bewildered.

'You missed your chance there Benjy,' said Amy.

'I think that's just something he'll have to live with, sweetpea,' Lucinda said sagely.

In the taxi it began to sink in what Amy had done.

'Thank God you guys were there. I mean, he wasn't the sex fiend type but you'd have thought I'd have grown up enough not to snog the first guy who crossed my path after Orlando Rock.'

'You're never too old to do stupid things Amy, just put it down to experience,' said Lucinda.

'Oh harken unto Clare Rayner here,' said Benjy. 'If I'd just made an itsy bitsy mistake like getting off with a complete stranger in a nightclub it'd have been a castratable offence.'

'Naturally,' said the girls in unison. You're a lone male Benjy, just leave it alone, for your own sake.

When Amy woke up the next morning she could smell cigarette smoke. Oh God it's me. Her mouth tasted very parrot cagey and oh no ... regression. It was the regression to that feeling when you've had one too many ciders when you're sixteen, you've snogged someone – you know that because your lips are cut – and you've kissed for so long that you've got kind of chillblains around your mouth, you can feel a nagging ache in your tummy, will he be at school on Monday? Did I give him my phone number? If you gave him your phone number not only were you braindead you also have to spend the rest of the weekend darting for the phone every time it rings because if your parents get it there'll be interminable inquisitions which will either take the form of: 'I think you're still too young to be going to discotheques, you're only sixteen.'

'It's not a disco mum, it's a club.'

'Precisely.'

Or alternatively, and much worse, 'Ooohh, Amy met a young man last night, Peter!'

'Tell us all about him, do you want to invite him to tea?'

'Dad, shurrrup.'

Occasionally the younger siblings became involved in which case you could guarantee that your diary would be quoted from at the breakfast table, and every visitor to the house from the person collecting for Christian Aid to granny would be greeted with the sing-song rendition of, 'Amy's got a boyfriend.'

'Bugger off.'

'Mum, Amy swore.'

Amy's stomach churned at the thought. And it was often worse if you didn't want to speak to Friday night's snog because they had spots and were in the third form.

'Amy, you can't just leave that poor young man on the end of the phone. Go and speak to him.'

'Mum, he's ugly.'

'Amy, I have not brought you up to be rude and cruel. Go and talk to him, NOW!'

Adolescence, thought Amy, suddenly putting all her

problems into perspective. I suppose it'll be the same throughout my life: the men you don't fancy send you flowers, phone you incessantly and can afford to buy you Hermès handbags. Those you do fancy are utter bastards and infidels. *C'est la vie.*

Chapter 22

As Amy was tickling the tonsils of her nameless consort in deepest North London, Orlando Rock was having breakfast with his director and great friend Bill Ballantyne. A hefty Scot, Bill was tucking into the full sausage, bacon and eggs whilst depriving Orlando of anything other than muesli and semi-skimmed.

'Bill, you're six stone heavier than me and you're having the works. Please, let me have just one sausage.'

'No way. If you come back from your shag-fest two stone heavier it is nae ma problem. I'm not the madman going in front of the camera.'

'Bill, come on, one sausage and I'll fix you up with that Anthea Turner,' Orlando promised.

'I said no. You had your oats for two weeks and now you'll have none.'

'I don't want porridge, just a sausage sandwich,' pleaded Orlando, starving hungry.

'Hush up, now, tell me about your lassie, what's she got that young Tiffany doesn't then?'

'Half a brain.'

'Come on Olly, Tiffany's a bright woman. You could do worse now Joanna's out of the picture.'

'Let's leave Joanna out of this. She's in LA doing her

157

thing and good luck to her. And can we leave Tiffany out of it too? Amy's nice, bright, funny, extremely attractive and that's it.'

'And I bet she's not averse to having her very own celebrity to take her out on the town.'

'Bill, Amy's really great.' Orlando took the opportunity to lean over and help himself to one of Bill's sausages.

'I know, but you could do worse than Tiffany. Good publicity too.'

'Bill, you're supposed to be my friend and you're beginning to sound like a pimp.'

'OK, but I like to get to know your young ladies. I've been in the business thirty years and you're a young pup who could easily be conned by some conniving young beauty dying to make it big.'

'Amy's already got a career. She's done very well in her life without you or me and you'll get an introduction when we get home. OK?'

'Och, don't mind me, I'm just a cynical old bastard. I'm sure you've done very well for yourself and I canna wait to meet her.'

Orlando was impressed at the resemblance between Dorset and New Zealand: grassy, rocky, enough sheep to keep you in chops for the rest of your born days, and the film set banter of English voices made him feel almost at home. But he kept remembering little things that he'd had in England. For instance he couldn't just nip round to Lily's after filming and trawl through the verbal archives of their childhood. The time they'd kissed at the age of ten and then not spoken to each other for two years. The time Lily broke her arm as they played circuses in the garden and she'd confused the seal part, standing on the ball instead of balancing it on her nose. All the adults kept saying, 'Poor Lily, what have you done to your arm?'

'I fell off a ball.'

'Oooh Terence, poor Lily fell off a wall.'

'No, it was a ball,' the tyrannical two chimed, time and again.

He missed Lily in the way that being thousands of miles from home makes everything seem much more acute. If someone said Marmite he melted; and every British television programme under the sun became a masterpiece of comedy or drama. *Are You Being Served?* was repeated once a week on satellite and Orlando would not move from the screen.

'Classic British comedy,' he'd mutter if anyone tried to disturb him, but try making him watch it in London and he'd have said TV was for sad people without lives of their own. So I think we can safely say he was homesick. But more than homesick Orlando was Amysick.

It had been a year since he'd had anything resembling a relationship with his ex wife Joanna but it was only recently that the press had cottoned on, probably because Joanna had started parading a string of handsome young men on her arm at every LA dinner and dog dance and none of them was Orlando. But that was past. There was absolutely no comparison between Joanna and Amy. Joanna was as hard as nails, which had turned him on when he was in his early twenties: Blonde Ambition, as every magazine article about her headlined. Orlando had been mad about acting, fresh out of drama school and she was great for him. But then she started inviting journalists into the house, telling all about their decision not to have children because they valued their careers too much, where they bought their sofas and the perils of a showbusiness marriage. Orlando had become increasingly uncomfortable with this side of his life. He couldn't take his wife out to dinner without the paparazzi collaring them and journalists asking the restaurant staff if he was a generous tipper. Eventually, he didn't really want to take his wife out at all; she had little conversation beyond herself and her latest role and he just began to find her very dull. He had a vague string of other women: models, costume designers, scriptwriters, all in the demonic world of stage and screen. The reputation kind of stuck, but he hadn't really been out with anyone for the past year, and didn't really want to until now. But Amy, different kettle of fish, he told himself. Or even soup tureen of fish, remembering their mad encounter in the Conran Shop. Amy was real. Real and bright and inspiring. She was also the kind of girl who once you'd got a look at nobody else seemed quite as strikingly beautiful. Other women stopped traffic. Amy stopped your heart. (And Amy was, at this very moment, squeezing the bum of a modelly looking guy in a nightclub.) It was such a relief to be with someone so completely natural and clever. She taught him things he didn't know, and didn't really need to know, but that was part of the fun. And he wanted to impress her, take her to places that she'd love. Show her that he wasn't just some showbiz himbo. It wasn't the acting he minded, that was his passion, his *raison d'être*.

It was the trappings, the interviews, the media. Clichéd but true, folks.

I want to take Amy and live in Brittany and she could write her novels and I could research parts and then, when I was away she could follow me with her laptop. We could just wear Breton shirts all day and cook marvellous dishes of roast onions and garlic and have horses (but not for dinner). Orlando didn't know quite how close he was sailing to a fantasy voiced by Lucinda not so long ago, and he didn't know how Amy had laughed off Lucinda's dream as ridiculous. But men are often hopelessly romantic creatures and forget to include the important extras into their day-dreams such as Harvey Nichols storecards and friends. Presumably they forget friends because they would spoil the sex-on-tap-twenty-seven-hours-a-day fantasy which men usually incorporate into their daydreams. And on Orlando went, sitting with his head in his hands in a far corner of the set. No one disturbed him because they thought he was getting in character.

'OK young fella me lad, your turn,' yelled Bill from his large seat behind the camera.

Orlando didn't hear.

'I said get your backside over here, lover boy.' Orlando sat up, startled and filled with nerves, as he always was before he trod the boards, as it were. Tiffany was waiting on set, her cloak and hood lending her considerably more mystery and appeal than her satin look.

'Have you told Bill then?' she cooed.

'Told him what exactly?' Orlando snapped. His Mr

Darcy was in fine fettle, charging away with the scene, except it was the wrong character for this film. But there was just something about that faux winsome thing that Tiffany did which brought out the curt, gloomy bastard side to his nature.

'Oh, come on Olly, I know you're a bit publicity shy but enough's enough. Everyone here can see that you can barely keep your hands off me.' (A painfully familiar phrase – could Amy have heard it at this moment she wouldn't have laughed it off with the incredulity and contempt it deserved – she'd have hit them both.)

'I haven't a clue what you're talking about, Tiffany. Please, can we just let it drop?'

Thankfully Bill interrupted their tête à tête.

'OK, now look at me, Tiffany, you've just found out that the man you love, the one who was going to rescue you from the Heath and your drab life, is going blind, you're destined to stay here for a long time yet,' Bill coached.

Lights, camera, action.

'Clym, what do you mean we can't go to Paris?' the actress looked distressed.

'I think we had better stay on Egdon for now, Eustacia. I can keep us somehow, there's always furze cutters needed this time of year.' Orlando's Dorset brogue was second nature and his acting impeccable. They carried on until,

'OK cut, take five guys,' said Bill, more than satisfied with the scene.

Orlando took a sip from his bottle of water and resumed his head in hands pose. This time though he was thinking of Clym Yeobright and his failing eyesight, and his increasing disenchantment with the demanding Eustacia.

'I think we really should sort this out, Orlando.' It was the ubiquitous Tiffany again. Orlando raised his head and looked at her with sheer disbelief.

'Just what is it you'd like to talk about, Tiffany?'

'Us.'

'Us?'

'Yes, you have to let me know whether we can go ahead with this or not. Do we let the crew know?'

'Do we let the crew know what?' Orlando sighed, knowing where this was heading but figuring that playing dumb was the best tactic.

'Well, I know that you've talked to Bill because, well because he called you lover boy earlier, and that's fine, I know he's a good friend of yours and you're entitled to talk it through with him first, but I think I also have a right to know where I stand.'

OK, Olly grab the bull by the horns, but gently now, there's a touch of the basket case about her, go easy. Look, Tiffany, I think you're really talented and beautiful but I've just been through a nasty divorce and ... no, that doesn't sound right. Can't use that excuse, she might find out about Amy and stick pins in her effigy. OK, here goes.

'Tiffany, I really admire you as an actor and you're a very attractive woman, but I think that you deserve better. And I make a point of never becoming emotionally involved with my fellow actors.' Orlando delivered his set piece and watched her turn from shrew to rabbit caught in the headlights, all hurt and wide eyed. Please don't cry, he thought, don't.

'Orlando, I know you're probably cut up about your divorce, but I've been there and I can help you out, show you that there's life after alimony.' There is if you're on the receiving end, thought Orlando bitterly, calling to mind his latest bank statement and the rent on a house in Bel Air he was paying for. This made his blood boil and Mr Darcy was resurrected.

'There is absolutely no point in you wasting your time with me, Tiffany. There is nothing going on between us and as far as I'm concerned there never will be.'

Wooh, you tell her Olly. Why oh why can't Amy be a fly on the wall right now, why is she instead lying sad and alone in Lucinda's spare room with only last night's discarded clothes and a cold cup of coffee for solace.

Orlando walked flushed into an interview with a journalist from a New Zealand women's magazine. He felt guilt-stricken about Tiffany and was sure that Bill would give him hell when he found out, which was inevitable because she'd tell everyone that he was numero uno bastard and then everyone on the film would blame him for dragging his personal life onto the set. No win situation was a phrase which sprang to mind. And now he had to go and answer questions about art, life, sex and his favourite type of pasta. He looked like an impoverished sheep farmer and knew that every detail of his mangy beard and bloodshot eyes would appear in print. Oh Amy, where are you when I need you?

Jane Sykes had a very short, tight skirt on and the kind

of spectacles only found on schoolmarms in Hollywood movies. She was just begging for them to be removed in true 'My God but you're beautiful Ms Sykes' fashion, but no one ever did.

'So, Mr Rock, let's get the formalities out of the way. I'm Jane Sykes and my readers would like to get to know you better, they want to feel they know you, so let's start in the bedroom department . . . what do you wear in bed?' Except she didn't say bed, she said bid, and she was brassy and fearsome and having her readers' best interests at heart was not going to be fobbed off by 'an old pair of pyjamas that my mother bought' which was the truth. Except of course when Amy was present. She wouldn't settle for anything less than 'nothing, except a condom'. (These are the nineties, Mr Rock and my readers like their sex symbols in the buff but with a social conscience.)

Orlando compromised slightly.

'Usually my silk boxer shorts but when it's hot, nothing,' said Orlando, playing the game as well as he could bear to.

'Veerry nice Mr Rock,' She leered over her hornrims.

'Call me Orlando, please.'

'OK, Orlando, would you say that the break up of your marriage was in part due to the outmoded and politically incorrect characters you play? For instance Mr Rochester, who we all know to be not only a sadist but a misogynist to boot'. No pussyfooting around for Ms Sykes, thought Orlando ruefully.

'I think that there is a certain element of charm in the character of Rochester, and indeed in my current role, as Clym Yeobright in *Return of the Native*. I think it's

the women who hold the dominant position in both
these films.'

'Come now Orlando, I would hardly call Thomas
Hardy a purveyor of sexual equality. Rape? Persecution?
I think he very much had it in for women.'

'Perhaps it was his age which had it in for women, and
not Hardy,' Orlando ventured, taking his life, or certainly
his manhood in his hands, for crossed Jane Sykes would
surely be an advocate of castration too.

'Let's move on to the subject of your marriage to
Joanna. It has been suggested that the problems between
you occurred because you weren't happy with her having
a career.'

'Nonsense,' snapped Orlando. Stop it Olly, the more
testosterone you can quell the nicer she'll be about you.
'What I mean is that our marriage failed because we were
both working on the opposite sides of the Atlantic.' He
smiled winningly.

'And it had nothing to do with your extracurricular,
and at times positively profligate love life, Mr Rock?'

'I beg your pardon?' She handed him a two day old
copy of the *Mail on Sunday*. Orlando looked at it and
turned almost as pale as Amy had when she'd seen it.

'Excuse me, Ms Sykes, I have a phone call to make,'
he said, dashing out of the room.

'Bugger bugger,' said Orlando dialling Amy's number
from the hotel lobby. He kept getting it wrong his hand
was trembling so much. Bill came along.

'Olly, what's the matter man?' Orlando thrust the
newspaper he was still gripping into Bill's hand.

'Great,' said Bill, 'Just what we needed, lots of smashing publicity.'

'Bill, don't you get it? Amy will have seen this. Look, it says we couldn't keep our hands off each other. Where do they get these lies?'

'Settle down, Olly. She'll understand, this kind of thing happens all the time.'

Orlando finally made the digits coherent but the phone just kept on ringing.

'Somehow I don't think she will understand, Bill,' he said despairingly.

Orlando tried and tried but no answer, bugger bugger bugger.

On set that afternoon the temperature was arctic. Bill was frosty because no one was working hard enough. The crew were possessed of a certain *froideur* towards Orlando because Tiffany had confessed her affection for him to them and they all fancied her. Tiffany was a walking icicle because she had been spurned, for the first time ever. And Orlando was Jack Frost himself for obvious reasons, and because he still hadn't been able to get hold of Amy though he'd tried Vogue House and Lily in Dorset to no avail.

The Big Chill.

Chapter 23

Gearing up for a big girls' night in Amy sat with her filofax open on her lap, phoning her way through those who told the dirtiest jokes, those who would dance naked on bars given enough vodka, those upon whose shoulders she'd shed many a tear throughout her life. In short, her best girlfriends.

'Charlie, hi it's Amy. Do you fancy coming round to supper on Thursday? . . . no nothing special, just haven't seen you for ages. OK, see you then.'

'Sal, I haven't seen you for ages. Come round on Thursday, Charlie'll be here and we can catch up.'

And so on and so forth. Amy went to the supermarket and bought two kinds of cardamom pods, a bottle of red wine, some fresh lemon grass and coconut milk. She rushed home and, with her Van Morrison on at full blast, skipped round the kitchen concocting the wickedest Thai curry this side of Bangkok. Now, whilst it doesn't always pay to put on a brave face, Amy felt that masking her misery was the healthiest option. And you know what? It was paying off. She only thought about Orlando every three minutes now and not all the time. He was there, of course, just under the surface of her thoughts, waiting to jump out at unsuspecting moments like when she cleaned

169

her teeth or thought about roast potatoes. Boo! But she'd dried her tears and was preparing a massive banquet for eight of her closest friends on Thursday. She chopped and diced and peeled and sliced, she licked wooden spoons and burnt her tongue, she choked on chilli powder and scraped her knuckle grating ginger. The smell was magnificent, creamy, spicy and tropical all at once. Yum, thank you Mr Floyd, she said, closing the recipe book and putting her pungent concoction in the fridge to work its magic overnight.

The next day Amy played the part of fashion editor with aplomb. She borrowed a pair of red satin Manolo Blahnik stilettos from Lucinda and swirled her way through the swing doors of Vogue House with the panache of a catwalk model. Today was her first assignment on her own shoot. Council estate glamour had finally made it to the studio. She'd booked her models and chosen the clothes and was about to launch her career in fashion into orbit. Is power a substitute for love or vice versa? Amy wasn't sure and didn't really care; she threw herself headlong into her downbeat darlings. Her models were real women, which meant that they had breasts, and her clothes hung on rails, a violent mixture of psychedelic and Bet Lynch. Brash, brazen and loud.

Amy took the whole shooting match in a mini-bus to a particularly grotty student hovel where she'd lived with three college friends one summer. She felt authenticity was imperative for her first assignment and since the council had condemned the property the whole team were able to clamber through the boarded up bathroom

window. Though the make-up artist claimed that if his
union ever found out they'd sue Amy for all she was
worth. Not very much, ha ha, let them try. It all came
flooding back to her. Her summer of contentment. Not
a man in sight. They were all meant to be encased in the
library like hothouse flowers, pounding out their disser-
tations on the modern novel – *mais non!* The sun streaked
into the library windows and Nabokov lay abandoned
on the desk where he would sit all day until five o'clock
when the library was about to close and they'd charge in
and pack everything away until tomorrow. Inspired by
Lolita, they spent their days wearing mules and barely
there shorts, trotting up and down the high street.
They'd lie in the long grass in the churchyard, reading
magazines and laughing lazily. They went through their
local Oxfam with a fine-tooth comb, unearthing fabulous
kaftans and a series of books enticingly called *Silhouette
Desire*, obviously the raunchy seventies cousin of Mills
and Boon, their favourite of which was *Renaissance Man*
which they took it in turns to read out to one another and
which involved many a brush with 'pulsating manhood'
on cream shagpile carpets. They searched for David, the
open-shirted medallion bearing hero of *Renaissance Man*,
on the streets of the town but he'd obviously fled to
St-Tropez for the summer. They lived on Eccles cakes
from the bakers round the corner and as a concession
to dreaming spires polished off a bottle of Pimms daily.
One day they abandoned even the pretence of the library
and took their kaftans to the beach, buying whisky and
sausages on the way, and building a bonfire to cook on
and keep them warm, spent the night beneath the stars.

Hair was dyed in the kitchen sink, a range of shades from magpie black to reddest henna. Thinking about that summer Amy felt restored beyond measure, secure in the knowledge that life had been heady and perfect once and surely would be again.

She directed the models into mouldering corners of what was once her sitting room, the peeling sixties wallpaper clashing fantastically with the model's lilac negligee. The overgrown roses in the garden they'd never even ventured into as students were the perfect backdrop for the models to have a neighbourly chat over the garden fence, fags dangling, rollers resting neatly atop of heads. In fact all went remarkably well. On their drive back to London everyone was declaring what an outré idea it was and how fabulously the shoot had gone, 'The girls looked so slutty, it was heavenly,' mused the make-up artist.

'Thanks a lot,' a model groaned busily removing a roller that had got stuck in her hair.

'Yeah, thanks guys, what a buzz eh? Who needs men when you've got a career and friends?' Amy bolstered herself.

'Oooh, I do. I always feel like a man,' the make-up artist pouted.

'That's because you are one you idiot,' said Amy, and the bus collapsed into laughter and school-trip renditions of Boney M songs. Amy felt a once familiar glow return, the warmth of being pleased with yourself and feeling the sky very high above. Yes, she could get by without Orlando Rock, or anyone else for that matter.

*   *   *

That evening she returned home and in imitation of many an executive woman on television commercials kicked off her shoes and rested exhausted but fulfilled on the sofa. Her stomach still let her down by fluttering wildly every time the phone rang but logic fought equally hard. It's only one of the girls phoning to say they'll be late or mum phoning to say hello, she told herself firmly, refusing to even entertain the thought that it might be Orlando. After her token gesture to the exhausted career woman in her, she padded into the kitchen and boiled up a paddy field of basmati rice, not wanting her guests to go hungry. She gently simmered her coconut curry as instructed and ignoring the stirring frequently part, decided that it was better she look the part than cook the part. So she showered and dressed, taking care to keep that 'at home' feel to her attire. Looking for a cardigan, she came across one of her infamous kaftans. Amy, you can't, yes I can, they're my friends and they'll think it's great. So she abandoned her 'at home' look and popped the electric blue Oxfam number over her head and was transported to her past life. Airy, summery and carefree.

The doorbell rang to life at eight o'clock and a stream of familiar faces trailed in, all ecstatic to see one another again and wildly admiring of Amy's kaftan and the lovely smell. Eight old girlfriends in your kitchen is a recipe for instant joy, Keith Floyd or no Keith Floyd. Their laughter rattled the neighbour's chandeliers and their elephant patter shook the floorboards (just as surely as did her antics with Orlando Amy allowed herself fleetingly). The conversation was manifold. Like a perfume there was a basenote of 'well I never, did you hear about . . .' and a middle note of work-a-day exchanges, 'yes, I'm in publishing you know' and then the top note of hilarity and hysteria, 'Oh, we're not really going out, it's just a sex-thing'. Amy decided that her news about Orlando was not fragrant enough to be included in this general hubub, it'd have to wait until a few bottles of red down the line.

The curry was declared a success and faxes of the recipe promised to at least three friend's offices the next morning and the gathering of the clan transported itself to the living room.

'Amy, I can't believe you've got this great career now, you were always the flakiest of us all and look at you – high flying and living the glamorous life.'

'Don't be silly Alex, it's so unglamorous that you wouldn't believe it. Anyway I only earn about five pence a year.'

'Which is more than I get in publishing,' moaned Charlie.

'Yes, but at least you get to meet people with functioning brains,' said Zoe who'd just started work in the City.

'I wish. Just lots of lecherous poets.' Charlie tossed her hair back and longed for an office full of stockbrokers to take her mind off books, 'Who would be in your fantasy workmate league?' she asked Zoe.

'Definitely Ken Livingstone,' piped in Sally, 'For sheer loveliness value.'

'Oooh yes, I'd be very happy to share my printer with Red Ken.' Charlie smiled.

'Oh come on girls, what about someone younger?' Zoe

said, topping up each glass as though it were a party trick to fill each to the brim.

'Sting,' Alex thought. 'Something about the English teacher in him, d'you know what I mean?' They did and nodded agreement.

'Chris Evans. You always need someone anarchic in the office.' Charlie had made her choice.

'Yeah, but wouldn't it piss you off after a while?' Amy said, piling the plates up in the middle of the table.

'I think we need someone more decorative too,' Sally decided, reaching over to take the last chicken breast before Amy whisked it away to the kitchen.

'Tom Cruise.'

'God such a hackneyed choice Alex, what about someone British?' said Zoe. 'What about Rufus Sewell. Or whatshisname, the intense looking one?'

'Which intense looking one?' Amy was about to run to the kitchen as she knew what was coming next, but something glued her to her chair. She changed the CD as a compromise.

'Orlando Rock?' asked Alex. At which point the music stopped. Amy hiccuped in the corner.

'Don't go any further with that one,' she said. They were all looking at her now. What to say? She couldn't bear to hear anything said about Orlando in her own living room, it would be weird beyond belief. And part of her still had a longing to talk about it. To cast it to her friends like a frisbee and see what they made of it all. She tried to play down the anticipation which was just hanging there. 'Oh it's nothing really, just that, well, I was kind of seeing Orlando. I mean, I'm not anymore, so it doesn't really matter what you say about him. But, I just thought you should know.' She reached for her glass.

'Not Orlando Rock, Orlando Rock,' Sally squealed, just checking. Amy nodded.

'But didn't I see him in the paper the other day, with what's her name Swann?'

'Tiffany Swann,' Amy tried for the casual approach.

'That's the one.'

'Yeah, I'm not really sure what to think. Maybe it was innocent, but still . . .' she trailed off, not wanting to share her humiliation with so many people just yet, and most of all not wanting any sympathy. If they started to cluck and fuss she'd probably cry.

'Wow, lucky you,' said Sally admiringly. Yes, lucky me, thought Amy drily.

'So?'

'So what?' asked Amy.

'So tell all,' pestered Alex.

'Well, we met in Dorset, and I saw him in a play, and then bumped into him on a shoot and then the Conran shop . . .'

'Spare us the boring details Ames, just tell us the scandal.'

'Nothing, except he took me on holiday to Australia and I thought it was going well but . . .' Amy's eyes began to well up. Stop it Amy, you're stronger than that. The girls sensed her discomfort and rallied to her rescue. Old chestnuts fell thick and fast but she began to feel better.

'There's plenty more fish in the sea.'

'What a rotten bastard, men just can't help themselves can they?'

'Anyway, he's not such a great actor. He got a terrible review for something in *Time Out* the other day.'

The vitriol flowed along with the wine and soon turned to mirth as anecdotes about the general inferiority of the male population were volleyed back and forth. They were momentarily interrupted by the doorbell but Amy slipped away to answer it and the battle raged on.

'Hang on a minute,' she yelled down the stairs. But she couldn't remember anyone ordering a cab so maybe it was someone's boyfriend come to infiltrate the ranks on the pretext of being a lift home. She opened the door and nearly shut it again. Orlando. Her heart soared. This was not something that had ever happened to her before. She'd imagined it was just a thing that happened in bad fiction. But here it was going on inside her ribcage. He looked so tired and beautiful she almost couldn't help herself. But what was he doing here? She couldn't remember him ever having left his record collection so he couldn't be coming to collect it. Kiss him? No! Smile? No! Give him hell? The only way to teach them I'm afraid.

'Amy.'

'What the hell . . . ?'

'I've come to explain.'

'You're supposed to be in New Zealand.'

'I came to see you, I tried for days to get through but . . .'

'I was away . . . staying with friends.'

'Look, do I have to stand here all night or will you invite me in?'

'It's a bit awkward, I'm having a dinner party . . .' So much for giving him hell, darling. Amy could scarcely believe that here he was large as life on her doorstep, Orlando Rock. The last time they'd seen one another there'd been tears in their eyes and the weeks couldn't pass quickly enough until they were together again. But now – now Amy was in heightened single mode, he'd abused her loyalty and (let's ignore for the minute her own minor aberration in the nightclub) just what was he doing here?

A face appeared round the wall behind her.

'Come on Amy, you're missing all the juicy bits about Sally's Ann Summers party.'

Alex fell stone silent as she saw Orlando Rock standing in the doorway, barely recognisable behind his tatty beard and oldest overcoat. She sloped off back into the living room and within seconds the laughter upstairs stopped, replaced by expectant silence. Amy and Orlando looked at one another and she realised that he was in fact fantastically handsome and his eyelashes were all spiky and little-boyish, so she let him in, just to hear what he had to say mind you.

'Guys, I'm just going to go upstairs with Orlando for a bit of a chat. You know where the wine is, help yourselves. I'm sure I won't be long,' said Amy to an expectant room of surprised faces. Well imagine how you'd feel if you went for supper at your friend's house and Brad Pitt turned up on the doorstep only to be whisked to the hostess's bedroom moments later, without so much of a how's your father. They didn't blame her though, really, they knew it was important and that ordinarily Amy wouldn't blow out her mates for a man, even Mel Gibson. So with a few of the psychic thought waves that girls, like dolphins, are so adept at they wished her well and she thanked them.

'It's this one, isn't it?' Orlando hesitantly pushed open Amy's bedroom door.

'Oh, I really wouldn't expect you to remember, the amount of bedrooms you have to visit I'm sure they all start to look the same after a while.' Amy was on fighting form, bolstered by the telepathic moral support waves coming from the living room. Orlando pretended not to hear the bitterness in her voice and launched into the monologue he'd been planning since yesterday morning when Bill decided he wasn't any good to them on set because he was behaving like a big girl's blouse, so put him on a plane to England for a few days' sabbatical.

'Amy, I know how it must look and I can't begin to imagine how you felt when you picked up the newspaper and saw that picture . . .'

'Plural, Orlando, I picked up four newspapers and saw that picture.'

'Amy, please, can I just explain. If it had been me I'd probably never have spoken to you again, but you have to believe me, nothing happened between me and Tiffany Swann. Absolutely nothing. She's been quite persistent but I'm not remotely interested.'

'Have you any idea how humiliated I've felt? How one minute I'm supposed to be going out with the great Orlando Rock and the next he's carousing around the world with some . . . some slut of an actress for my friends, colleagues, even my mother to see!'

'Amy, stop just one minute. Do you believe me?'

'Do I believe what?' Her voice was so loaded with

venom that he instinctively recoiled, reminded of his constant battles with Joanna. But this is different, he told himself, she has every right to be angry.

'Do you believe that nothing happened, that it was just an unfortunate moment, but perfectly innocent nonetheless, and just happened to be captured on film?'

'Then why didn't you phone me when you saw it, let me know all this instead of leaving me to think that if you gave a damn you'd phone and tell me there was nothing to worry about?'

'Amy, I did phone, I left two messages on your answerphone telling you to call me back. When you didn't I presumed you didn't want to speak to me.'

'Which is why you flew all the way here, because you thought I didn't want to speak to you. That makes sense,' she said sarcastically. Lowest form of wit, Amy.

'No, I flew here because I like you a hell of a lot and wanted you to hear my apology. I couldn't just sit around thinking of you being unhappy.'

'Anyway, you can't have left any messages you liar. No one told me.'

'Hand on my heart Amy, I left two.' He sensed that her anger was abating a bit and tried to catch hold of her hand, but she snatched it away.

'Don't come here with your acting and try to get round me. I'm not stupid, you know.'

'I know you're not stupid, darling, but I need to know if you believe me or not.'

Darling, thought Amy, he called me darling. It had the same effect as a wink does on some people. Ooh I rather like that, she thought, suddenly seeing his passion in all its

wuthering glory. Hmmm Rochester, very sexy. So it was
not because of Orlando Rock's powers of reasoning or
persuasion that he managed on this occasion to win Amy
around, although he thought so. Rather it was because,
for an instant, in the dim light of her bedroom he looked
so like her arch-hero Mr Rochester that . . . well, she was
putty in his hands.

'Yes, I believe you.'

'Really?'

'Yes.'

Orlando's stomach did cartwheels and although he
sensed that he hadn't quite heard the last of it, that there
would be the odd revisiting of his alleged misbehaviour,
he was too relieved to care right now. Amy sat there
looking as appealing as she could muster in her kaftan,
and Orlando leant over and took her hands. She kissed
him and thought, wow this is much nicer than the sweaty
Australian kiss, and he thought, thank God I'm here with
her and not tormenting myself in deepest New Zealand.
And they both forgot about the guests sitting downstairs
running out of red wine.

Until . . . there was an outbreak of frenetic coughing
at the foot of the stairs and only after it had been going
on for about five minutes did Orlando and Amy notice.
He could tell she'd noticed because her kiss turned into
a smile and she slid away shyly.

'Oh heavens, I forgot about my party.'

'They'll be fine sweetheart, I'm sure they can let
themselves out.' Ever noticed how men will blatantly
lie, cheat or kill to keep the object of their desire in bed
once they're there? No? Try interrupting at half time and

your normally honest lesser spotted male will turn into a cross between a member of MI5 and Captain Caveman, all scurrilous deception and macho insistence. Just an observation.

'I can't just leave them there,' said Amy, scurrying round on the floor trying to find her kaftan. 'They might need me for something.'

'And so might I,' said Orlando to himself as she drifted out of the bedroom.

Her friends stood in a cluster at the bottom of the stairs and were both relieved and impressed to witness her crumpled state.

'Glad to see someone's been enjoying themselves,' said Alex with a wink.

'Oh, I'm so sorry, really. Have you had a horrible time?' Amy's hostess-guilt reared its head and, knowing that if they stayed they'd be in for a ceaseless barrage of apologies and 'I'm so terrible's, they decided to leave forthwith.

'No, Amy, it's been fun. You must all come to me next time.'

'Yes, none of you have seen my new place – maybe I'll have a soiree.'

'Byee Amy, thanks a lot.'

'Yeah, the curry was lovely, don't forget to fax me with the recipe.'

And they were gone. Scarpered. Every last one. Silence reigned and Amy went back to her room and the dulcet tones of Orlando's snores.

'Poor baby, he must be exhausted,' whispered Amy. I think we can also take it from that he was forgiven.

Chapter 24

It didn't really occur to Amy and Orlando to wonder why she'd never got the messages he left on the
answerphone; they were too giddy with bliss and relief
to care. Perhaps had they had half a brain between them
they could have saved a little heartache later, but we have
to make allowances for love and hope that the lesson they
learn won't be too painful.

The flat monsters were just getting ready for work as Amy
ventured into the bathroom. Keeping Orlando secret
became a full scale military operation. She closed her
bedroom door firmly behind and hoped that Orlando
wouldn't have a sudden urge to shave or shower. No
cheery 'top o' the mornings to you' in this household,
that's for sure. Thank God. Amy tried not to act suspicious as she squeezed back into her room, balancing two
cups of coffee on a tray, through a crack about half an
inch wide. She'd made it, she'd been over the top and
was safely back in the trenches.

'Let's go out tonight, somewhere really special,' said
Orlando, his head propped against the pillow sipping
his coffee.

'Sounds lovely. Where to?' said Amy bending over the

bottom of the bed looking for the magazine section of the newspaper.

'I don't know, we'll think of somewhere.'

'Orlando, I'm just going to nip down and phone Lucinda, have a quick chat.'

'Why not ask her and Benjy out with us tonight?'

'How do you know Benjy?'

''Cause he's Lily's older brother, we've known each other since we were knee high.'

'Of course, I forgot. All that whinging I did about you in their kitchen, he's not a very loyal friend to you – he just agreed with every insult I hurled in your direction.'

'Probably had more sense than to argue with you, darling,' Orlando said placatingly.

Amy threw the travel section at him and went to phone Lucinda.

'Luce, it's Amy. I didn't wake you did I?'

'No, I was just leaving for work.'

'Oh God, it's Friday, I thought it was Saturday.'

'Someone had a good night then,' said Lucinda, glad to see old Amy back on form.

'Luce, I'll probably be a bit late for work . . . Orlando's here.'

'What? Where?'

'In my bedroom.' Amy giggled sheepishly

'Oh my God, you old fox, what's going on? One minute you're cooking curry to mend a broken heart, the next there's a strange man in your bed!'

'He turned up, just like that. It was all a mistake that newspaper story Luce, really,' Amy reassured her friend.

'I'm glad, but why didn't he just phone? Did he come

all the way from New Zealand to tell you that?'

'Yup,' said Amy, proudly ignoring the first question. 'Look, we were wondering if you wanted to come out with us tonight, dinner?'

'Love to. You arrange it with Orlando and tell me when you get into work . . . shall I expect you at lunchtime?'

'Okaydokey.'

Amy went to the kitchen and squeezed some oranges and in the absence of any random fresh croissants poured two bowls of shreddies instead. Can't have it all ways, she thought, spontaneity and preprepared sophistication don't go hand in hand.

'You mean you don't always have ready-made post-coital breakfasts prepared just in case?' said Orlando as she told him of the quandary he'd put her in.

''Fraid not. If you will turn up on my doorstep at eleven o'clock at night you can eat your shreddies and be thankful.'

'I think not. Get dressed and let's go out to breakfast,' he instructed.

Glamour, thought Amy, wondering if people still wore twinsets to Claridges for breakfast.

'Where to?' she asked hopefully.

'There's this amazing greasy spoon in Balham. Let's splash out and take a taxi.'

'God, you really know how to woo a girl, Orlando Rock. You'd better be careful or I'll sell my "Mean Love Rat only bought me Breakfast in Joe's Caff" story to the *Sun*,' Amy laughed.

So they hopped in a cab and the taxi driver insisted on opening the glass flap.

'You're that Rock bloke from the papers, aren't you?'

'Something like that,' obliged Orlando.

''Ere, that bird you was with in the paper the other morning . . . very tasty,' he said approvingly, seeming not to notice that Amy was a living, breathing, thinking individual. Or maybe he thinks I'm Orlando's sister, we do look quite alike. Like those narcissistic lovers who go out with their spitting image. No, we don't look remotely alike. Miserable sod, she cursed the driver. Orlando squeezed her hand and kissed her cheek reassuringly, then he slammed closed the cab driver's window, not really caring about the inevitable tales that would be bandied around every passenger from here to kingdom come about the 'bit of a miserable git really that Oliver Rock'. Amy trembled at his moodiness and was glad to be on the receiving end of his devotion. Mr Darcy strikes again, only this time Amy witnessed him in all his splendour. God he's sexy, she thought, placing her hand firmly on his thigh.

They arrived at the Bridge Diner in Balham and Amy feigned delight at the authenticity of the ketchup stains on the table. She was tempted to order just black tea, as she was dubious about the entire contents of the kitchen, with milk top of that list, but Orlando was so proud of his discovery, pleased as punch at the grottiness, that she really had to oblige and order full breakfast. Funny the things you'll put up with early into a relationship that six months down the line the man gets screamed at for just suggesting – 'If you expect me to go and sit in that greasy hole and come out reeking of chips . . .' etc – including a multitude of horrors, such as standing on the sidelines of a football match or eating pizzas and watching golf on TV. 'It was romantic,' the men warble; 'I must have been out of my mind,' the women realise.

Amy tried to get into the spirit of grot. She's a girl who can appreciate the seedier side of life, as witnessed by her sortie into downbeat fashion, but she felt much more at home with it when she could be sure of the pedigree of the sleaze. If it came with a hand-sewn silk label declaring that it was a Hamnett or Galliano or was a café carefully distressed by the cleverest stylists in the business, she felt a little more at ease, positively at one with the grime. Orlando was just a bit wide of the mark in terms of the right thing to do, she thought fleetingly, never mind, she'd bring him round.

'So where shall we go for dinner tonight, my love?' she asked, a wealth of possibilities and grand entrances into glittering restaurants doing alluring arabesques through her imagination.

'Somewhere lovely and intimate, somewhere quiet,' he said dreamily. Blakes, she thought, she'd heard that it was lovely, a haven for lovers not wanting to be seen by cuckolded husbands and jealous wives, and if they felt like it they could book into a room, each one was decorated differently, pricey, but what the hell. Lucinda and Benjy could take a cab after dinner and leave love's young dream to enjoy passionate sex in a Moroccan interior, and a breakfast of . . .

'There's this place in Chiswick I've heard about, it's meant to be the best Thai around. It's getting fantastic reviews.' Hmmm, good reviews, bound to be a chic crowd. Amy was in the mood for a little glamour, in case you hadn't guessed. She'd narrowly escaped the smelly jaws of grunge and had emerged with most of her friends and boyfriend, so was determined to rouge herself up to the cheekbones and replace that bloody Tiffany Duck or whatever she was called as the stunning companion on Orlando Rock's arm ... Thai sounded perfect, a demonstration of her prowess with chopsticks and the delicate flavours of oriental cuisine, her silk mandarin dress ... great.

'Sounds lovely, what's it called?'

'I don't think it has a name, it's just this place which is a lorry drivers' caff during the day and serves Thai food at night, formica tables and all, foodie heaven,' Orlando said, proud that he was so *au fait* with the gourmet cuisine and could discover such rare gems in unlooked for places. Formica. Amy's heart sank and her Japanese dress went back into her wardrobe. Foodies. Fat bloaters with red veiny noses and napkins tucked into their shirts, not a Georgina Von Etzdorf scarf in sight, not a camera man within a mile of Chiswick. Oh.

'Maybe Chiswick's a bit far for Lucinda and Benjy, they live in Notting Hill, you know.'

'Oh, I'm sure they won't mind travelling for this unique gastronomic experience,' he said confidently. Amy was a little quiet as she gingerly prodded her sausage, remembering documentaries about sheep's eye-balls and stuff that went into your average sausage. She couldn't quite bring herself to tackle her fried egg either so generously donated the contents of her plate to Orlando.

'Aren't you hungry?' he asked.

'It must be all the excitement of you coming back,' she said smiling. White lies.

'You know that's the problem with New Zealand. It's all so healthy, so clean, and the only time I got near a sausage was when Bill was flaunting his breakfast in front of me.'

'Who's Bill?' asked Amy, glad to change the subject from grease caked meat.

'My director and best friend, he's dying to meet you. He's a really good bloke, Scottish, you'd like him.'

Amy's mind was thrust back to the film set and New Zealand. 'So, what were you doing at this party? I always imagined you'd be filming way into the night and were too exhausted to socialise. That's what you told me, anyway.' Amy was feeling piqued. Not enough sleep and no food made her even more irritable.

'You wouldn't believe me if I told you, honestly. I was made to go by Bill, part of the actorly duty.'

'As long as I'm not around I suppose,' she sulked.

'Amy, I wouldn't want you within a mile of the press, you're too nice and too precious right now. I've already lost one wife because of that sort of thing, I'm not about to lose you too.' Amy carried on sipping her milky tea as she took in the remark. One wife. To lose one wife is unfortunate, to lose two is careless. Could that mean? Wow. Me. Wife. Same sentence. Part of her was thrilled, the other wanted to put his sausage up his nose for being so insensitive as to mention *her* in the same breath as Amy. Amy tested the water,

'I saw your ex-wife in a magazine the other day.'

189

'That's not surprising since she spends her life courting them.'

'She's very beautiful.'

'Yes.' Orlando, you're supposed to say, 'Nowhere near as lovely as you though, darling', but you're a guy and you're honest so it doesn't occur to you, you've got a lot to learn.

'Oh, I see.' Churlish.

'Amy, come on, she's much older and nowhere near as pretty as you.'

'I don't want to be pretty, pretty's boring.'

'Amy,' he pleaded in exasperation, but it was too late, he'd missed his cue to flatter her and lift her from her bad mood and now the coaxing and reassuring was going to take at least fifteen times as long. When will they ever learn?

'Oh, darling don't, you know that you're wonderful and that you're worth more than ten Joannas.' Nice work Olly, keep going. But then a Meatloaf song came on the jukebox and served to remind Amy that she wasn't in Claridges but the Bridge Diner, best just remove her from the scene of the crime as swiftly as possible, Orlando and start again. Take it from the top, the ten times prettier bit.

Amy and Orlando went their separate ways after breakfast, Orlando to wash and shave and Amy to fill up on muesli bars and wash up after last night's curry, but before she went home she had to pay a visit to the family planning clinic. She'd been putting it off for weeks and as usual was down to her last pill. She wandered down King's Road and through the doors of the clinic. Curiously this was one of her favourite places, all brown carpets and filing cabinets. The women were grey-haired matrons, pioneering women's rights since women had rights. They were matter of fact and lovely. As Amy took a seat a girl ran through the doors pink in the face and desperate.

'Can I have an appointment?' she panted.

'Run out, have we dear?' The matron looked up from her desk.

'Yeah.'

'Take a seat then.'

This always happened. It made Amy feel practically organised to have thought of coming here two minutes before the eleventh hour rather than after it. She picked up a magazine, but it was *Country Life* so not very interesting. Rather than walk across the room to get another she waltzed off into the never never instead. I wonder what they'd think if they all knew I was sleeping with Orlando Rock, she thought of the assembled family planees. Probably give their right arms, if not their Marvelon for the joy. The joy of sex. He was good in bed, Orlando. Very expert, I wonder where he learned all those things, she worried for a second. Her name was called and she was whisked away and weighed. Her blood pressure was pronounced,

'Nice and normal, dear,' and she was propelled back into the waiting room and the front desk. Here an array of pinks and blues and whites, all carnation colours, sat like packets of sweets, with butterflies etched on the side and licensed to thrill. The girl in front of Amy asked for extra condoms and they were doled out like lemon bonbons in a sweetshop. Amy's pill was in a comparatively dull yellow foil wrapper but before she had time to complain she was packed off with six months' worth in a white paper bag. She was Scheherezade with her thousand and one nights tucked away in her handbag. Oh the possibilites . . .

It was the most beautiful spring morning. The kind that put a smile on the face of most mortals. The kind that sent Amy into raptures. The trees were just budding in the early sunshine. Winter was behind them and something new was round the corner, the spring in Amy's step was unmistakable. She had that indefinable yet irresistible new-love-thing walk. Men on newspaper stalls smiled at her bottom in the same way that she had smiled at the sparrows splashing in a puddle. All was well with the morning. Strolling past the backward spinning clock outside Vivienne Westwood's shop in World's End she wondered if her relationship with Orlando would outlast her contraceptive supplies. One can but hope she thought. But let's not take things too quickly. Twelve hours is a long time in love and Amy could barely believe the transformation in her life. But she hadn't had time to digest it yet, let it sink in that her love god was back, all the way across the world to see her, to put his reassuring arm around her shoulder and apologise.

Amy walked back over the bridge to Battersea past the houseboats. It seemed a long time since she'd been there with Toby, holding his hand and wishing she'd been with the actor from the party. God, fate is a funny thing. She smiled goofily. A bus sailed past and she contemplated running to catch it. But if she'd sat on a bus, she would have been in danger of being arrested, all lunatic smiles and little endearments practised under her breath. You know, you've been there. At least if she walked innocent citizens could choose to cross to the other side of the road. Arriving home pink-cheeked and glowing, yes glowing, she decided to make a start on some spring cleaning. After washing up she plumped pillows and straightened duvets in her bedroom. She buried her head in the pillow and smelled Orlando on it. A lovely musky smell of hair and leather, warm and comforting. She felt quite guilty about being so ungracious over breakfast. Now she could sit back and distill essence of Orlando, now she could uncork the little bottled-away events in her head and breathe in their heady aroma, she felt practically in love. She picked up the offending newspaper photograph from her bedroom floor and, blotting out the Duck woman, looked wistfully at the picture of Orlando, handsome and yet so reserved, and he was hers. Yippee. Then she remembered she had to be at work three hours ago so put on her trainers and ran.

Orlando went home to his, if the truth be known, lonely flat. He unpacked a few things and had a shower, splashing on lots of the leathery smell and wondering why Amy seemed a bit out of sorts today. Imagine reaching the age of thirty and not realising that a woman in love is little more than a series of moods in flux. He presumed she was still a bit sore from the Tiffany fiasco and chided himself for not being firmer with Bill on the night of the party. Still, he thought, I've got a few days in London to make it up to her. And he couldn't think of a better way to do it than with a few intimate dinners and quiet days alone. Benjy and Lucinda were OK, they were friends, but he wasn't about to share her with anyone else. No siree, this was one relationship he intended to keep to himself. So perhaps we can forgive him for being a little insensitive to Amy's needs, for not noticing that quite naturally what a girl wants to do when she's just landed herself a plum heartthrob is to take him on the town, show him to the world and his dog and bask in her kill. Perhaps we'll let him off his slight obsession with all things anonymous and all places quiet. But the question is, folks, will Amy let him off?

Amy wasn't really mulling over that point right now, she was racing along on the tube towards work. When she arrived she was yelled at in full view of everyone by the bitch Nathalia and sentenced to two hours of sewing on buttons. Lucinda crept in after lunch and gave her a sympathetic hug,

'So where's the big event tonight?' she asked.

'Some place in Chiswick, supposed to be great Thai food,' said Amy, having sided with Orlando since her muesli bar and pause for romantic reflection.

'I think I've heard of it, it's got great reviews. Now, tell me all about last night.'

'God Luce, it was amazing, really weird. There we were in mid-slag-off-Orlando-session when the doorbell rings and he's just standing there.'

'And?'

'And we left everyone to it and had this amazingly heavy chat about it all. I was furious but then, when I realised it wasn't really his fault, couldn't help but forgive him.' No, Amy, when you saw his brooding actor sexiness you couldn't help yourself.

'And that was it?'

'Yup, and this morning we went to this greasy spoon place and had breakfast and caught up a bit.' Amy's grease phobia deserted her and she painted the scene anew in her head, plastic spoons, sugar cubes and hand holding in a kitsch fifties milkbar-cute way instead of chip fat and discontent.

'So how long's he around for?'

'No idea. A few days, I suppose. He said he just couldn't stay in New Zealand whilst he knew I was unhappy, isn't that lovely?'

And so on and so forth, Amy was grilled like the proverbial sausage and the buttons were left unsewn as they worked themselves up into a lather of excitement and outfits for the evening ahead.

Chapter 25

They took a taxi to Chiswick and the infamous Thai restaurant. The diners were a mixture of adventurous foodies (adventurous in that they would take their palates to West London rather than the tried and tested establishments of Fulham Road and the Conran Empire) and locals making the most of the newly discovered cult status of their local. As they walked into the small room and the name 'Rock' was uttered in low Shakespearean tones by Orlando in response to the maitre d's 'What name is that booked under sir?' heads turned and eyes were on the small party. Amy felt a rush of pride and reached for Orlando's hand so everyone could see they were together. It wasn't exactly the entrance she'd planned with flashbulbs and red carpets but it was thrilling nonetheless.

'So, how are the folks Olly?' asked Benjy casually.

'Fine. Mum's well, dad's much the same as ever. They potter in the garden and I still haven't persuaded them to come and see me on set, so nothing changes.' Amy pondered ma and pa Rock. Were they cruel as Amy's mother had said, for calling their child such a name, and why hadn't they come to see him on set? Obviously negligent parents, she decided.

'Why won't they see you, Orlando?' asked Lucinda. More intelligent to ask before assuming that they locked their child in a cellar from an early age and fed him nothing but gruel.

'Oh, they're terrified that if they come, they'll jinx me. Mum once came to see me rehearse the fool in *Lear* when I was at college and I fluffed my lines on the opening night so she's never come near me at work since.'

'How adorable,' said Lucinda, laughing. Amy reformed her opinion for the time being but wasn't convinced of their lack of humanity on the name front.

'So dish the dirt on one another's childhood antics then,' Amy instructed the boys.

'Benjy used to bite people.'

'Rubbish!'

'Absolutely true, the Sweeney Todd of toddlers. We were all convinced you were a changeling child, and had been switched at birth. Lily was an angel with her little halo of curls and daisy chains and you just ate your fellow infants.'

'Orlando, you're talking utter rubbish!' Benjy insisted. 'What about you when you were losing at football and you used to hide the ball?'

'I don't remember that. Anyway the girls were probably far more scandalous as nippers than we were, girls always did more outrageous things.'

'Do you remember when Lily did cartwheels without her knickers on?' asked Benjy laughing.

'Scarred me for life, I think. Ok, who wants wine? Are we ready to order?' The waiter appeared and filled his pad with soups and garlic prawns and a rainbow of curries, green and red and birdsnests of noodles and rice.

'I'm ravenous. If they don't hurry up I'll eat the formica,' moaned Lucinda.

'If they don't hurry up Benjy, our resident cannibal, may eat us all,' Orlando said.

'So, Orlando, tell us about *Return of the Native*,' said Lucinda, vaguely imitating an interviewer.

'Very little to tell. I thought it was a good bet to make a film in Dorset, so I could be in the country for more than five minutes at a time and catch up with the parentals and stuff, but now I'm in New Zealand I'm cursing the day I said I'd do it. It's a good script though, and the team's good.'

'Except Tiffany Swann,' said Amy chippily.

'Goes without saying, my love.' He ruffled her hair and her feathers perked up, all pigeony again. She had a swift glance around the tables to see if anyone had witnessed that moment of affection. If they had they pretended not to have.

They saw the wine bottle replaced several times and relaxed into an easy pattern of laughter and banter.

'I actually thought this place would be horrid,' Amy confessed to Orlando.

'Charming of you to say so, darling.'

'Oh my God,' Lucinda attempted to whisper but was too drunk to lower her tone.

'What?' asked Amy.

'You see that guy who's just walked in with the seventeen-year-old on his arm?'

'Yes,' they chorused.

'It's my father.'

'Bloody hell,' whispered Amy. They sat huddled, their heads almost touching, all staring in the direction of the leather jacketed man who had his back to them and was helping some honey-thighed beauty into her seat. He turned towards the maitre d' and they all turned away, pretending not to be looking.

'Don't I recognise him?' Amy asked.

'Very probably, he used to be quite famous.'

'Quite famous, he was my total idol when I was seventeen,' said Orlando, stunned with admiration.

'Luce, you didn't tell me it was HIM! I can't believe your father is so amazingly famous, I thought it might be Bill Wyman but I never thought it would be him,' said Amy.

Four are flabbergasted in a restaurant, as Enid Blyton would have it. Except it was only two. Benjy, of course, was the only other party to this secret on the face of the planet, but even he was having trouble dealing with the idea as it was standing there in the flesh. Lucinda was mildly amused by their reactions to her errant father and quite proud too. There, one glass of wine and her secret was out. The idol slid into the seat and looked every inch the jaded star. Amy could just see Anita falling for those famously coloured eyes. Yes indeedy, who wouldn't travel to the ends of the world for a night in bed with him. Men and women alike had. Good old Anita, thought Amy. Cool, cool Lucinda. Amy silently wishes her father were a rock star but try as she might all she could envisage was a Cliff Richard and the Shadows-type figure, she cringed at:

'Orlando Rock, meet my father,' and a figure in a leather jacket and Buddy Holly glasses stepped forward.

'Do you think I should say hello?' asked Lucinda hesitantly.

'When was the last time you saw him?'

'When I was about fourteen and he bought me a pony.'

'Did you call him dad?'

'No, course not!'

'Wild.' The others were awe-struck and Lucinda, as if realising for the first time what a big deal it was to have such a father, began to feel rather nervous.

'Let's just forget it,' said Lucinda, nervously returning to her green curry. 'It's all a bit of a head-fry.'

So they tried to forget it but kept sneaking glances at snake hips and honey thighs in the corner.

'And I thought Orlando was supposed to be the famous party here tonight,' said Amy.

'Do you suppose he's sleeping with that child?' asked Lucinda, obviously distracted by the paternal presence.

'That would be too disgusting,' Amy said.

'Sounds like a wonderful thought to me,' said Benjy. Lucinda kicked him under the table and stored the comment up for argument later. Orlando refrained from agreeing. He didn't have the security of a three-year-old relationship from which to make outrageous remarks like that.

'Why do men think that they have to be clever and handsome to sleep with young nubile girls?' asked Amy. 'Don't they realise that any idiot with half a Ferrari can pull?'

'It's because they're witless; whereas women wouldn't want to spend the evening listening to a seventeen-year-old boy talk about skateboards just so she could press his pecs later, men don't care, conversation is not a priority,' Lucinda replied bitterly. Bitter with her lothario father and cross with Benjy for being nothing short of a pervert.

'You only have to look at her breasts to answer that question,' said Benjy. Boy was he heading for trouble later on, and he just kept on courting it. Next time they go out to dinner Benjy will have to give the wine a wider berth, it seems.

From the breasts of an adolescent the conversation cannot stoop much lower. They chit-chatted and lapped up the remains of the soft mango ice cream and dripped the last of the wine into their glasses and the time came to leave. Benjy and Lucinda were straining for a fight in a pointed, veteran relationship way and Orlando and Amy were straining for each other. Amy slid off her shoe and wriggled her toes over Orlando's ankle. Amy watched Orlando's lips seek out the last droplets of red liquid from his glass and stroked her toes up his leg towards his knee. He winked at her and, courage taken, she slipped her foot up further, replicating a thousand seduction scenes, feeling her way between Orlando's thighs. His head moved instinctively back and eyes closed for a fraction of a second, long enough for the maitre d' to note the untowardness and look away. Amy bit her lower lip and wiggled her toes. Delicious, she thought. Orlando contemplated the logistics of a quickie in the Ladies but they had company so, ever the gentleman (not that he had much choice), he allowed himself to be ushered into a cab with the others. Libido responds to danger as much as to audience, or perhaps it's the very fact that you always want what you can't have. So, when constrained by decorum into sitting and chatting with friends, all you can think of is heady sex on the dinner table and hot kisses on your neck.

So cool and fruity as mango sorbet they toyed with one another in the back of the cab, Amy's hand easing up the inside of Orlando's thigh; Orlando slipped his hand up her blouse and stroked and teased her nipple, running his fingers over the satin soft skin of her breasts. They kissed whenever Lucinda and Benjy fell into conversation with one another and ached to be home.

'Your place or mine?' Orlando whispered as he kissed her behind the ear.

'Mine?'

'Fine,' he agreed willingly.

'OK guys, we're out of here. If we leave you a fiver that should cover the fare,' said Benjy, bursting into their erotic reverie.

'See you darlings, thanks for a lovely evening.' Lucinda kissed them both goodbye.

'I'll tell Nathalia that you've got food poisoning. Take Monday off,' she told Amy. Amy was too heady to appreciate the act of kindness, but Lucinda will undoubtedly get her reward in heaven. Just as surely as the poor inherit the earth and the meek are happy because the kingdom of heaven is theirs, there must be a clause for those who help the course of true love on the way. Blind Cupid. Kind Lucinda. Kindred spirits really. The arrow-struck couple took their taxi as far as home and thence Nirvana.

Chapter 26

They slept fitfully, mirroring one another's movements around the bed with the slight unease of new lovers. As they drifted off they tried to make their breathing patterns coincide, so fearful were they of slipping from their reverie. Amy was careful to keep her hair out of his mouth when her back was turned to him and he gently held his hand across her breasts. Like wood nymphs curled in some beachen haven, thought Amy as she lapsed into her dreams.

The next morning they woke to a sky of deepest azure and had no choice but to spend the day outside in the sunshine. Kew Gardens was decided on as the picnic venue and they made a trip to the supermarket where they cavorted amongst the isles, having light sabre fights with baguettes and filling their baskets with every variety of kitsch food ever invented: Jaffa cakes, Nutella, mini rum babas with green cherries on top and fake cream.

'God I love fake cream,' said Amy, cherishing a can with its plastic whipped peak.

Orlando thought he'd probably be able to find an erotic use for it later, I mean, with its hard nozzle and frothy contents, it was practically begging to be squirted over Amy. 'Let's get some of those plastic cheese slices too,' said Orlando, heading for the dairy products.

'And Pringles,' added Amy, remembering with joyous irony the night she'd binged on two whole cans to suppress her misery. She grabbed his hand and kissed it hastily.

'What was that for?' he asked.

'Just because.'

Just because she was relieved that it had all sorted itself out, that here they were, enjoying each other's company and getting along like oldest friends, bed was a treat and they laughed easily together. What more could a girl ask for? (Premieres cartwheeled through her mind but she dismissed these with a 'they can wait'.)

They made their way to the drinks and picked out green cream soda and little bottles of cherry-flavoured pop with polar bears on the label.

'You do realise that we'll be high as kites for a month with all this tartrazine and sunset yellow stuff,' said Amy.

'Yeah, who needs drugs when you can overdose on food colouring?'

They stopped off at an old-fashioned sweetshop on the way to the park and bought lemon bonbons, sherbet pips by the quarter and some pear drops. As they were about to pay Amy dropped in a walnut whip for good measure.

'Whatever happened to Spangles?' they wondered as the door creaked shut behind them.

They paid their entrance to the gardens and, as it was almost twelve o'clock, felt that they must have lunch, if only to relieve them of the burden of several carrier bags full of food.

'Let's go over by these bushes.' Amy led the way to a spot she'd singled out but on closer inspection the ground was wet. Instead they found a bench and sitting at either corner, like a pair of book ends, spread the garishly coloured feast out between them.

'It's so beautiful with all the spring flowers around and the birds – like a morning out of Chaucer.'

'And pray tell what is a Chaucer morning like?' Orlando asked, taking a teeth-marked bite out of a slice of orange cheese.

'Well, just lots of flowers in bloom, ready for the May queen to make her entrance and always lots of bird noises. Can you imagine what England was like in Chaucer's time? So many trees, my God, wolves still roamed the land.'

'I could never get to grips with *The Pardoner's Tale* for A level. I just cheated and read the crib notes,' Orlando confessed.

'God no, Chaucer's great, the bawdiest stories imaginable. That's the whole joke, if teenage boys had known that they were all about farting and sex you'd all have got grade As at A level.'

'But I couldn't understand it.'

'Just a matter of time. Persevere, he's worth it.' So Orlando made a mental note to pick up a copy of the *Canterbury Tales* when he was next in a bookshop. In the way that we've all at some time or another, in those early days of love, decided that there was after all some merit in the cinematography of *Apocalypse Now* or that

Hemingway could be enjoyed by women too. All utter lies of course, but love is a powerful broadener of horizons for all of five minutes.

They grazed their way through the assembled rainbow of nibbles, a pear drop here and nectarine there. Orlando picked up a strawberry and squirted the foamy cream on to the top of it.

'For you,' he proffered. Amy opened her mouth and he popped it in. Tess of the D'Urbervilles at long last, she thought.

She made up a sandwich of banana and nutella, promising it was the most heavenly thing Orlando would ever eat.

'No, it sounds revolting,' he protested.

'Trust me, you'll love it.'

He screwed up his face and opened his mouth, as if preparing for a spoonful of castor oil.

'See, it's gorgeous,' she said. He remained unconvinced and washed it down with a huge gulp of cherry soda.

Finally, they packed their wrappers away into a plastic bag and rested bloated and groaning against one another.

'Do you think we're bulimic?' asked Amy.

'No, just greedy.'

'I feel so sick,' she moaned. Orlando prodded her tummy.

'Bleugh! Get off!'

They sat there emitting wailing noises and vowing they'd never eat another sweet as long as they lived until Amy finally decided that enough was enough and there was a hothouse to visit. She pulled Orlando up from the bench and they strolled into the steamy glass-house.

'Come on fatty,' she teased him, patting his stomach.

'People in glasshouses shouldn't throw stones,' he said, relishing the opportunity.

'You are so unoriginal. What am I doing with you?' She shook her head in mock despair.

'We should go to Brazil sometime, see the real rain-forest, canoe down the Amazon and live on sugarcane.'

'I've had enough sugar for a lifetime. Rio would be great though, they all wear g-strings all the time, that's the only problem.' Man rose to the bait.

'Let's go tomorrow darling,' he said, squeezing her bottom.

They wandered through green dewy leaves and strange flowering flytraps, breaking off for the odd damp kiss.

'This is so lovely, I usually spend Saturdays doing mundane rubbish, shopping, ironing; it's so nice not to do anything. But still I have this guilty feeling that I should be doing something.' Amy was delirious and rambling.

'You are, you're busy falling in love,' said Orlando, taking the back of her head in his hand and easing her fringe behind her ear. Love? Amy was silent inside. A huge word that seemed to fill the greenhouse, fill her head. Was that a casual 'love' or the enormous rare variety? If in doubt play dumb, a clever female adage.

'Am I?'

'I am,' said Orlando, his blue eyes looking so carefully into hers that she lowered her lashes and held her breath. Six feet of darkly beautiful Orlando Rock was standing before her, telling her he was in love with her (at least, she thought that's what he meant, she was too dithery to think). She felt the full force of his actorly passion, his stage managed intensity and romantic hero status. Except this wasn't film, it wasn't the cornfield kiss in *A Room with a View*, it wasn't the safe page-turning romance of Jane Austen, it was flesh and blood and less than a foot away, no ecstatic embellishments needed.

'Me too.' But she asked it rather than telling it. She was face to face with the most romantic encounter of her life (sex doesn't really count, that was much easier) and its proximity left her terrified. But just wait until I tell Lucinda, she thought, suddenly happier.

The rest of the afternoon was a haze of April drizzle and easy kisses, they held hands and poured over snow-drops and daffodils, hiding under willow trees when the rain poured. Amy was happy to be outside, the hothouse encounter had left her flushed and in need of time to herself, but this was much more relaxed, more fun now he wasn't quite so intense. Back home later on, when Orlando had gone to sort out a leaky washing machine in his flat, Amy alternated between hopping around her landing and feeling terrified of being IN LOVE. Was she? She'd always thought it would take much longer, and Orlando was divine, it was immensely flattering but? BUT. There had to be one but, things like that didn't just happen, and, well, he could have been acting, he must be so used to telling women he loved them, practically did it for a living. This thought made Amy a bit happier; he was obviously very fond of her but maybe just a bit dramatic to call it love, yes, that's it, the words just come easier to him. I'm sure once I've spent a bit longer with him I'll be in love too.

Orlando was on the phone to Bill.

'See the thing is, Bill, she's just lovely, so normal, so funny and everything, we can just go to the park, the supermarket, McDonald's and no one even bothers us.'

'Och, it sounds great but doesn't the wee lass want to go anywhere more exciting?'

'No, Bill, it's really exciting just being with her, doing everyday things. After all those years of *Hello!* interviews it's like heaven.'

'Take my word for it, she'll get bored pretty soon if you keep on harping on about being such unexciting things. You're bloody obsessed with being Mr Average, Olly.' But Orlando was too in love to heed Bill's words. And he was in love. He loved the romance of Amy, her spark and imagination, for him it made even a bus journey seem like an Odyssean adventure, her vision was inspiring and refreshing. And he loved the way she bit her lip when she was thinking. Yup, he did love her, he thought, as he scattered tea towels all over the wet kitchen floor.

Chapter 27

Amy had been coaxed over to Orlando's on Saturday night where they'd got a video out and howled with laughter at *Roseanne*. Sunday morning lay in front of them like an unopened present and Amy filled it with excitement in her imagination, a meander through Camden market and coffee in a café brimming with beautiful young people, all buzzing with gossip and the entrance of a famous actor. Or perhaps lunch at Daphne's. It was fun when she did it with Lucinda, to share lettuce with the man you were in love with would be even better. And then they could mosey through the cool marble floorspace of Joseph looking for his and hers outfits, a tweedy jacket and soft chenille scarf for him and some ice blue hipsters and a tiny t-shirt for her. Sheer glamour. And she'd even managed to think through her anxieties about the L word. She'd just never said it to anyone before, she could jump willy nilly (if you'll pardon the expression) into bed with men she fancied, she could suck Strepsils out of the bellybuttons of any number of adoring beaus, but she'd never really been in love. Read about it? Yes. Fallen in love with love in films? Yes. Longed for Lenny Kravitz to write 'My Love is Gentle as a Rose' for her? Of course. But been there done that? Not yet. But she was overcoming her fear, trusting Orlando beyond the actor front and was confidently awaiting the paralysing blow of cupid's arrow.

'You've got the most adorable lips,' she told him, confirming her opinion with a kiss. He smiled and seized the opportunity to kiss her and trail his hand across her stomach. Hmmm they both sighed, and Amy, planting soft lips over his chest, moved down to his stomach, feeling its muscles tighten beneath her, his legs instinctively parted and he reached down and held the back of her head, gently easing her towards him, and then the phone rang . . . the phone rang, yes, 'fraid so. Orlando struggled to ignore it but they were both distracted and Amy flopped back onto the bed in resignation.

'Better get it darling.'

'Who the bloody hell's that?' he spat crossly, stubbing his toe on a chest of drawers as he ran downstairs. No room for cheeky sexy fun here, she lamented. If he had a phone by the bed, he could answer it gruffly and Amy could carry on regardless, licking him as though he were a raspberry cornetto, sucking gently at his tip, and cradling him carefully in her hand, and he would moan and shudder and not be able to think about the person on the phone who would feel piqued and suspicious. Maybe it would be a woman, his ex-wife checking on alimony or something, or just an admirer and all he'd want to do was abandon himself to Amy's womanly power over him. Oh well, she'd have to save that part of her sexual repertoire for another time when the phone's beside the bed.

Drifting out of her dream blow job scenario, she heard Orlando shout. Not mildly irritated toe stubbed crossness. Terrifying angry shouting. She pulled on his towelling dressing gown and went out and sat on the top step listening to his conversation. He saw her and shook his head in despair, listening intently to the voice on the end of the phone.

'Bill, why the fuck don't you just sack her, what the bloody hell was she thinking of?' He listened scowling for a while longer and then slammed the phone down.

'Come on my love, we've got to go,' he said so firmly and sexily she wanted to jump back into bed with him.

'Go where?'

'It's in the papers, that little bitch Tiffany, I've no idea what it says but we have to leave the house.' He walked over towards the windows at the front of the house and looking out, screamed a string of abuse unpunctuated by sense.

'Darling, what's wrong?' Amy felt a surge of fear at this outburst and was panic stricken as to what was in the papers.

'She's told some wretched bloody magazine all about me, what a misogynist, etc. etc. I am, how I've no idea how to treat women, and they've got my bloody ex-wife giving her thoughts and feelings on the matter . . . Shit!' He ran up the stairs past Amy and pulled a canvas bag out of a cupboard.

'You'd better come with me, you won't be safe on your own if they get wind of us.'

'Where will we go?'

'A hotel somewhere, a big one, they're better equipped at keeping the bastard press out. Look, they're crawling all over the street!' Amy took him at his word and wandered towards the window to have a look. So they were. Lots of men in jeans and leather jackets hanging around sipping coffee from polystyrene cups. Bastards seems a bit harsh, she thought, trying to peer at them discreetly though a crack in the curtains. They saw the curtain twitch and discarding coffee reached for their obscenely long lenses. Amy looked at her towelling dressing gown and recoiled in horror at being splashed all over the papers in it, her hair unwashed and teeth unbrushed. She'd look like some ageing fat actress in the Betty Ford Clinic she thought. Can't have that. So she ran a bath and soothed Olly as much as possible. She made him tea and holding his hand said she couldn't imagine that anyone could say anything too nasty about him. And besides, he had her. They'd be fine, she'd tell them that he was a darling.

'You won't say anything to them sweetheart, you can't trust any of them. Just stay well away. Look, you have a bath and I'll sort things out, a taxi and book the hotel. I'd better speak to my agent too.'

Amy cradled her tea in her hands and disappeared into the bathroom. I'm sure I could convince them that he hadn't done any of the things they're saying he's done, she told herself. As she stepped into the bath she gave an interview to herself: 'But what about the allegations of mistreatment of women that have been levelled at Orlando Rock?' asked a voice.

'Well, Orlando and I have been together for about two months now and I can categorically say that he has been nothing but wonderful to me, he's been supportive of my career and behaved like the perfect gentleman.'

'And what is your career?' said the voice, urging Amy to talk more about herself.

'Oh, I work for *Vogue* as a fashion editor.' Nobody would bother to query the minor details, editor, assistant, all the same, she thought.

'So you lead a very glamorous life and are obviously very beautiful and talented but do you think Orlando would still love you otherwise?' Amy cleverly anticipated this question and delivered what she thought was an eloquent and deft reply.

'Orlando and I have a very profound love. It is more than a façade of film star glamour, we live a life of celebrity only in parenthesis; our love is very real and we connect on an intellectual as well as a very physical level.' Don't let them think he only loves me for my brain, she thought. It'll be obvious from my vocabulary that I'm clever. No, I have to get in the sex angle too, put all those hormonally crazed fans off sending him their knickers in the belief that he doesn't get enough already.

She rounded off the interview in a dignified but charming manner, leaving the journalist besotted and willing to write all manner of obliging things about how she was softer and prettier in the flesh than in her photos and how it was obvious why Orlando was in love with her, what man wouldn't be, frankly.

Then she realised she hadn't washed her hair for two days so shoved it under water and gave it a thorough shampooing. Oh why hadn't she brought her thicker fuller hair stuff, Orlando just had some medicated gunge lying around and she'd end up smelling like a bathroom cabinet. Oh well, the paparazzi wouldn't get close enough to smell her, as long as she looked OK. She went into Orlando's bedroom and surreptitiously coiffed her hair; she did a little beehive thing at the back and thanked her lucky stars she'd remembered her sunglasses – Jackie O. That was it. Perfect. *Bellissima*. The tragic woman, the limelight shy beauty. She looked stunning, if she did say so herself. Orlando trailed back into the room with a few carrier bags and she quickly flipped her sunglasses to the top of her head, no point in showing her ace until she was in front of the paparazzi, and she knew he'd probably think sunglasses a little too media tart-ish and tell her to put a baseball cap on instead to defy recognition, no way José, she was going the whole hog, hog heaven.

The taxi pulled up outside the house and they stood in the hallway with their bags and contemplated the dash. Amy tried to avoid the plastic carrier bags screaming Sainsburys and took the canvas number, it wasn't Vuitton but didn't clash too horribly with her outfit.

'OK, darling, now or never, I'll go first and just stay close behind.' He took hold of her hand and led her out of the front door into the fray of cameras and polystyrene cups, Amy held her breath, waiting to be beset, but instead they just kept their distance and snapped away, almost casually. She held Orlando's hand and, sucking in her cheeks and pouting subtly, tried to stop him going so fast, just in case they didn't get the picture she wanted to see. The black and white grainy look of Orlando Rock and his mysterious beauty, who is she? they will ask, where does she come from? In the back of the cab Orlando looked down at his feet and held her hand with such ferocity she saw her fingers start to turn blue. And here she was, the mercurial *femme fatale*, weaving a web of intrigue about herself, the cherished lover of a famous, much desired actor. Orlando felt sorry for her, guilty at dragging her into this topsy turvy world of celebrity.

'Thanks for being such an angel,' he said, believing her the one good thing in his life right now. When they arrived at the hotel they were hurried through the lobby by a silent man in a green peaked cap who took their bags and ushered them into a lift. On the fifth floor they stopped and he led them to their room. But room was not description enough for this lavish suite. Cloud nine, thought Amy. More soaps and shower caps than she could wish for, white bathrobes, one for each of them, and fresh flowers. She swirled around as soberly as the decorum of the situation allowed, concealing her delight beneath,

'Oh well, if we're to be kept prisoners by those wretched newspaper people at least it's a comfortable cell.' Amy unearthed the champagne in the ice bucket – until now she had believed champagne in hotel rooms to be apocryphal, the preserve of honeymooners in holiday brochures and lotharios in Hollywood movies, preparing to get the dame at all costs. As she rubbed condensation from the label, Orlando was busy scanning the front pages of the newpapers laid out on a coffee table.

'Oh my God, I can't believe they've said all this.'

'What have they said?' Amy sat beside Orlando on the sofa, looking over his shoulder at the pictures, one of Tiffany in a dress tighter than a tube of toothpaste, one of Orlando and Joanna together at some long ago award ceremony.

'She's quite beautiful,' said Amy generously. She felt she could afford to be generous now she had Orlando alone, on the right side of the paparazzi, and besides, she was feeling buoyant, but in a strictly tragic sort of way. Dignified, that's what she would be, yup, dignified was good.

'She's not beautiful, she's a bitch,' said Orlando flatly as he scanned the paragraphs beneath the photo.

'"Rock frequently ignored the other members of the cast, choosing instead to spend his evenings in his hotel room, virtually snubbing his co-star Tiffany Swann who tried many times to break the ice with the reclusive star. 'Eventually I just gave up. I think Orlando Rock has a problem with women, finds it very difficult to talk to them. Some people would say he thought women inferior, good only for one thing,' says the strikingly beautiful Swann ..." I can't believe what rubbish this is.' Orlando grasped his head in his hands and shook his head in despair.

'Oh my God, look at this, they've asked that stupid journalist cow what she thinks: "defensive, sexist and difficult" and Joanna: "Orlando and I often clashed about work, he wasn't happy having a wife who was more successful than him." Bloody bitch!' Orlando stood up and paced the room quite obviously racked with misery. Amy suddenly felt quite sorry for him. How could they say things like that? He was so amazingly fair and kind. Poor Orlando.

'Amy, you don't believe them do you?' He knelt

at her feet as she sat on the soft magnolia-coloured sofa.

'Of course not, sweetheart. Look, they don't know you, it doesn't matter what they say. We're stronger than that, and we've got each other.' It sounded suitably filmy and she touched his hand for sincerity.

'It matters because now you're involved. Now nothing you do will be private either, to a lesser degree. They won't rest until they know what your father does and how many times a night you like it. Poor child, it's going to be hell for you.' Hell indeed, thought Amy, my father's a chartered accountant. Why oh why can't he be a fabulous rock star like Lucinda's father, that would make for much better copy.

'Olly darling, don't worry about me. I'd better give mum and dad a ring and warn them about all this, though.'

'Yeah, just dial nine for an outside line,' he said, distractedly riffling through the assortment of broadsheets, just in case.

'Hi mum, it's me.'

'Amy, thank heavens, we've been trying to get hold of you all morning. Some man came round to the house, wanted to know all about you, asked if that young actor had ever been here for tea.' Her mother sounded bewildered but not terribly concerned, Amy thought. Mum had probably invited him in for tea and fruitcake.

'Mum, what did you tell him?' Amy tried to sound a bit anxious for poor Orlando's sake.

'Oh I didn't speak to him love, I was in my gardening clothes you see. Jake spoke to him.'

'OK, can I have a word with Jake then?'

'Jake, Amy wants a word. I'll be off then, darling.'

'OK mum, love you lots, see you soon.'

'Amy?'

'Jake, what's been going on? What did they say?'

'Well, I guess you're about to get your fifteen minutes' worth, sis.'

'My what?' said Amy, her brain scrambling through nerves and excitement.

'Your fifteen minutes' worth of fame. I was just sitting here picking my nose when this bloke from the *Express* turns up on the doorstep. It's OK, he was much shorter than me, I could have hit him if I'd wanted but he was quite polite, just asked about your boyfriends and stuff.'

'Jake, what did you say? You didn't tell him anything did you?' Amy felt sudden panic that one of the mangier specimens from her past had been exhumed for public consumption, perhaps some art student or ... oh God that hairdresser she went out with for six weeks with pink hair ... please God no.

'Of course I didn't, I've got a reputation to think of too, those blokes were bloody awful and after reading the papers today I don't think much of that Rock bloke either, sounds like a bit of a ...'

'Yeah, OK Jake, but don't believe everything you read in the papers eh?' she chided.

'Yeah, look I've got to go, I've got rugby training, I'll give you a call later.' And he rang off.

'Patience of a gnat my brother,' said Amy fondly, for had he not just protected her from the hooded claw, from the death by humiliation which was the

small legion of long-ago undesirable men in her life?
Phew.

Orlando came over to the bed and put his arm
around her.

'Can I get you a drink or something?'

'I know it's not really a time for celebrating but we
could have champagne. Never look a gifthorse in the
mouth, eh?' she said rather glibly, feeling sure that
champagne must also be drunk at salubrious funerals.
It couldn't just be the preserve of celebrations, surely?

'Well, OK, I suppose a drink might steady my nerves
a bit,' he agreed.

Amy cracked open the champagne and tried to cheer
Orlando up a bit. She stroked his beard and kissed his
ears; she reminded him of the time they'd been on the
beach in Sydney and had shocked the old lady to an early
grave, but Orlando only smiled weakly and responded to
her physical advances with the kind of pats and strokes
designed for pets, not lovers.

'Orlando, I feel like a cat,' she said, grumpily because
she felt a bit rejected.

'Oh, it's nothing personal, I just feel distracted. But
it's so good having you here, I don't know where I'd be
without you, really. I know I'm a bit bear with a sore
head-ish but this is so awful, and I know when I see
what they've written about you I'll have to smash some
bastard's face up.' How romantic, thought Amy.

'Pistols at dawn,' she mused. Orlando was silent. He
toyed with her hair and after a few minutes she wriggled
away and went to the window and looked out over
Knightsbridge.

'Do you think anyone would notice if we went shopping?' She was already feeling quite bored hiding out.

'I think it's safer to stay here for a while, we could watch some telly.'

'Yes, and have some more bubbly.' She felt renewed. Don't forget the glamour, she told herself. Here I am, hiding out like some shadowy Greta Garbo figure, not to be seen for days.

'It's a bit like that line from *Henry V* isn't it, "being wanted I may be more wondered at"?' she said, to no one in particular.

'Sorry?' Orlando said, puzzled,

'Well, in some ways, the more rare you are the more spectacular it is when you're finally seen. You know that's what Prince Hal said when he was hidden away with his drinking buddies.' She was proud to be able to quote Shakespeare on this occasion, and rather aptly too, she thought. Oh the multitude of uses for an education. She poured him another drink and relaxed a bit.

They watched MTV, dancing a bit when the Bob Marley vintage video slot came on and stumbling around on their second bottle of champagne, Amy fell onto the very plush sofa.

'"In order not to let the crushing burden of life get you down you must be ceaselessly drunken,"' she mumbled.

'What?' said Orlando, crashing down on the sofa next to her.

'Baudelaire,' she informed him.

'Thank you very much rent-a-quote,' he hiccuped.

'Champagne is lovely, isn't it? I think we should drink it more often.'

'Oh, give me an ice cold beer anyday.'

'You're just a pseudo working-class boy aren't you? Downmarket aspirations?' she said, quite lucidly for her degree of inebriation.

'Don't be silly, I just overdosed on the high life for a while. It's not all it's cracked up to be, you know.'

'All the same I'd quite like to make that decision for myself. I guess I'll just have to compromise myself and write an erotic blockbuster so I can buy a house in Monte Carlo.'

Orlando suddenly became quite coherent too.

'Amy, I don't bore you do I? I mean I know maybe I go a bit overboard on trying to be normal and stuff, but if you want to do more, we could work something out, especially now you're out of the closet, as it were.'

'What?' It was Amy's turn to be dumb. Her afternoon as Lily's lover flashed into her subconscious.

'Now that you're the official girlfriend, you've served your apprenticeship, made it to the front pages and the new woman in my life and maybe now the hounds will stay away from our door.'

Amy lightened at the thought. She hadn't really looked at it that way, and her new status was rather grand. She felt privileged and also quite safe with Orlando. Orlando the god. Orlando my boyfriend. She wasn't sure which she preferred most at the moment. It was probably neck and neck, with the boyfriend just winning by a nose, because they were having a really nice time. How many boyfriends could you lock yourself away with in a hotel room and lurch drunkenly to Bob Marley with as though you were with your best friend? Not many that

I've known, thought Amy, relishing the closeness that she'd often despised. Yes, maybe we're getting there in the love department, she thought.

'Tell you what, let's eat in the grand dining hall tonight, let's put on our best togs and play the showbiz couple with aplomb.' He suddenly lit up.

'Really?' Amy was rendered satisfied. Wow.

'Yup, why not, you've put up with my crap for long enough, let's have some fun.'

Bill's words had reverberated in Orlando's head for a while and he was determined not to let Amy pass him by. Anyway he would probably enjoy a night out, as long as the cameras could be kept at bay.

'I know it sounds corny but I haven't got a thing to wear,' said Amy suddenly realising that all she had were the jeans and grubby jumper she stood in.

'Not a problem.'

'Actually I think it is. That's the thing about girls, they can only go out if they feel right, and I'm not an exception to that rule.'

'I know,' he said matter of factly.

'So, I can't borrow your shirt really can I?'

'No, but there was one of those horrid little boutiques in the foyer downstairs. Let's go and buy you something gold and glittery, you'll still look amazing no matter how tacky.' Amy recalled the horrid little boutique. Very expensive Italian horrid boutique actually, she was going to end up in some gold glittery number costing more than a small car. Oh well, if he insisted.

So in sunglasses and baseball caps the camera dodging pair stole into the bijou arcade of cool marble hotel shops selling jewels and golf clubs and umbrellas and Swiss watches.

'Oh darling, I've just remembered, I've left my rubies at home, I absolutely can't wear my emeralds with my scarlet ballgown, I simply must have these.' She put on her best American oil baron's mistress in London voice and pointed to a string of shimmering stones with a price tag whose noughts ran into next week. This was taken by the shimmery, terrifyingly smart lady behind the counter as an everyday request to buy her wares, so Amy and Orlando had to scuttle off before she realised they could no more afford a ruby necklace than they could afford to run for the American presidency. Once inside the expensive Italian bolthole they squinted at the brightness of sequins and gilt buttons and tried to hide their distaste. Eventually Amy's well-trained fashion eye alighted upon a red Indian number, sort of leather strands and suede. Orlando raised his eyebrows dubiously.

'Are you sure?' he whispered.

'Trust me,' she said.

As they entered the grand dining hall of the restaurant all eyes turned to witness the dazzling couple. The management kept the paparazzi firmly outside the hotels revolving doors and Orlando was happier and prouder to be on show in public than he'd felt since his first review appeared in *The Stage*. Amy dazzled, quite simply. He held her hand and she turned to him.

'Are you sure I don't look like Pocahontas?' she said quietly, her pale caramel coloured thighs darting through the strands of softest suede as she padded silently across the dance floor.

'You look wonderful,' he reassured her, needlessly. Orlando by her side was equally striking. His hair curled gently over his collar and he had shaven his beard off again, leaving the blunt contours of his jawline to vye with his navy blue eyes for attention. They were suddenly beyond. Beyond the reach of every person in the room, beyond everyday beauty and charm, they existed in some realm of moon dust and glamour reserved only for those immortals come down from the olive groves of classical myth for the evening. It was an old-time Hollywood entrance, an entrance that you think only occurs in the mind of some journalist or social chronicler with an overactive imagination and one too many brandies, but this was real and those who saw it committed it to memory and never quite forgot it. It was the essence of youthful romance. And yes, we should envy them, we should wish ourselves them for this one fleeting, magical moment, for they're fantastically happy up there on their cloud. Lucky, lucky them.

And the cup of love and the cup of happiness brimmed over. Their chatter chinked along with the glasses and flowed as easily as the bubbles rising to the surface of yet more champagne, the food was tender and delighted the palate but was barely registered as they slipped easily into one another's eyes and revealed their heart's desires. Amy laughed as high and hard as a sugared almond and the rich timbre of Orlando's voice sunk deep inside Amy's head, saying exactly what she wanted to hear.

'It's been a struggle, an ill-fated path at times but we got here,' he sighed.

'Not too much of a struggle, I hope?' Amy was eager to ease all his worries.

'No, just the Tiffany Swann thing, the media, me and my reluctance to socialise, but nothing could beat how good this feels.'

'To us.' Amy raised her glass to meet his.

'Too right,' echoed Orlando.

And the other diners watched with the same blend of joy and envy as we watch them, but this time neither really noticed or cared. The staircase to their room seemed eternal that night and with the ease of dripping honey they explored each other's bodies in a familiar yet ecstatic way. It was at least two o'clock in the morning before Amy remembered that they were under siege and that she still had her public to face.

Chapter 28

The breakfast tray clattered on the bed and the orange juice flooded the scrambled egg.

'Shit,' muttered Orlando. It always seems quite blasphemous for the first word of a new day to be of the Anglo-Saxon variety, especially if the sky is blue and the evening before can only be described as heaven-sent. But Orlando had a hollow tummy and his hangover was merciless so we will forgive him.

'Mmmm, toast.' Amy's nose twitched to life at the smell and she lifted her head to investigate the rest of the breakfast.

'Morning, my love.' Orlando leaned over and kissed her forehead, narrowly missing upsetting the teapot. Amy scrabbled up and, pulling on a T-shirt, eyed-up the bacon.

'Do you remember the pig incident?' she asked thinking back to the early hours of their acquaintance in the woods in Dorset.

'Am I supposed to?' asked Orlando, fearful of being negligent.

'When we were on the shoot and that woman Nathalia told me off for giving her pig sandwiches. Old trollop,' said Amy, feeling a million miles from her career in ironing.

'Vaguely. Was she the hard faced one?'

'Yup indeedy,' said Amy, reaching for the newspapers, tabloid naturally, who could manoeuvre the broadsheets before midday she wondered?

'Orlando.' She froze on the front page of the *Express*.

'Hmmm?' he quizzed, squeezing another butter drenched soldier of toast into his mouth.

'Orlando, isn't that us on holiday?' She registered it gradually. He put his tray to one side and leant over the paper.

'How the bloody hell?' he asked, seeing a picture of himself and Amy wearing very little on a beach in Sydney. It was one that they'd done on self-timer, running into the picture as the button popped. Amy tried to make sense of the article. 'Orlando Rocks his Lover all Night Long.' What? Oh my God, Amy caught sight of two names, Catherine Hastings and Kate Chapman. Who? she thought at first. Then. Click. Flat monsters.

'Orlando, oh my God, it's my bloody flatmates, they've done this.' But Orlando wasn't listening, he was devouring the contents of the piece. Amy looked too but could only make out . . . I was his sex slave . . . Ozzie hideaway . . . exclusive photographs . . . six times a night. No, please God no thought Amy. Orlando stayed silent until,

'Amy, I think you'd better explain this to me.' Oh my God he was fierce. Headmaster's study fierce. Amy couldn't bear it. More than anything she refused to be told off.

'Explain what?' As if you didn't know, Amy.

'This.' He pointed calmly but firmly to the newspaper. Amy thought it was the bit which said, 'My Night of

Passion with Rocking Romeo,' but she couldn't be sure, maybe he just meant the whole thing.

'I really don't know what makes you think you can talk to me like that, Orlando Rock, but in case it had escaped your attention I'm free to come and go as I please and won't answer to you . . . not when you're treating me like a five-year-old on detention.' Deflection, Amy, oldest trick in the book when you're guilty. But it won't wash with Orlando, sorry.

'All I want to know is if you told the papers and if not how they know all this crap, and how they got our private holiday photos.' Amy worked though the problem in her head. Kitchen table. Gossip gossip. Tell us more. Bitches, she concluded, and I bet they nicked the bloody photo. But still he can't talk to me like that.

'You can't talk to me like that and get away with it you know.' She leapt out of bed and sought out her jeans.

'Amy, I just want to know what's going on.'

'No, you're practically accusing me of selling my story to the newspapers and I won't stay here and listen to it.'

'I'm not accusing you of anything, I just want to get to the bottom of it. Just answer my question. How did they get hold of all this?'

'I've no idea, but you seem convinced that it was me so I'll just leave you with that delusion and go.'

'Amy, I have to know I can trust you, don't you understand?'

'I understand that you're paranoid and that if I carry on going out with you I'm doomed to spending the rest of my days like Persephone in the underworld, darkness and misery. I might as well just take the veil now save us both the trouble.'

Orlando was lost. Veils? Persephone? He just wanted to know what was happening and how a photograph of him in his swimming trunks came to be on the front of every national tabloid and one broadsheet.

Once safely ensconced in the back of the taxi Amy wasn't quite sure where she should go. She hadn't thought of the consequences of returning to the nest of vipers at home; she was sure that if she saw either Kate or Cath she'd club them with a blunt instrument. Orlando's, her other safe haven, was most definitely off bounds and all she could think of was Lucinda. She checked her watch: Lucinda and Benjy never went in to work earlier than ten. Would she make it? Amy took the chance, directing the cab to Notting Hill. She piled onto the doorstep with her carrier bags.

'Hi Amy,' said Benjy without blinking at her red puffy eyes and backwards-through-a-hedge look. Suppose he's used to it by now, thought Amy, hoping at the very least to have caused concern or a minor stir.

'Is that Amy?' Lucinda brayed from inside the house. She came tearing out, oozing the worry and maternal anxiety Amy longed for. 'Darling where have you been? We've been trying for days to get hold of you, you do know what's happened don't you?' She lifted all Amy's carrier bags and ushered her into the house. Amy erupted into tears.

'I've left him,' she sobbed.

'Where?' asked Lucinda, slightly confused.

'No, I've left him. We had a fight about the papers, about my flat monsters.' Amy was incoherent so they just sat her in a large armchair and intravenously fed her camomile tea with whisky in it until the little hiccups of tears and misery abated.

'What have I done?'

'I don't know darling, what have you done?' Lucinda sat on the arm of the chair and stroked Amy's shoulder.

'We had a really nice night. I was just thinking I might be in love with him but then he snapped because of all the newspaper stuff, practically accused me of kissing and telling so I left,' Amy spluttered.

'I saw the pieces. You have to admit, sweetie, it does look as though you had a hand in it, all the photos and stuff about you guys on holiday.' Lucinda suddenly regretted saying this and, noticing Amy's shoulders beginning to shake again at the mere mention that she might be responsible, she retracted it.

'But of course we know it wasn't you, it was those awful bloody bitches and when I get hold of them I'll throttle them. I'm just saying that you can't be too harsh on Orlando. He's had a rough time with the press over the past few years, he's bound to be oversensitive.' At this Amy cried all over again. The shoulder stroking and camomile teaing continued for some hours to come.

Amy woke up with bloated froggy red eyes from crying too much and lots of crumbled bits of tissue stuck in her hair. She was lying on top of a rosy sprigged duvet in the spare room at Benjy and Lucinda's and it slowly came back to her that she was Orlando-less. And they'd had the most amazing evening. Quite simply she'd never been happier, and things were never usually very simple for Amy, so this was nothing short of miraculous. But now she'd pissed him off and couldn't go back. How could he accuse her of that, she smarted, and her blood ran hotter at the very thought. Didn't he know her better? So for a while logic escaped Amy; she didn't stop to analyse in her usual way the fact that he had said nothing of the sort. Guilt, my dear, guilt.

Chapter 29

On the creamy, inch-deep carpets of the Knightsbridge hotel Orlando Rock sat with his back against the wall, the day's newspapers scattered about him. He tried to read the horrors in print but kept returning to the picture of Amy in her bikini on holiday. He remembered how much they'd laughed and how much they'd eaten, how he had to tell her that if she ate another prawn she'd turn pink and start swimming backwards in the bath. And last night, last night with its glow almost too bright to look at just yet, he could only feel the soft tassels of Amy's dress brushing his skin as he touched her, remember how ethereal she had looked with her fading tan and almond skin. How much lovelier than any woman he'd known. But what could he do? She'd told someone about them, that was for sure. And she'd told whoever it was things he couldn't imagine telling anyone, not even Bill. Logic told him that women had different codes of revelation and discretion amongst one another than men had, but to talk about their jokes, their feelings, the whole kit and caboodle? And although Orlando knew this, he didn't feel an awful lot better. Well, let's face it, would you if your sexual prowess had been turned into a series of trite one-liners mostly pertaining to Rocks or Rock 'Ard or something for the nation to digest over breakfast, on building sites and in hairdressing salons? The more he thought about it the more furious he became.

And so they sit at opposite ends of London, not really understanding each other but longing to forget the whole thing and just kiss and make-up without the intervening postmortem. *Mais non.* Star-crossed lovers were ever thus, their love shines brighter but when extinguished there's no finding your way in the darkness. Amy didn't really understand what all the fuss was about. So what there was a bikini shot on the front of the newspapers? It was quite nice, not a spare tyre in sight, she thought with relief. And it was pretty embarrassing for her mother and old maths teacher to bear witness to the fact that she had rather a lot of sex with a famous actor, but it could have been worse, they could have exhumed one of the exs. Small Mercies!

Amy was naïve in most matters tabloid. She knew about magazine distribution and could tell her *Vogue* masthead from a sub-editor, but the logistics of dishing the dirt escaped her. But not for long, folks.

Lucinda pushed open the door of the spare room,

'Amy, are you awake? I've got to go to work in a min. Are you going to come in?'

Amy groaned to life. Actually she'd been awake since four o'clock in the morning, feeling sick and terrified of never seeing Orlando again, but she'd forgotten about the demon work.

'I guess so. Can I borrow some clothes?' Lucinda

handed over an outfit she'd prepared earlier, safe and black and baggy. What a gem.

As they were squashed up on the tube with frizzy hair and dandruffy shoulders serving to remind them how horrible the human race was they were rendered even more misanthropic by a glance at a headline in the *Sun*. Lucinda saw it first but she didn't have her contact lenses in, so squinted in a bid to make out the bold type of AMY AND AMIABILITY, rather charmingly literary for the *Sun* you have to admit. Amy saw it and were it not for the grainy topless shot of her underneath she would probably have been flattered at the aptness of it. But right now her attention was drawn to her left breast. She would have screamed had she not had a mouthful of commuter's elbow as the train jarred into the station. Her knees went weak and continuing the Jane Austen motif she felt faint. She would have run mad too, had she had the space. Imagine your horror. The breasts that you are familiar with only in terms of having a bath with them and the odd squeezing into a wonderbra, you've tried to keep them half hidden even when trying on some divine garment in a shop changing room, you've looked anew at them at the beginning of relationships and hoped they would pass muster, then realised they must do or the relevant man wouldn't give them the time of night. And so they are forgotten again, those wonders of womankind. Until they appear on the front of a newspaper being read two feet away from you on the underground. Then you feel very peculiar indeed. Especially if they weren't teased to peak perfection by some ice-cube wielding photographer for rather a lot of money, but instead recorded by some rat ex-boyfriend for five minutes in his monochrome Battersea flat. Bloody hell. Rat. Bastard. Traitor. Cad. No word was strong enough, no implement sharp enough or blunt enough to club him about the head with when she saw him next. But what was she to do? She couldn't go to work and have everyone see that. Oh my God the men in the postroom, the security guards. Her editor. The man standing next to her. Surely he could see the resemblance between the shadowy figure with breasts protruding from his briefcase and the girl stood in front of him. Amy had to get hold of a copy. She had to lock herself in the loo and cry with horror at herself looking like a star of *Emanuelle II* for national delectation or even worse and, more likely, she concluded, ridicule. All this time she was holding onto Lucinda's jacket sleeve, her mouth open, her face frozen in horror. Lucinda was oblivious to the full catastrophe, being as she was deprived the salient image due to her shortsightedness. Amy mouthed various swear words at Lucinda but no words came out. She motioned noiselessly at the paper but made no sense. Eventually they got to their stop and Lucinda had to steer Amy over the gap onto the platform. They sat on a broken plastic bench.

'Amy, what is wrong? Tell me what it said! I was half tempted to wrest it from that man but thought you might keel over!'

'I . . . it's me,' spluttered Amy.

'I know, sweetheart, but what did it say?' coaxed Lucinda.

'It was me . . . with the photographer,' Lucinda was

none the wiser and the way Amy was staring at the peeling Holidays in the Sun poster on the other side of the track thought it best if she steered her away from the train part of the station altogether. She knew of Amy's penchant for Tolstoy and didn't want an Anna Karenina drama to deal with, thank you very much.

'Darling let's see if we can make it into work and then we can sit somewhere quiet and talk about it.' Amy glued herself to her seat like a toddler refusing to go to playschool.

'I can't, Luce.'

'Come on, whatever it was couldn't be so bad, think of what poor Orlando has been through and he's still standing.' Amy was thinking of Orlando, but not poor Orlando. Bloody Orlando, if I'd never met him ... But she wished he was there now too. Couldn't decide whether she loved or loathed him. Hither, thither, which way next?

'Luce it was me ... without my top on.' Amy was in denial, the topless part she was coming to terms with, the fact that there was a shadowy figure of a man lurking in the same picture, the fact that she was actually having sex in print seemed not quite to sink in.

'But how darling, was it another holiday snap?'

'No, it was the photographer.' Lucinda was getting nowhere with her line of enquiry so pulled the dead weight to her feet and marched her military fashion along the platform and up the escalator. Outside the station she picked up copies of every tabloid and left the change of her fiver with the fortunate vendor. After a frogmarch down Hanover Street and a difficult negotiation of the revolving doors of Vogue House the girls found a quiet corner of the beauty cupboard and Lucinda extracted two plastic cups of tarry coffee from the machine and set about making sense of Amy's rantings.

'Here's some coffee, now let's see what this is all about,' said Lucinda, opening the offending *Sun*.

'No!' Amy reached over and tried to cover the headline with her arm but was soon defeated. 'I suppose everyone's going to see it soon enough.' Lucinda scanned the paper with barely concealed amusement.

'Darling, how on earth did they get hold of all this? Was this Toby's idea?' Amy shrugged her shoulders feebly.

'It's really not funny, Luce. Look, this bit here says you can buy the video for £11.99 on their hotline. They can't do this.'

'Darling, they are doing it, but don't worry, it'll be a one-minute wonder. And anyway, if I had boobs like that I wouldn't care if they were on *News at Ten*.'

'But it's not just that, it's the fact that Toby's there too, God it's disgusting. It's so sordid. I feel so violated Luce, it's horrible. I don't want to see anyone. What am I going to do?'

'Well, Toby actually just looks like part of the mattress he's such a dark shadow so don't worry about that too much. And you're going to feel shit for a few days, your parents will disown you for a bit and your answerphone will be overflowing with offers from *Playboy* and then it'll die down and you'll wonder what the fuss was all about.' Amy remained singularly unconvinced. Of course she did. AMY AND AMIABILITY, and it wasn't just about how nice she was to animals and children, it was liberally strewn with phrases like insatiable and curvaceous, free-thinking and even, heaven forfend, wait till her mother sees it, a bit of a goer. No! thought Amy. I can't bear it. She couldn't sit still and she couldn't go anywhere. If she looked at the papers she felt sick, but if she didn't read them she imagined the reports as ten times more crass than they actually were. She was embarrassed even in front of Lucinda but couldn't bear to be on her own. Oh God, she thought, what am I going to do? For a moment she was struck with empathy for Orlando. Now I know how he felt, she thought. But she quickly forgot about him. She was more concerned with herself right now, more terrified of her fate.

'Oh well, look who it isn't. I had no idea you were moonlighting as a porn queen, Amy.' Nathalia flashed into the room, her silver puffa jacket setting off her ski tan and her 'helped' blonde hair lent her that fresh from Klosters look.

'Come on, Nats, Amy's having a rough time, she can do without that,' said Lucinda, firm but fair.

'Darling, if I were to prostrate myself naked before a video camera it would be naïve to think that it was going to end anyway other than messily.'

'Piss off and leave us alone,' Lucinda snapped, her fair aspect vanishing behind a cloud. Nathalia picked up a pair of shoes fresh from a high street fashion shoot and with a wrinkling of her nose and a cursory, 'Cheap rubbish,' walked away.

Amy bit her lip and tried not to cry. Lucinda decided that it was time to take action.

She picked up the phone.

'Who're you phoning?'

'I'm going to get hold of Orlando. There's no way you can go through this on your own, darling.'

'Luce, that would just be too embarrassing. Besides, he was awful to me, accusing me of all sorts of things, I wouldn't ask him for help if you paid me.' Defiant, she was. She was also deeply worried how he would react to her recent excursion into pornography. Whilst he may have forgiven her for blabbing to her flatmates (although she wouldn't give him the chance), she could see she'd have problems explaining away her top shelf antics. And bloody hell, I'm a grown woman, if I want to experiment with sex I will, it's none of his business. Amy was defiant, if distraught.

'Yup, I'd like to speak to Orlando Rock, I believe he's in room ... Amy, which room is it?' Lucinda was on fine form.

'Can't remember.' Stubbornly.

'Amy, which room is Orlando in?' she shouted.

'Fifty-nine.' Surly.

'Yeah, he's in room fifty-nine, I'm a friend. What do you mean his agent, I'm his friend, please put me through,' Lucinda bellowed. But she persisted, agent's number from directory enquiries. Dial dial,

'Yes, I'm trying to get in touch with Orlando Rock, his girlfriend needs to speak to him.' Contempt on the other end of the line.

'Look, he doesn't pay you to be some moral judge, so just tell him to call Amy as soon as possible. If you don't there'll be hell to pay. What do you mean you don't know where he is, just tell him, OK?' Lucinda hung up.

Amy was mortified. She may be Miss Big Happening Girlfriend in her head but in the eyes of the world she was Miss Kiss and Tell Sleazy Sex Scandal. I'll show him, she thought.

In an unconscious mirroring of Orlando's behaviour yesterday Amy sat on the floor in the corner of the fashion room with the papers about her, deep in thought. Orlando, however, had braved it out of his room and was sitting in the hotel dining room sipping black coffee when he encountered Amy's proud breasts half obscured by a bowl of cereal. AMY AND AMIABILITY. He couldn't believe it either. Firstly he couldn't believe that she'd ever have let herself be filmed having sex with some social climbing photographer, secondly he felt incredibly sorry for her. But decent though he is, Orlando could not help countering his sorrow with the hope that there'd be a chastening lesson in there for her. And let's face it, this could happen to anyone, Orlando knew only too well, he'd been caught in a few clinches in his time. But despite this he didn't feel as philosophical as he should. There was a glint in her eye, he'd seen it in his wife on many an occasion. Amy may not be solely responsible for yesterday's tabloid fest, but she wasn't opposed to it and was quick to dismiss his anxieties as paranoia. Maybe now she'd have a bit more sympathy with his plight. He also still wanted to hug her though, wished she hadn't been so wretchedly stubborn and would call him. With the perspicacity only marriage to an actress can bestow, Orlando realised he'd just have to give Amy time if he wanted her and let her work some things out of her system, so when he packed his bags to return to New Zealand later that day it was with a sagacity and patience often granted only to Buddhist monks.

Later on in the day Amy was smuggled out of Vogue House under an Isaac Mizrahi parka, its furry hood over her head and a pair of Raybans obscuring her eyes. This was at her own insistence. She'd decided that the ponytailed couriers littering the pavements of Hanover Square were in fact paparazzi in disguise. Lucinda had tried but failed to take a firm stance.

'Amy, these guys don't even bother to disguise themselves when they're lurking outside Princess Diana's balcony at Kensington Palace trying to catch her in her rollers and La Perla. What on earth makes you think they'd go to such lengths just to snap you leaving work on a rainy Tuesday?'

'Because I swear to you, that one down there, the one with the label with CFP Couriers on his back, the bald one with the ponytail, he was definitely outside Orlando's flat and he was also outside the hotel. I'd know those beady eyes anywhere, I even had a nightmare about them last night.'

'Darling, don't you think you're being just a bit melodramatic?' said Lucinda, Orlando may be being saint-like in his patience but Lucinda could feel her halo sliding.

'Lucinda, I'm telling you, just let's find something that doesn't show my face and certainly not my body, and then we can call a cab and have the security guards radio up when it arrives.'

'Look, I'm sure you'll be perfectly safe on the tube, it's

not as though you'll be topless is it?' Lucinda instantly regretted her cheap jibe but after approximately five hours of being barricaded into a room in Vogue House with Amy and her bruised yet recovering speedily ego she felt rather worn.

'Lucinda, I need my friends for support, how can you joke about it?'

'Sorry, sweetheart. Look, here's a lovely coat to hide your face and some glasses, *et voilà*, nobody will look twice at you.' But of course they did: in her fashion conscious, raybanned-eskimo-in-April attire she presented a strange sight even for those accustomed to beholding the curios coming and going from Vogue House. But if they stared they merely saw a prettily dressed fashion editor, her glossy locks skimming her shoulders in an immaculate bob, escorting someone who was clearly off their trolley, but who was certainly not to be recognised as this morning's Stunna from Surrey. So, almost sadly, Amy had her anonymous way.

Once back at Lucinda's they endured the six, nine and ten o'clock newses, just in case in the 'and finally ...' section an item on the latest love of Orlando Rock had been slipped in by some duty manager with a sharp eye for detail and penchant for firm 34B breasts. *Mais non*, of course. Lucinda was not too miserable about the news-watching part of her care in the community duties as she had a bit of a crush on Peter Sissons. Ever since she'd seen him in a moment of national crisis and he'd furrowed his brow and asked scarily intelligent questions to government ministers she'd found him disturbingly sexy. But that was another story, and one which she'd rather keep to herself. What she did mind, though, were Amy's worrying sojourns into the world of media prostitution.

'Do you think maybe I should get an agent, Luce?'

'Why do you need an agent?' Lucinda's 'darlings' were noticeably absent.

'Well, to ensure my privacy, and also, well . . . if people want to talk to me, well it seems more professional for them to go through an agent, really. You know, money is quite vulgar.'

'I've always thought money far from vulgar,' chipped in Benjy, who darted into the room to extricate some cigarettes from down the side of the sofa.

'Oh God darling, can I have one?' begged Lucinda.

'You're supposed to have given up.'

'Needs must and all that,' said Lucinda, gesturing discreetly towards Amy who was engrossed in last week's *Hello!* It's enough to make a grown girl cry, she thought.

'How much do you think they pay Fergie for appearing in here?'

'Bloody fortune,' said Benjy, heading back to the safety of the kitchen.

'Really?' Amy's eyes shone, 'If they pay someone like her so much, someone *passé* and outmoded who never really did anything but get married and have Titian hair, well then, I'm sure the sky's the limit for someone, y'know, a bit cooler, younger, fresher.'

'Anyone in mind?' asked Lucinda tetchily, taking a lungful of heavenly tar.

'No, just thinking out loud really.' Lucinda could barely stand any more. People deal with shock in different ways, she told herself, they do all sorts of funny things, you don't just faint and turn white, you say all kinds of weird things. Perhaps I should be more understanding.

'But I suppose if I were to be asked, I mean I would be stupid to turn it down. Just a bit of posing in other people's clothes. I've heard they don't even use your own house, just some plush hotel and fill it with your own stuff, at least then I wouldn't have to have the flat monsters sitting at the kitchen table looking homely.'

Heaven forfend. Bollocks to understanding, she needs a big kick up the backside.

'Amy, don't you think you should call your parents? I mean they're bound to have seen all that stuff and they'll be desperate to get in touch with you, to make sure you're not too upset.' Upset? I don't think so, after all tears don't photograph well do they, thought Lucinda.

'Maybe I'll call them tomorrow, they'll be in bed by now.'

'Yeah, well, I think it's past my bedtime too. Do you think you'll be OK if you're alone, not too upset or anything?' sniped Lucinda.

'Oh, I think I'll be all right. Besides I need my beauty sleep too, and I'm still utterly miserable about Orlando.' Like hell she was. She'd barely given a thought to Orlando since the prospect of fame in her own right writ large appeared in her sights. Her eyes should be like those cartoon characters but instead of pound signs she just had popping flashbulbs and *Hello!* covers. Without another word Lucinda tripped off to bed feeling like a bad troll lurking under the bridge, but she couldn't help it. It's not much fun watching a friend transform into the picture of Dorian Grey before your eyes.

The next morning saw the bathroom door slammed in the face of Lucinda and Benjy from six thirty until they could wait no longer.

'Amy, I've got to pee!' Lucinda knocked.

'Won't be a mo, I've just got to chip this facepack off, five minutes OK?'

Lucinda crossed her legs in the bedroom and cursed Amy.

'I just can't believe it. If she'd show some bloody remorse about Orlando, it'd be more tolerable but she's totally forgotten about him. I can't believe what a self-obsessed cow she's being.'

Only Amy knew that as she pondered the joys of celebrity, the lunches in nice restaurants, the mantelpiece bowing under the weight of party invitations, the column inches devoted to her latest hairstyle, there was one thing missing: Orlando Rock. She may have had trouble saying she loved him but she couldn't eliminate the warmth she felt as she saw his head on the pillow beside her, the pride she'd felt walking into the hotel with him, the fun they'd had on their normal dates. Even the greasy spoon had taken on a romantic glow. Still, Orlando had questioned her integrity and she'd been humiliated, but also, as we know only too well, guilty. He'd trusted her and she'd spilled all their beans at the drop of a hat to people she didn't really give a damn about. So what could she do? Her rationale, apart from vengeance towards his snide agent, was that if he saw her looking glorious in the papers with some handsome man on her arm he'd be so overcome with jealousy that he'd have to have her back, sacrifice his pride and ride in on the proverbial white charger and kidnap her, Sir Lancelot fashion. Prove his love once and for all. For where was romance if not in jeopardy? But Amy darling, how could you get it so wrong? Think about it. Can you really see Orlando running open armed back to you just because you prove yourself incapable of behaving like a grown-up? Does being on the front page of a newspaper addle the brain?

Chapter 30

Amy was reconciled with the flat monsters. She was quite cross at Lucinda's recent frostiness and they proved good listeners. Even if they stored it up to mull over and pull apart later, she couldn't really give a stuff right now. She had her career to think of. Oh, girls, how we moan when we see bright, happy, highlighted-haired wonders transformed from just-another-weather-girl into the flavour of the month with a Chanel suit. How we hate to see the wife of a rugby player elevated to cover girl status because of her saintly ability to smile through her husband's infidelity. How we despise the cult of the model who becomes super because she suppresses her appetite behind a wider smile than most women can endure. Oh la la, how bitter we are. Which of us wouldn't throw in the towel of self-respect if presented with stardom on a silver platter? Well, Amy would, for one. The flat monsters sat at the table with her, limpet-like and sycophantically providing her with camomile tea. I wonder if I could get sponsorship, she thought? Is there a camomile marketing board who'd be happy to have a vivacious spokeswoman? Maybe not, camomile wasn't really a product she wanted to endorse, not terribly glamorous, enjoyable with hot water but a bit too organic. Her free love reputation was already nudging at the boundaries of hippydom, one had to watch one's public image.

'Amy, here's one that doesn't sound too bad.' Cath passed her an envelope with a News International logo on the back, she was quite *au fait* with that one now.

'Life story to the *News of the World*, no, that's just a bit too flat, too one-dimensional, I'm looking more for magazine features, something topical.'

'Here, be on that debate programme with the tanned dishy bloke, they want you to talk about being in a dysfunctional relationship.'

'God no, too parochial, they'll set wronged housewives from Berkshire onto me and call me a slut, way too embarrassing.'

'Oooh, a private view at the Saatchi gallery.'

'That'll do, would you mind rsvp'ing a yes to that, Cath. You can come along too. It's really good gallery space, perfect for seeing and being seen.' The phone disturbed Amy's masterplan to be that most coveted of phenomena, famous for being famous.

'Ames, it's that Marquesa woman again, the one from *Hello!*'

'Oh good,' said Amy, running to the phone. 'Marquesa hi, yes let's do that. OK. Friday two o'clock. Bye.' Amy had just secured a preliminary interview with the woman who wielded the *Hello!* pursestrings.

'God, it's harder than getting into Cambridge, she'll probably ask me what I think of Tolstoy's narrative style,' she bewailed, wondering which of her now depleted (she hadn't seen Lucinda for a week) cache of outfits to choose from for the interview. But there was tonight to get through, a book launch. Amy had decided that if she were ever to sound like a legitimate celebrity she had to have at least one substantial string to her bow – literary glamour girl was her chosen specialist style. At least it would set her apart from the fashion crowd, and she'd once practically worked in publishing, and who knows Martin Amis might be there, very sexy voice, she'd once heard him on Radio Four whilst she was at the dentist. So she chose carefully, subtle and sober but with a flash of originality, she thought, some learned spark. She pulled out her trusty black suit and decided on a gold theme, some large bracelets, a gold body a model once left behind on a shoot and a shimmery bronzed look for her face. Standing back, she couldn't imagine that book people could be so dull so went for the final effect, some silk flowers sprayed gold – very messy and she had to soak her hands in nail polish remover to get it off – but good. Yes, the effect was Dionysian, she thought, lavish and opulent and excessive, bit like me, she winked to herself. Ohhh, how that tiny, frail ego we first encountered has started to flex its muscles, toughen up and take over the world. Pride comes before a fall, Amy, but Amy's effectively had a fall and come up if not smelling of roses, at least adorned by them.

It would be nice right now to be able to lift the top off Amy's head like a teapot and take a quick look around inside, stir up the tea leaves and see what was churned up – would she be sorry beneath all the gold and ridiculous notions? Wish that she was watching TV quietly with Orlando, falling in love with the way he looked at her and chucked her under the chin and nibbled his toenails when she wasn't looking? This is after all what she should do, fall in love with his showbiz image and come around eventually to the less than idyllic lifestyle, but love it warts and all because after all it's reality and she's in love with the real Orlando. But when opportunity knocks and you're standing at the door in your best frock with newly waxed legs it would seem foolish to shut the door and say sorry, I'm washing my hair. However, we don't have the divine Mr R waiting in the wings, perhaps then we'd tell opportunity to take a hike. Who knows? And does even Amy know? No, we should stick with her for just a bit longer, be the loyal friend she needs, tell her when she's getting wide of the mark but enjoy the good times too. As the Americans are so fond of saying, life's a learning curve; she'll get there in the end, it just might not be tonight.

Amy handed over her invitation at the door and bent down to avoid the low ceiling of breezeblocks as she entered what had once been a war bunker. That was the thing about literary types, they loved a theme. She supposed that the novel being launched was someone very old's memoirs, or maybe it was a romance with a war theme. She couldn't quite remember what the PR girl had said now, just that it would be attended by some of the biggest names in the literary world. Amy knew that when fashion people said that kind of thing they were usually lying, but this was literature, they had too much integrity to lie in a nice old gentlemen's business. She entered the room with Cath. Cath wasn't quite so ideal a companion as Lucinda, she wasn't as pretty, as engaging, as beautifully dressed or as witty, but who's the heroine here? In the absence of the lovely Lucinda she'll have to do. The bunker belied its façade and from behind a concrete pillar emerged a man brandishing champagne. 'This is more like it,' said Amy, taking one without orange juice. She looked around the room for familiar faces, but couldn't see anyone really, and they were mostly dressed in grey and all looked quite alike, even the women. There were a few with large heaving bosoms and red hair but that was about it. Besides, the only faces Amy could ever really recognise were those of long departed souls. She'd know Jane Austen by her dress if she walked in, she'd know Byron by his breeches and pheromones and Wordsworth because he was so boring everyone would leave the room (may God and my nineteenth-century poetry tutor strike me down), but with the moderns she was less familiar – Salman Rushdie was a doddle but the rest tended to blend into one clever-looking mass. As she perused the bunker and took a large gulp of champagne she thought she saw Martin Amis, but he was with someone terribly chic and sexy so she thought she'd wait until she was out of the way before she tried to make an *entrée* there. A young man in a tapestry waistcoat came and stood beside her.

'I think I know you. Terribly brave to show yourself in public after last week's little news item. Oh Ho, pardon the pun, I suppose you're rather used to showing yourself in public.' Ho bloody ho, thought Amy, what a wit. His voice was like thick toffee sticking to his teeth, he had to prise it open at every word in order to set his plummy vowels free. Where's Lucinda when I need her? She'd say something clever like, perhaps you need another half hour to prepare your next joke, shall I hold my breath? But Amy felt dull and her public image was at stake, and now she was in the middle of the room she realised how horrendously overdressed she was. What on earth had possessed her to dress in gold? The brightest colour here was black, the rest was grey. Even the chic Amis beauty was dressed in funereal splendour. Maybe book people just don't dress up. You'd think that after days sitting round in tracky bums writing they'd relish the opportunity to make like a peacock. Obviously not. And oh no, Amis was holding hands with the beauty. One of Amy's literary aspirations crashed down around her head and she put her empty champagne glass back on a roaming tray. Maybe this wasn't such a good idea. Cath was entertaining (if that's the word) the waistcoat and so Amy took a turn around the room. She wandered over to a table of books piled up in the corner and determined that even if she wasn't going to pull or get her picture in the papers she could at least find out what the launch was for. As she cast her eye over the blurb she felt a hand on her waist. Martin? She hoped. No, she turned round and saw a familiar shaggy bowl cut. Well, first of all she saw a bit of chest hair sprouting from under his shiny nylon football shirt, but swiftly turned her attention to the face that had launched a million album covers. The face of internationally successful indie music, very nice, she thought, not about the face but about the meaning of the face. For it meant street cred, it meant fans, idolatry, greatness by association. Amy lifted her golden eyelids and grinned widely.

'Hi,' she charmed.

'Hi yourself,' he smarmed.

'Looks good,' she said, picking up the book as a conversation prop. She could tell just by the slightly vacant behind the eyes look that she would need it.

'Yeah.' He looked at her shimmering cleavage.

'Maybe I'll read it, I don't usually come to these kind of parties, but everyone seems very interesting, I wouldn't have thought you'd come to many of these yourself, what with all the excitements of the music industry, in fact I'm surprised it's your scene at all.' She was jabbering.

'Nah, I quite like books.'

'Yeah, me too.'

'You want a drink?'

'Could kill for one.' He whistled to a passing waiter and deposited the remains of his cigarette on the champagne tray, picking up two glasses with one hand.

'Cheers,' he muttered.

'Cheers,' she echoed.

'What do you do then?' he managed between glugs of champagne.

'I work in fashion,' she said, disappointed that he didn't recognise her.

'Also been known to take her top off occasionally.' The waistcoat arrived by Amy's side. The pop-star's eyes reverted to her cleavage.

'Would you mind telling me who you are?' she said bravely to the waistcoat. A bit of cockiness always went down well with pop-stars, she imagined.

'Joshua Bennett, *Times* diary.' He chewed his make-believe toffee.

'Shaun Madden, Lucifer. Fuck off.' That's who he was. Amy couldn't remember the name of the band. Lucifer: it sounded like a parody of a seventies heavy metal band but those guys were seriously cool, not really her thing but big time. The Bennett Waistcoat person made for Martin Amis, and Amy and the pop-star sniggered conspiratorially.

'So what's all this topless vibe then, a babe like you's a bit clever to be taking her clothes off for a living,' he flattered.

'Not for a living, more an accident, but I don't regret it. It was quite liberating actually; there's not much else they can do or say to touch you when you've done that.'

'Don't you believe it.' His casual delivery belied the astute intelligence of the remark (intelligent for Shaun that is), so Amy just pouted instead of listening.

'So why are you here?' she asked.

'Oh y'know, just thought it might be a laugh, and I read lots of poetry and stuff, great inspiration for lyrics.' Amy thought this might be a good sign.

'Oh, who do you like?'

'Well I reckon Sid Vicious was a bit of a poet, and Bowie, man, he's an all time great.'

'Oh, I didn't realise Sid Vicious wrote his own stuff.'

'Yeah, course he did. Anyway, I've gotta go, I've got a gig at ten but let's go out, somewhere flash. What's your number?' Amy jotted it down on a cigarette packet for him and he pushed it into his pocket, then he kissed her and felt her bottom. Not a proper kiss but definitely a proper grope, and with a crackle of nylon static he was gone. Amy was about to bemoan the unoriginality of pop stars and think how vulgar and all of the same mould when Cath came running over.

'Oh my God that was Shaun Madden. He's so gorgeous! Did you get his autograph?'

'Cath, I'm twenty-four, I'm not getting anyone's autograph.' She was about to add,

'Especially not some hairy, ignorant git who should have the decency to realise he looked like a football fan from some lesser known European city,' but shut up. Be your own best self-publicist she chanted. 'We're going out to dinner.' Cath flapped around like a trout on a sandbank for a while and whispered to the waistcoat and then proudly escorted Amy to a taxi. Oh well, at least someone thought the pop-star was worth writing home about. Amy certainly didn't.

Maybe he won't ring, she thought as she sat waiting for the Marquesa in a neat Brasserie in Fulham. Of course he will, they always do when you don't want them to. And she didn't really want him to. I mean, of course she did, but she didn't too. Do you know what I mean? No? Well that's probably because Amy doesn't know what she means. The Lucifer bloke was not her dream bloke, Orlando was. And anyway, imagine taking someone from Lucifer home. Her mother thought Orlando Rock was a horrid name; she'd invite the local exorcist round and have Shaun Madden doused in holy water before he set foot on the Welcome mat. But Orlando just seemed so clean and lovely in comparison, he was clever and funny and good in bed and . . . oh shut up you can't have him, he's not part of the masterplan and he's not speaking to you anyway, she told herself firmly. And where was Lucinda when you needed her? Off sunning herself on some exotic Caribbean holiday that's where. She probably went there to get away from me, thought Amy, knowing full well what a boring cow she'd been for the past few weeks. She was starting to tire of the incessant flat monsters. God she couldn't even open her cereal packet without finding one lurking somewhere, outside the bathroom door, by the phone as she planned her celebrity, hoovering under her feet as she watched late night TV (just keeping an eye out for Lucifer). Amy even contemplated calling Anita for a woman to woman chat but didn't know the number. Was it too much to ask for someone intelligent to talk to? The answer, it seemed, was yes. If you burn your friends like boats as you set sail onto the choppy and murky waters of fame what can you expect? Media-tarting is OK if you want to shag a pop-star but not so great for good conversation and loyal companions.

But later Amy concluded her conversation with the Marquesa most satisfactorily and secured a four-page spread about her pain and hurt and extensive wardrobe. She felt good as a wheeler-dealer. This is the life, she thought, quashing her need for intellectual stimulation beneath a cheque weighty enough to buy her a Prada outfit. Now I know why I suffer, she reassured herself.

Chapter 31

And so it was in her new Prada ensemble that she stepped out with Shaun Madden. Stepped out because stepping out was what one did with pop-stars and Amy had to get it right. There'd been some sniping in the press the other day about her being a callous opportunist who should stick to hemlines, but the thumbsize photo of the journalist revealed her to be quite bovine looking so Amy neatly put it down to jealousy. Still, though, she had to be careful not to seem like any old trollop but a discerning woman with a life of her own. Easier said than done. They went to the Saatchi Gallery and mingled in a space made for posing, vast open white floors and warehouse expanses. Mick and Jerry were holding court further along in the room and Amy pretended not to stare but couldn't help but check out Jerry's hair and leopard print. Mick was sexy and wore a frock coat; even with his used look he was indisputably gorgeous.

'Scrotum face,' the pop-star declared. At least he hasn't got bollocks for a brain, Amy was tempted to retort but instead smiled in pretend amusement.

'Let's go and look in the room over there.' Amy nodded in the direction of a darkened room and the pair wandered off, yet more champagne clutched in their hands.

But Amy should have known better, amongst the strange distorted faces and spooky sounds of the exhibit she felt something on her bottom. Part of the overall effect of the artistic installation designed to inspire surprise and delight? No just a hormonally overactive Shaun.

'How about it?' he smirked, pointing to the darkest corner of the room behind a fine piece of conceptual sculpture. Amy's sense of propriety gasped in horror.

'It might be just a bit risky, we could get mistaken for a work of art,' said Amy casually, as though she always had sex in public but just didn't feel like it today. The only merit she could see in the plan was that Mick Jagger might take his clothes off too and join them.

'Aw, come on, it'll be a laugh.' Amy could think of funnier things than bonking a hairy singer with a limited vocabulary in a public place.

'Maybe later eh?' she said making for the light and safety of the main hall.

At dinner he was equally tedious. He tried to remove her knickers before they'd sat down at their table and she had to keep up a constant wriggling motion to prevent him from catching hold of her.

'You're not frigid are you?' he laughed.

'No, of course not. I just think maybe we should wait until later.'

'You're not Christian are you?' He looked worried.

'No, and just as well since I'm practically having a date with Lucifer.' She laughed at her feeble joke to try to persuade the blood swirling round his groin to depart for his brain.

'Yeah,' he laughed blankly. 'Later then eh?' And so it

continued. Amy writhed like an eel and he didn't quite get it together to have a conversation. Towards dessert she started to yawn huge enormous yawns.

'Oh deary me, I must be tired.' She sounded like her mother as she put down her knitting before bed but had stopped caring how she appeared.

'Will a line of charlie sort you out?'

'A line of . . . ? Oh, no, really thanks, I'll be fine. Thanks for the offer though.' Always refuse drugs politely – it was uncool not to seem grateful for the fantastic offer you'd just passed up – was one of Amy's diehard rules. But then she became transfixed by his nostrils, noticing the red raw insides. Should have known, she thought. Well I'm definitely not going home with some sex-crazed drug fiend. Steady Amy, he's just a bloke who likes the odd snort, but Amy had found her excuse and it fitted like a glove. Yeeha! I don't have to sleep with him, he's a drug addict. Whatever you say Amy, we're just innocent bystanders.

So the dessert was munched. She thought back to Orlando and the tiny thimblefuls of chantilly cream and raspberry meringue they'd shared over their last dinner, the dusting of icing sugar and kisses. She compared Orlando's crisply rolled back shirtsleeves revealing tanned and strong wrists, to the medallion rings and hairy knuckles of thingummyjig colliding noisily with everything in sight. Well, they're not colliding with me, she thought firmly. She'd been off the champagne since they left the gallery and had stoically adhered to lime and soda. No slip ups with monkey man she thought. Oh Orlando, I think I loved you. Then just as the said hand disappeared under the table, in pursuit of underwear probably, Amy drew on all her reserves of acting skills. Not since fourth form drama classes had she shown such outstanding skills at histrionics.

'Oh my God!'

'What's wrong babe?' said Shaun, his hand still lurching around under the table.

'Killer headache.' She started to cry. Well, if she'd just have whined a bit he might have thought she wanted sympathy and just groped her. As it was he reacted just as predicted by Amy.

'Come on, it's only a bleedin' headache!'

'No, it's a migraine,' she sobbed.

'You'll be all right.' He didn't know where to look. How embarrassing he thought, out to dinner with some bird and she starts to cry. Finally he brought his hand up for air.

'I think it's best if I go.' Amy stood up and picked up her handbag. 'Thanks, I've had a lovely night.' Neither did he stand up, offer to pay for a cab home or kiss her goodbye. Mission accomplished, she thought as she bounded into the street and waved a cab. It was only then that she saw the lurking paparazzi. Oh well, too late she turned round and flashed them a smile but even with her new improved ego knew that she wouldn't make it into the papers without Shaun Madden on her arm. Some you win . . .

As she lay in bed that night she felt relieved but sad. In fact she cried. Properly cried. Not headachey crying, not I'm-so-offended-Orlando-Rock-how-dare-you-suggest-such-a-thing crying. But real crying. Real sad, I

266

miss him and wish he were here now and I could tell him all about my disastrous date and we could laugh about it together crying. She also cried with relief. She hadn't had to snog the pop-star. That would have been so horrible she couldn't bear to think about it. Sometimes when you get what you want you don't want what you wanted at all she thought sagely. And again, You can't always get what you want, but if you try sometimes you just might find you get what you need. It was amazing how these old proverbs comforted her in hard times. Even though she knew the last one was a Rolling Stones' song and not a proverb, it still seemed to have a certain rustic purity. Bloody hell, compared with Shaun Madden, Mick Jagger seemed like a gentle shepherdess. She wished she could share her hideous evening with Orlando, but she couldn't as he was thousands of miles away and hated her, so she cried again.

Chapter 32

He was actually closer to home than she thought. But not that much closer. For unbeknown to Amy he was on the self-same Caribbean island as Lucinda and Benjy. Shooting had been postponed due to torrential New Zealand rains and he'd taken a breather from everything, returning to a place where he and Lily had once had a holiday. It was thus that Lucinda and Benjy found themselves there.

'You absolutely must go there,' Lily instructed. 'In fact, if you could bear the intrusion I'd love to come too.'

'You've got yourself a deal,' Lucinda agreed. She knew that wherever Lily led good times and fun would follow. So it was on a distinctly more exotic beach than the Dorset one that Lily and Orlando met again. Lily was lying splayed out on a towel with her walkman for company.

'I'd recognise those legs anywhere,' Lily said, screwing her face up into the sun as Orlando stood above her. Yelping and hugging followed and when Benjy and Lucinda returned from their absailing lesson they found the two sipping pina coladas from half coconuts and looking like a scene from a tacky postcard.

'Orlando,' Lucinda shrieked in surprise.

'All right mate?' Benjy was more sedate and, knowing his sister, was less than surprised. Murphy's law – she always ran into someone she knew. They all sat under a straw canopy and after several pina coladas had got over the small world element and progressed.

'I can't believe how beautiful this place is. Why don't we just come out here and open a bar?' said Benjy.

'If you can make cocktails like this I'll be beside you all the way, darling,' said Lucinda.

'And Olly and I will be bouncers if you like,' Lily volunteered. There was a gap where Amy should have been. They all noticed but only Lily asked.

'And where does Amy fit into all this Olly?' she asked boldly.

'Always rely on Lil to get to the heart of the matter.' Orlando smiled.

'Olly, what's the story?' she urged.

'Well, your guess is as good as mine. I haven't seen her since the day we were in the hotel and she left. I keep seeing her mentioned in the papers, and I saw that cover story about that video thing, poor love. How is she, Lucinda?'

'Unbearable, but irresistible as usual. I haven't act-ually seen much of her this past week. She was a bit into the whole media thing to be honest, I got a bit pissed off.'

'Yeah I could see that coming, but the way things are going I guess it won't last long. She's a bright girl and she'll get pretty sick of it soon,' said Orlando, more hopeful than prophetic.

'Poor Olly, she's the nicest woman you've ever been

out with. Don't worry, sweetheart, she'll be back soon,' said Lily, slathering her stomach with sun cream.

'I really hope so,' said Orlando.

'So that's the plan is it?' asked Lucinda, 'Clever, I have to say. Amy's not the kind of person to be immediately attracted to what's best for her, but she does come round eventually. A stroke of genius, Mr Rock. You may be the first guy our Amy has ever really fallen in love with.' Orlando held up his hand to show crossed fingers and sipped his pina colada through his straw.

'So what about you guys, when are you going to get married?' Lily continued her onslaught.

'Oh you know, the longer you go on the less you need to get married. We're all right, aren't we?' Benjy leaned over and took Lucinda's hand.

'Yeah, we'll be around for ever, but no wedding bells just yet. I haven't really got a thing to wear for a wedding.' They dissolved into laughter and turned their attentions to Lily.

'Oh, I'm going to be one of those old spinsters with lots of cats. The village children will think I'm a witch and I'll buy a broomstick just to scare the hell out of them.'

'No one special lurking in your coal shed then, my love?' Orlando asked.

'Nah, my last encounter was with Amy and you stole her from me, Mr Rock, so I'd just keep your counsel and stop asking questions before I start to cry.'

'I suppose you could share her,' suggested Benjy, ever one for a novel solution to a problem, particularly if it involved risqué sex.

'Yeah, she'd love that,' said Lucinda. 'It would make

her feel like a lead part in a Noel Coward play, *ménage à trois* and all. Maybe you could suggest it.'

But right now the only part in any play Amy felt like was the back of a horse in a pantomime. She was missing her other half and missing her friends. She hadn't even asked Lucinda where she was going. But she had to get on with things, today was Wednesday and as any secret *Hello!* fan knows but will refuse to admit to knowing, the aforementioned publication has its debut on the newstands on that day. Amy thought it was all a bit bizarre actually, dressing up to buy pictures of herself dressing up. But it had to be done. Imagine if the man in the newspaper shop recognised her and she looked as bad as she felt. That was the thing about Tracy Sunshine-style celebrity, always look as if you've won the lottery and been invited to the best party in the universe, even if you're boyfriendless and miserable. That's what people love you for. A mascot. A happy shining smiling groomed mascot. The nearest affinity Amy felt to any mascot was to one of those gonks you put on your desk during exams, but folks, the show must go on. I've made my bed now I have to lie in it, thought Amy, wheeling out some more proverbs and curling her eyelashes for that Bambi look.

She strolled down the street and the spring sunshine made her feel much happier. No one would have guessed she'd been awake half the night crying. She sought out the largest newsagent within walking distance and made her entrance, but the only people in there were an Indian lady and her daughter who sat behind the till not really noticing anything at all, least of all Amy and her *Hello!*

lifestyle. The new issue was still tied up in a bundle on the floor which was a bit embarrassing because she had to ask for a pair of scissors to undo it, and even if you regularly grace the pages of this glossy creation, you're still hard pushed to admit that you actually buy it rather than steal it from the doctor's waiting room. So, blushes and scissors aside, Amy hastily purchased it and scuttled out of the shop. Life'll be so much easier when I have someone to do my embarrassing shopping for me, she sighed. It was only then that she realised that it wasn't her on the cover but some horsey looking European royal. This was quite a shock as in her mind she'd always imagined that it would be her on the cover. Perhaps that picture with the nice yellow Versace jacket she'd worn, or the one of her with the cat, – they'd found it outside the back door and borrowed it for a while, – that would have been a perfect cover. But no, so she tried to juggle looking famous (sunglasses always help) with walking along the street and trying to find herself in a magazine that she was trying to seem as though she wasn't reading because it was not *Vogue* but a naff magazine. Oh dear. Her debut seemed to have got lost somewhere amongst those pictures of massacres and world tragedy and the accompanying sensitive prose. All very distasteful really but Amy fought on valiantly. Eventually she found herself, tucked between Gary Lineker's baby and Sharon Stone's brother. A double page spread: '"My Hurt At Media Lies" Former Lover of Actor Orlando Rock Tells Of Her Pain And How Life Can Never Be The Same Again'. She scanned the text and was utterly embarrassed. On nought to ten, if buying *Hello!* was embarrassing how about appearing in it. Way off the scale, she thought. Somewhere between fifteen and seven hundred and eleven. She looked like Julie Andrews in the yellow Versace number, like a bloody plastic daffodil she thought. With the cat she looked like she was in the advanced stages of alzheimers and the rest were too pitiful to look at. And all this victim bollocks. Oh I can't bear it. Amy didn't know whether to laugh or cry. If only someone were here to share this with me, if only Lucinda and I could curl up on the sofa and wet ourselves laughing about it, if only Orlando had been around, he'd have said something sane like, 'I don't really think it's a good idea sweetheart'. If only she'd listened. The flat monsters would just read it and snipe even more when she wasn't around, cows that they were. She returned home and found they'd all gone to work. Work, that was another thing. She was still employed but hadn't made it in for a few days now. She'd assumed celebrity leave was a bit like compassionate leave, everybody would be really understanding and put their arm around you. But now she was plunging back to earth without her parachute she began to see that actually she might be in trouble, would have to face the music sometime or other. Anyway she was sick of daytime television, Richard and Judy were OK but there were only so many gardening slots and recovering anorexics one could bear and when it got to lunchtime she was totally at a loss for what to do. Aussie soaps reminded her of Orlando (no apparent reason other than the Australian connection) and she could never be bothered to go to the supermarket or out, ostensibly because she might be spotted, but really because she hated having to put so much make-up on in the maintenance of public image, and mothers with pushchairs depressed her. What goes around comes around I suppose, she told herself.

If a parrot were to have flown over a particular Caribbean beach right now he would have seen four young, tanned and delightful people. Two girls in swimsuits were lying flat out on sun loungers, flipping the pages of an inexplicably popular magazine, their heads together. They hadn't the heart to laugh at the pictures; being good friends they winced.

'What on earth possessed her to do it?' asked Lily.

'Oh God, this is the act of a desperate woman,' said Lucinda.

'What are you girls crowing about?' Orlando picked up a towel from the sand and rubbed the water from his body.

'You don't want to know,' Lucinda said bluntly. She was sickened by the photographs, Amy looked so smug and ridiculous. And how dare she take Orlando's name in vain. Lucinda wasn't one to slag off her friends readily but, God, Amy was pushing it. Orlando presumed it was some magazine article about whether size mattered. He picked it up and sitting on the edge of Lily's sunlounger flicked over the pages. He stopped.

'Fucking Hell.' You said it Orlando.

'She looks like a plastic daffodil,' noted Benjy leaning over Orlando's shoulder and not wanting to be left out. There was a sense of communal horror. They were afraid for her, afraid for what she might do next. But what does come next? Humiliation on breakfast television? An exercise video? Why not just have done with it and put yourself in the stocks, Amy. That's a more direct way of inviting the public to throw rotting tomatoes and bitter insults at you.

'Orlando, I'm really sorry.' Lucinda sat up and watched Orlando's stony expression anxiously. Lily and Benjy had become engrossed in some article on Pamela Anderson in the *Express*.

'Christ, Lucinda, it's not your fault.' He shook his head, reading through the article, 'I just really can't believe she's done this.'

'I knew she was a bloody liability and should have warned you sooner. She was like an idiot possessed with all her talk of agents and journalists.'

'Why do you think she did this?' Orlando looked so desperate, so miserable. Lucinda didn't know which way to go. She couldn't bear that Amy had behaved so badly, dragged Orlando into all this. But neither could she bear that he was so hurt. Her mother looked after hurt animals, Lucinda inclined towards hurt men.

'Do you think I should call her and get her side of the story?' He was longing for Lucinda to give him some excuse, some reason for him to forgive Amy.

'I think her side of the story is pretty clear, Orlando. Look, it's here in black and white. "I felt there was great sadness in Orlando's life." She's the only sad thing in your life,' said Lucinda, who was having trouble blunting her pique.

'I think you're both over-reacting. What she did was tasteless but she's only a child, you can't blame her. Anyway, this guff won't last more than three minutes.'

Lily waved her hand dismissively at the European Royal on the cover of the magazine. 'I think we should call her, tell her to pack her bikini and come over. You can talk it through when she gets here. Olly, you can pay.'

'Thank you so much for the kind offer Lily,' Orlando said sarcastically, but inside excitement was splintering and crashing around. God it would be so good to see her, I'd fly her to the moon if I had to and what better excuse than this island with her friends. But then he looked down again. 'We had a fantastic holiday in Australia. We stayed in a lovely little house in Sydney and just spent days on the beach. Orlando was a wonderful companion.' Well wouldn't it make you want to throw up? But for Orlando the issue was a little deeper. A lifetime with Amy might not turn out to be any different to a lifetime with Joanna or any number of other women who couldn't get enough of this crap. He'd thought she was different but obviously not. And how bloody dare she do this without asking him? This was big time betrayal. Orlando decided that Amy should suffer a little bit more, that she shouldn't win him back just yet, that the more pain she had the more joy she would feel, vain and mean maybe but we think Amy deserves it. But then again maybe Lily was right, maybe if he saw her he'd understand.

'How about you just give her a call, don't tell her I'm here? Lie, say something like you'll pay through work expenses.'

'Don't be ridiculous, she'd never fall for that.' But she did. Amy was so accustomed to freeloading after just three weeks of celebritydom that she wouldn't think twice about a gratis holiday in the sun.

'Lucinda, hi, where are you? I thought you were on holiday.' Amy was thrilled to hear the familiar rounded vowels and endearments from Lucinda.

'Listen, darling, just put a little case together and book a flight, let us know when you'll be arriving and we'll sort accommodation out this end. *C'est parfait.*'

'OK, sounds lovely, but I'm not being gooseberry, am I, Luce?' Lucinda mopped imaginary sweat from her brow in relief. The little tell-tale signs that Amy was back in the land of the thinking were beginning to surface, and not a moment too soon.

Amy pulled at the foil on the peanut packet with her teeth and they spilt out on her lap. The man in the seat next to her smiled sympathetically. She darted her gaze away. There was no escaping people on aeroplanes, the sooner the flight was over the better.

'The fasten seatbelt sign hasn't been switched off yet, madam.' The air hostess pointed meaningfully to Amy's midriff. God she was sick of people getting at her, she felt so victimised and exposed. Paranoia maybe, but it was miserable. She had nearly resorted to theft when she saw a copy of the offending *Hello!* sticking out of some woman's travel bag in the departure lounge. The woman was now sitting just two rows in front of her and Amy was convinced that she and her husband kept turning round and looking at her whilst pretending to be seeing if the loo was free. It was horrible, she felt really misanthropic and fed up. And what's more it was all her own fault; she'd gone to the press not vice versa, she didn't have anyone to blame but her stupid self. As soon as the dust had begun to settle, she'd stopped feeling quite so embarrassed about her bad outfits and started to fret for Orlando instead. What a bitch I am. He goes to all that trouble to be careful not to talk to the press, and then I come along and bugger it all up. I'm no better than his ex-wife, in fact I'm worse. She was consumed with self-loathing. And Lucinda. How can she bear to be so sweet to me after I've been such a cow?

To the schmaltzy music of the hotel lobby they planned how best to surprise Amy. Benjy and Lily pushed for maximum shock factor, like having Orlando push his way out of the wardrobe as Amy unpacked in her room or perhaps have him disguise himself as a hairy German and chat her up in the disco. Orlando however decided to go for maximum punishment and keep himself concealed until the eleventh hour. He'd begun to have doubts about the wisdom of this plan. Reading over the interview again he'd started to doubt if Amy was at all interested in him anyway. Maybe he'd totally misjudged her, Lucinda certainly seemed pretty down on her and she was supposed to be her closest friend. Maybe she loves being headline news. She certainly looked happy in that yellow dress. Maybe I shouldn't go through with this.

So when Amy walked in through the doors of the hotel there was no welcoming committee, no flags, no friends. There were, however, an abundance of women who had decided that Orlando Rock was to be their holiday romance. Though most of them had no idea of his celebrity he was by far the most fling-worthy man in the resort, thus he was the basis of many a fantasy and the cause of a drain of the hot water supplies when at six o'clock the women would leave the beach en masse and make for their boudoirs where they would shower away the day's sand and sexy thoughts, and perfume, blow dry and drape sarongs for optimum flesh exposure and maximum Rock appeal. Then they'd sit at supper fiddling oh-so-sexily with the straws in their cocktails until Orlando Rock fixed them with the stare to end all stares and dragged them in a fireman's lift back to his room . . . oh how they wanted him. But Amy knew nothing of this as she walked up to the reception desk and brushed sand from her smooth, long legs, her silk slip clinging alluringly to her dusty, hot body. She had no idea of the strategies that were being hatched to have her eliminated from the competition for Orlando, Immac in her shampoo, steal her foundation, etc. For surely this languid beauty was a threat to their plans for a steamy holiday encounter, and they watched and resented as she remained luscious and oblivious.

Amy unpacked her bag and showered away her dusty taxi ride and still there was no sign of Benjy and Lucinda. They'd probably gone sightseeing or to the beach or something, she imagined. She pulled on her bikini and finding traces of sand in it thought of Orlando with that kittens-drowning-in-her-stomach feeling, nerves and regret and nostalgia in a handful of sand. She pulled her hair into a ponytail and headed down to the swimming pool area, she could maybe have a swim and a drink and then catch up with the others later. It was very sweet of them to think of her, she thought, albeit briefly. Amy stretched out on a sunlounger and decided that the pool was not going to be the place to be. It was deserted save for a couple of remarkably mahogany Swedish girls and an old man doing laps of the pool. But Amy wasn't too concerned about being in the right place right now, she'd had rather enough of that and much preferred reading Virginia Woolf by the pool without a Hermès handbag or television personality in sight. It was like being able to breathe again, she thought. She meandered around Bloomsbury in the early part of the century, walking through St James's Park and watching ladies with hats and rooms with fluttering gauze curtains, then she drifted from Virginia Woolf into a light doze, the bright sun grazing her skin and turning her face and chest pink.

'You'll need something cool on that later,' a voice traced fingers over her burning chest. Amy shivered awake.

'Orlando,' she said softly, half believing the voice to be in her head, but the fingertips were cooling and she turned her head to see him, crouched down beside her sunlounger, an iced glass in his hand. 'Oh my God, Orlando, I'm so, so sorry darling. What are you doing here?'

'Someone has to keep you out of trouble,' he said, leaning over to kiss her on the lips. With the other hand he teased an ice cube out of his glass and dripping freezing beads of moisture onto her skin ran the ice cube slowly over her lips. She shivered, and her lips parted instinctively, he ran it along her inner lip and let it flicker on her tongue. All the while drops fell from his hand onto her scalding chest.

'Someone has to teach you to keep your cool, darling.' He wore just shorts and his chest was bare and lightly covered in blonding hairs. He took the ice cube and never moving his eyes from her lips let it glide down her neck, trickling into each crease and the hollow of her breastbone, Amy was silent except for a slow gasp as he pulled down the strap of her bikini and took the now much smaller piece of ice along her ribs, over them one by one, slowly until his fingertips reached into her bikini and lightly rubbed the freezing cold hard nub over her nipple, again and again. Then he kissed her again his tongue warming her chilled lips. Oh my God, she thought. She wondered if the bronzed Swedes were still there and she could certainly hear the splash, lap lap of the old man in the pool. Orlando's cool hands trailed across her burning stomach and down to her tiny bikini bottoms. He can't be going to do this here, she thought, not moving or even breathing, but his hand remained, firm on the front of her bikini. He flicked the elastic with two fingers and let it snap gently back, taking her hand instead. They kissed and Amy was burning up inside and out. Stretching his palm out to match hers he folded his fingers through hers and eased Amy to standing position.

'My room, do you think, before the others find us?'

'Orlando, I don't really understand,' she said, reeling from one of the most erotic experiences she'd ever had, well, by a swimming pool and in public. 'Do Benjy and Lucinda know you're here then?'

'Why do you think you're here, if not for me?' he asked picking up her drink and placing it in the hollow of her back.

'Orlando, that's cold,' she said skipping away from the shock.

'Just call it punishment,' he said.

'For what, you bastard? As I remember you were the one who did the throwing out.' But she didn't really care. She was here, Orlando was here and they were going to his room, it's what one might call a lucky day. As they walked into what was a mirror image of her room he locked the door and just as she was about to take her usual spin around checking out soaps and mini-bars he slid his finger down the back of her bikini bottoms, letting the elastic flip back again. She froze and turned around.

'Ow,' she said without a flicker of pain in her voice, but looking up just saw his eyes and beard. In her mind she could already feel it scratching her face, longed for it to graze against her stomach and be buried in every crevice.

'There'll be no impunity, I hope you realise?' he smiled tantalisingly.

'Vice versa darling. I believe in the crime fitting the punishment,' she retorted swiftly and as huskily as she could manage.

'So.'

'So?' she asked. So he took a step towards her and bending to kiss her bit her lip.

'Ow,' she yelped, digging her nails into his arm. They stepped back towards the bed, a tug of her hair for him, a pinch on his leg for her, until they fell onto the bed and swallowed one another's ouches, exchanging them for sighs and gasps and ahs and as Orlando pulled down her bikini and she slipped off her top and eased his shorts down. They were drawn together in two short thrusts. There they were, reunited in bed and in love, Amy supposed, if she had time to suppose, as he pulled her smooth thighs apart and she slid them up his legs to join behind his back, locked in a pact of pleasure, of pain. Orlando was scratched and Amy was bruised, small pink marks on her arms which would turn the pale lilac of his discarded shorts later on. His lip bled and they collapsed post-battle on the top of the bed in exhaustion.

'Welcome back darling,' Orlando said.

'Glad I could make it.'

They dozed as the sun filtered in through the slats in the blind, naked and moist with the sweat and scratches and tiny drops of blood. Delicious, she thought. Polarity is a divine thing, there can be no pleasure without just a touch of pain, and touching a mark on her upper arm fell back into sleep.

'Orlando, are you there?' A knock followed by Lily's voice.

'Mmmm, I'm here,' he shouted gruffly.

'Olly, we can't find Amy. I think she's here 'cause she left a note, have you seen her?'

Orlando got up and pulling on his shorts walked to the door. Amy could just hear the exchange in whispers but not make out the words, then the door closed and Orlando came back and sat on the bed.

'Is it OK if we meet them all in a couple of hours

downstairs?' he asked, running his fingers over her sunburn.

'Yeah, sure but what shall we do till then?' Disingenuous does it, Amy, you should know by now, nothing gets a man quicker than letting him think it was his idea, his seduction. Well it worked with Orlando as he pulled off his shorts and buried his head in Amy's pink chest, worked a treat.

Amy was seen by one of the admirers leaving Orlando Rock's room in his white Armani shirt and nothing else. She padded down the corridor like a furtive pervert in one of her beloved *Carry On* films and Orlando tapped her bare bottom as he saw her out of the door.

'Don't! Someone might see,' she panicked. After the swimming pool it was rather academic but this was not a university entrance exam and Amy's brain was scrambled by morality and hormones again. She skipped barefoot through the corridors and by the time she was back in her room showering and applying councillor to her sunburn but not her battlescars (let everyone see my trophies, she thought proudly), the word was out on the hotel grapevine that a scrappy, sunburnt, mousy hairdo, very badly dressed, probably English girl had been seen leaving Orlando's room. The hotel was alive with the sound of hopes dashing like broken plates on stone floors. But still the make-up was applied and the sarongs slung slinkily and the hair blow dried carefully and still a chink of optimism remained in their minds, based on the fact that Amy didn't seem to possess a hairbrush, let alone a hairdryer and mousse and that she may have cellulite free thighs but that didn't constitute international style, which they had and she didn't.

But Amy was oblivious to the sneers as she came down the swirling staircase into the lounge with parrots and huge palm trees framing her entrance, free of her labels and *Hello!* accessories and wearing just Orlando's shirt and a pair of loose cotton trousers. Orlando stood up from the white leatherette sofa and kissed her gently on the lips.

'Hello beautiful,' he said. 'Drink?'

'Whatever you're having,' she said, sitting down a little painfully, for was an intense stint in bed not as physically taxing and muscle-ache inducing as a hefty workout in a spartanly sadistic gym? Amy looked around as Orlando went over to the bar and was surprised to find about twenty pairs of eyes flick away from her own. Wow, they all fancy him, she clicked in a nanosecond, well, who wouldn't with that edible little bottom, she thought. But more importantly she wasn't thinking anything at all. We've just witnessed a seminal moment in Amy's development: she watched Orlando, not everyone watching her watching Orlando. A slight difference but it means everything, and it would have meant everything to Orlando had he known. But it was fleeting and it didn't stop her, on realising she was the envy of each woman in the room, from flashing lustrous eyes at her beau and then self-consciously running her fingers over her lightly bruised arms. She wanted them to detect the pain and detect the precursor to the pain, namely tempestuous sex in his room upstairs, oh how they'd hate her, she thought with perverse pleasure. But

her daydream and status as a vamp were interrupted by
three burnished figures crashing down beside her on the
sofa and ruffling her *froideur*.

'Hi, you old trollope are you better now?' said Lucinda,
loudly hugging her.

'What do you mean?' Amy pretended not to know
she'd been a royal pain in the bum for several weeks.

'The *Hello!* piece was horrid wasn't it?' said Lily with
genuine sympathy, as though it was a mistake we could
all make at the drop of our bra straps.

'Hiya Ames,' said Benjy, kissing her on both cheeks.
Their exuberance was exhausting and as they bounded
around like puppies, she abandoned all pretence and
slurped down the seabreeze Orlando had just brought
her, and snorting with laughter put paid to her image
as a glamourpuss. And good riddance, she thought, as
she showed her friends and inadvertently the rest of the
bar her dramatic white bikini marks branded into her
lobster skin.

'Gruesome isn't it?' she giggled as the Orlando admirers
looked on in horror and renewed hope for their own
chances with the god.

But none of them got him that night, nor for the
next week, because Amy was on fine form. She was her
funniest and liveliest and it became her mission to shock
her fellow hotel guests. She and Lily snogged over the
breakfast table as Orlando looked on and smiled. She
and Orlando replicated a fair few ice cubes and other
love aids scenes by the pool and she and Lucinda made
the rest of the holiday a fashion show of high camp and
vulgarity. All of this was watched with bewilderment and

contempt by the tastefully Gucci-ed set in the hotel and would be related at European cocktail parties and county shires horse trials for months to come.

'Orlando Rock was terribly charming whenever he talked to me, but the people he was with, no better than louts, no idea what he was doing with them.'

Chapter 33

So the stories travelled and Amy and Orlando were separated again, more tears in airports but not so hideous. As filming was over and he was just helping Bill with the post-production bits in LA, he'd soon be home and they'd be able to get around to some serious dating back in London. Alleluiah thought Amy, we can be together and cook dinners for friends and go for walks in the park and I can meet his parents and we'll have beautiful children. It's early days so we won't worry too much about all that silly talk, she'll get over it, but still Lucinda teased her as they had lunch one day in a quiet noodle bar in Knightsbridge.

'Do you remember that day when you said you wanted glamour and hair-free legs in your life, not monotony and Sunday roasts?'

'It's not the same though, Luce, I really love Orlando. And he's very handsome.'

'But he's very ordinary, you know he'll never go to casinos in Monte Carlo or buy a boat.'

'So?'

'So just pointing out that fact.'

'It doesn't matter, I love him.' Amy was adamant.

'So the fact that he's as famous as Cornflakes has nothing to do with it?'

'Absolutely not. I've had my brush with glamour and couldn't give a damn about it, had my fingers burnt. Anyway, why are you asking?'

'No reason, only that we got a postcard from Orlando this morning saying that he was coming back next week—'

'I know that,' Amy interrupted.

'And that it's the premiere of his film, and would we like to come.'

'Who, me and you?'

'No, me and Benjy.'

'What?' Amy shrieked, letting her noodle drop back into her miso soup and splash her clean shirt. 'Why didn't he ask me?'

'Presumably because you've done such a great job of convincing him that you're now limelight-shy.'

'Yes but I'm not Lord Lucan, I do intend to be seen again.'

'But the press will be there.'

'Yes, but I don't care, I'll just wear jeans or something and then they won't want to take pictures.'

'And Tiffany Swann.' There's nothing like a bit of competition to heighten one's sense of occasion.

'Well then, maybe they'll be silk jeans or something.' Amy smiled wickedly. 'And maybe they'll be fitted and I might just go to the hairdressers first.'

'And get a seaweed wrap,' added Lucinda.

'And a pedicure. God, I can't go out without a pedicure.'

'And maybe a tiny weeny collagen injection in your lips, just to even them out.'

'God yes, and whip out a couple of ribs, just to emphasise my minute waistline.' The girls exploded with laughter and their noodles plopped and splashed and a piece of sushi was knocked onto the floor in the fracas. The waiter looked disapproving and they laughed even more.

But whatever Amy said she had meant. As she wandered down King's Road looking for a pair of shoes worthy of a premiere, she didn't think I must look nice for the cameras, she thought I want to look nice for Orlando, I want him to think my feet look so unutterably perfect in these shoes that he just has to kiss my toes one by one and then work his way up, I want him to lose concentration talking to all those famous people because I'm there and he can't take his eyes off me. I want him to love me more than anyone or anything, more than beer, she smiled wistfully. So he was an actor of Olivier proportions, so he was possibly the most handsome man she'd ever set eyes on, he was also in love with her and no amount of public adoration or designer freebies could match that for her. It was a buzz and a headfry and it was the first time she'd felt like this. She hadn't told him that she loved him yet, but she would, when the time was right.

The car would be arriving at seven so she had two hours. There hadn't been time for the rib removal but she gave herself a homemade facepack and fluffed around in a cloud of Chanel No 5. She lay in the bath and remembered a trick where if you hypnotised yourself and imagined your breasts were growing they actually would. She didn't want to be outdone by Tiffany 'Tits and Bum' Swann, so she thought swelling breasts for all of three minutes until she got bored and decided she'd have to be content with what God had given her. If they were good enough for the *Sun* they couldn't be the small bee stings her mind's eye perceived them as. She put heavenly smelling soap in places she didn't know she had and wiping the steam from the bathroom mirror looked at herself in her new underwear, white and bright against her now pale caramel coloured skin. She thought it most becoming, and indeed herself most becoming. Tiffany Swann may have the assets but Amy could go as *au naturel* as women ever did and shine with wit and charm instead.

Yes, there was no knocking her confidence tonight. In the wake of the *Hello!* fiasco, she'd learnt that she was not a hallowed babe. She would never be. Elegant? Yes. Well-dressed? Yes. Lithe? Yes. She could think of a million adjectives but babe wasn't one. To be a babe you had to have tiny plucked eyebrows and pneumatic boobs, tiny T-shirts and high heels. Amy was too tall for high heels for a start and she couldn't laugh at men's jokes if she didn't find them funny. No matter how rich or gorgeous the man. So long babe. Hello Amy, she thought, winking in the mirror at herself. Tiffany Swann would have to do the gin-and-limelight party queen bit tonight. Amy just wanted to see her man act his socks off and then take him home and get his kit off. Why couldn't things have been this simple from the start, she thought, burying the buttock-clenchingly cringy moments of the last three months beneath her excitement at seeing Orlando again. She wondered if he'd shaved his beard off. She also wondered what Bill would think of her. He was coming in the car with them, Orlando had told her on the phone from LA, and was dying to meet her. She'd have preferred to have him in the car by herself, limousines were practically an invitation to licentious behaviour on the back seat and now she'd have to shake hands and make do with air kisses. Should she practise her vehicular exit, she wondered, thinking of all those terrible actressy pictures of exposed knickers and spilling breasts. The last thing she wanted was to be on the front of the newspapers in a *crise d'* underwear. Finally she was ready. She sat on the stairs of her flat and checked her toenail polish one more time, wondering what Orlando would wear and say tonight.

'Heaven, I'm in heaven,' she sang quietly until the doorbell rang and she pattered down to find the sleek ridiculously long limousine blocking her road. God how embarrassing and naff, she thought locking her door and trotting to the car. It's obscene.

'Orlando, darling!' She did kiss both cheeks. My God, he looked sexy, crisp clean white shirt, black-tie, beardless and tanned. He smelled of lemons and musk and soft dark leather and as she was about to squeeze his bottom Amy noticed a hefty man in a dinner jacket sitting in the backseat too.

'Amy, this is Bill Ballantyne.'

'Bill, Amy.'

'Pleased to meet you.' He reached a hairy paw out and Amy shook it,

Clare Naylor

'You too,' she lied. I'd rather shag senseless in the backseat, she thought cheerfully.

'So how was Los Angeles?' she offered her conversational opener and sat back to watch Orlando's mouth as the two men exchanged anecdotes and jokes, made for eating oysters and women an interview had once said of his mouth. Perfect description, she agreed.

'So, Amy, are you looking forward to seeing your young man's crack at Thomas Hardy?' Not as much as I'm looking forward to seeing the crack of his bottom.

'Oh yes, I can't wait.'

'And have you read the book?' Which book? Why was this Scottish voice bothering her every five seconds, couldn't a girl fantasise in peace?

'I studied it for A Level actually,' she replied. Now shut up and let me think about his pulsating manhood. Finally they arrived at the cinema and Amy was unprepared for the long red carpet she had to trail down with her consort. This wasn't fun, this was terrifying, why on earth she'd wasted her days wanting to shunt up and down vile coloured carpets she couldn't begin to understand. Help! Orlando did help, he took her hand and led her from the taxi, whispering softly,

'If you get through this I'll do anything you want me to do to you later.' Amy's face lit up in a smile and she felt totally desirable and confident and fabulous.

'Anything?' she asked. He nodded and smiled in just the right direction and with just the right amount of starriness. She hadn't a bloody clue where to look, she was either grinning like the village idiot or looking like her goldfish had just died. Her face flickered from one expression to the other like a broken television set. Smile grimace, grimace grimace smile. Help. She was consumed by admiration for Orlando's easy manner and when they finally got inside the doors was sweating and shivering.

'God that was horrible,' she said.

'Don't worry darling, you were beautiful,' he reassured her, and oh what perfect timing, there behind them to hear his adoration were the heaving bosoms and expanses of flesh that denoted Tiffany Swann. Amy looked closely at her face as she talked to Bill. She's a babe really, isn't she? she thought, examining her thinly arched brows. Well bugger that then, I couldn't compete if I tried, and neither could she. Amy's head was swimming with faces and shining gowns and the whirr of chatter and laughter and it was an enormous relief when finally they were shown to their seats and sat down to watch the film. She gripped the inside of Orlando's thigh as the credits rolled and only when she saw his name did she realise the enormity of his penis ... no of his fame ... Stop it, Amy, put those hormones away. There are words for women like you she chided herself.

Then she was suddenly transported to the wilds of Egdon Heath, to windswept heather and bleak Titanic skies. To interweaving fates and sorrows and missed opportunities, to Eustacia's love first for Wildeve and then Clym Yeobright, Orlando. There he was, ohmigod, there he was with his striking eyes and breathtaking body, he was wearing first a smart Parisian outfit and later some dashing thigh high boots and trousers, his chest bare and broad, he was sensitive and in love with Eustacia but she treated him so badly, such a wronged man, such a handsome man. There was no way she'd treat him like that if she were Eustacia, she thought, as her eyes pricked with tears at the thwarted love, and his mother hindering his happiness by forbidding the banns in church, how could she? Amy melted into the celluloid and made the characters' emotions her own. She pricked with pain and oppression as they did and was struck by love for the weak but well meaning Clym, for after all here was a man who understood daydreams, who knew that life was more perfect in the imagination. Here was a man who understood her, Amy, sitting in her cramped red velvet seat with a tissue drying her eyes. She was desperate for the film to stay there, not to finish but to wind on beyond the end to engulf her in it. God how tragic. Clym I'd never have treated you so badly, she thought.

As they all filed out of the cinema and the buzz filled her head, the night air was as cool and reassuring as the breeze across the heath, the soft enveloping carpet a floor of heather, Amy could think only of Clym; she wanted to live on Egdon Heath with him in his furzecutter's cottage and tend to his failing eyesight like an angel of mercy. She'd make him broth and help him take faltering steps from his dark room onto the lichen steps of their cottage. She wouldn't desert him by cruelly drowning herself. No, she'd stand by her man to the death, she'd kiss him tenderly on his full, sad mouth and restore happiness to his life, they could have children and maypole dancing on the heath each spring, she'd . . .

'So what did you think my love?' Clym asked, oh but not Clym, it was Orlando.

'I think I'm in love,' she said as the cameras popped in their direction and they walked out into Leicester Square and the midnight blue sky overhead flickered with flashes of stars. She was dazzled and saw only the moon over Egdon and a distant bonfire beside which she and Clym could stand and talk long into the night.

'I love you too darling,' he said kissing her forehead not caring about the cameras or the paparazzi yelling,

'Give 'er anovver one, Olly!' Amy blinked in all the light and thought, yes, Clym I love you too. But what about Orlando, Amy? Well, yes I love Orlando as well, but then that's the more glorious thing about all this, I get to have my cake and eat it. For once I get to sleep with my hero and my boyfriend, interchangeable romance and reality in the same bed. Just the thing for me, thought Amy.